Cleo's Fabulous Adventures:

THE REALM
OF THE WOODS

Cleo's Fabulous Adventures:

THE REALM
OF THE WOODS

Anne Pollard

Blue Ink Media Solutions

Printed in the United States of America
ISBN 978-1-64133-926-1 (sc)
ISBN 978-1-64133-929-2 (e)
ISBN 978-1-64133-928-5 (hc)

2024.07.30

Blue Ink Media Solutions
1111B S Governors Ave
STE 7582 Dover,
DE 19904

www.blueinkmediasolutions.com

DEDICATION

When I started my writing journey, I was drawn to a book that is still my favorite. But I could not have foretold the impact this book and its author would have on my life.

The book is *Animal Spirit Guides* and the author is Dr. Steven Farmer. This book opened my eyes to the incredible world of animal spirits and what a profound message they can send to all of us, if we are willing to listen. But more than that, it allowed me the greatest honor of working with Dr. Farmer as my mentor and friend. He helped me discover so much more than animal spirits; he helped me discover my authentic self. And that is a gift for which I can never thank him enough.

His inspiration and his book spawned the idea for *Cleo's Fabulous Adventures: The Realm of the Woods*. And his guidance and encouragement through the writing of this book were priceless.

And so, it is with the upmost gratitude and humility that I dedicate this book to Dr. Steven Farmer. There are no words that can express the impact you have had on my life. Thank you for your grace and thank you for everything you do for our animal kingdom and Gaia.

INTRODUCTION

This book is meant to be read on several levels. It is the reader's choice on how you choose to enjoy it.

You can just read the story, as is, and enjoy a fantasy journey of meeting some amazing animals through Cleo, the main character, and Bacchus, her black panther animal guide.

However, there are deeper meanings, if you choose to discover more. Each animal in the book has an animal spirit, or personality, that is explored to engage Cleo in new ideas, new ways of thinking and on a path toward enlightenment. But even deeper, each animal is named after an Archangel, an Ascended Master, an Enlightened Being or a spiritual name. The personalities and teachings of that angel, etc. are also woven into the animal's story. The traits of the animal and its sacred name are always similar in their message.

At the end of the book, there is a Reader's Guide Section. That section outlines the animal spirit and the associated name. You can choose to look through the Reader's Guide before, during or after reading the book. Whatever you decide, I encourage you to review the Reader's Guide for a more immersive experience.

Also, at the end of the book, there is an Acknowledgement Section. This section references all of the various ideas that Cleo learns and the main inspiration for that knowledge. So, when you find a chapter or two that resonates with you, you can check the Acknowledgement Section to find out more about that topic or that technique.

This life journey is meant to be fun, to explore, to raise our own awareness and to learn to love ourselves even more. My wish is for you to find one take away from the Woods Realm that means something to you. Then, follow that forward. Learn, research, play and discover what's out there that you may not even be aware of. Just imagine. Suspend your disbelief and open your heart.

CLEO

Cleo loved to walk in the woods. It was always a great way to connect to nature and calm her down, especially if she was having a bad day. And it seemed lately that she was having a lot of them. She was thinking about her day as she got ready for work. She stood in front of the mirror and saw the face that she sees every morning. Her skin was a golden bronze and her eyes were a deep shade of brown. She combed her long hair, straight, and black, and mussed with her bangs to cover that scar on her forehead. It was a childhood injury that left its mark from her hair line, down her forehead, almost to her eyebrow. She hated that scar and was always embarrassed about it. She knew other people would stare and think how ugly she was. But she pushed that feeling aside, grabbed her coffee and started getting ready to head to the office. She had a lot to get done, but she felt like she mostly had it all under control. Yet she couldn't shake the feeling that something major was going to happen today. It was her birthday, but that usually didn't mean much. She wasn't the type of person that went out and celebrated things like that. She would just spend a quite evening at home after work.

She gathered her usual stuff and jumped in her car. It was only a short ride to the office. She started the car and pulled out of the driveway. As she turned in to the street, a crow flew by, cawing loudly, and almost hit her car. Wow! She thought. That was weird. But she continued down the street.

As she was getting ready to turn out of her neighborhood, she hesitated for just an instant. She got a flash of something and slammed on the brakes, just in time to miss being broadsided by some crazy driver who just ran the red light going 60 MPH. Cleo's heart was racing, and she stopped breathing for a minute. Even though she wasn't hurt, the whole thing caused her to freeze, her hands clutched tightly on the steering wheel. She stayed like that for a few minutes to catch her breath and come back to reality. As she sat in her car, her feelings shifted from fear to sheer anger. She could feel it starting in her gut and pretty soon had taken over her body and her mind. She started shaking she was so mad. So, she just sat in her car, feeling all of the emotions that were rushing through her body. After about ten minutes, she pushed all of the feelings aside and headed to the office. When she arrived, the parking lot was full, since she was late. She ended up parking in the alternate lot and walked the rest of the way to the office. ARGH! This is going to be one of *those* days she said to herself. I can already feel it going downhill.

At least it was summer, so the weather was good and the sun was out. As she entered the building, she took the elevator up to the 4th floor to her office. Cleo was an office manager in a small but upcoming company. She had lots of various responsibilities depending on the day and had a staff of 12 people helping her, well at least most days they helped. As she got off the elevator, one of her staff members, Jonathan, ran over to her before she could even get into the office. "Cleo! Where have you been??? We've been looking for you!" Cleo was a little surprised because she was really only about 15 minutes late. She explained that she got delayed with traffic and asked what was so urgent anyway? Jonathan said that the company owner was in the office today and was looking for her. She wanted to set up a small meeting with the office staff to review some 'upcoming changes'. Oh boy, that's never a good sign.

Cleo and Jonathan walked in and found the owner waiting for her in her office. Jonathan eased away so he wouldn't have to deal with what might be coming, and Cleo went into her office and closed the door. The owner, Samantha, was a great leader and boss and she and Cleo got along really well. Samantha told Cleo that her small company was going to be bought out soon and things would be changing. At this point, everything would stay 'business as usual,' but they would be moving office spaces and that needed to happen sooner rather than later. Cleo took a breath and sighed. Thoughts started running through her head about whether she would have a job after the buyout was complete. Then she started thinking and calculating everything that would have to be done for an office move. The more she started creating that list in her head, the more she began to get anxious and stressed. Samantha was a good boss, but she rarely dealt with the day-to-day stuff and Cleo knew that would all fall to her. "So, are we talking like 90 days?" Cleo asked Samantha. "Well……. more like 45. This has all happened so fast and if I didn't act on it right away, they might have pulled the deal completely." They chatted about the buy out for a few more minutes and Cleo kept her composure like she always did. Then Samantha asked Cleo to set up an office meeting for everyone in the afternoon so she could announce the 'good' news. Cleo said she would, and suggested that they plan for 3:00 PM.

After Samantha left, Cleo sat down, drew in another deep breath and sighed. Yep, this is going to be one bad day! Jonathan saw she was alone and rushed to her office. "What did Samantha say?" he asked quickly and with some trepidation in his voice. Cleo said, "I can't really say now, Jonathan, but it's ok. We're going to have a meeting this afternoon and talk about some changes." "Oh no," said Jonathan. "It's bad news, isn't it?" Cleo smiled the warmest smile she could muster and told Jonathan that everything was fine and they would talk about it later. Jonathan did not return the smile, but headed back to his desk.

Cleo was the office support person and 'counselor'. When someone had a problem or needed to vent about something, Cleo was always the one they went to. She knew that was a good thing for them to have someone who would just listen, but sometimes it was really draining for her. But she never turned anyone away. And that usually translated into some long days.

She worked through the morning, starting to get the plans set for the meeting in the afternoon as well as the 10,000 other things she had on her plate. She was still shaken from the traffic 'near death experience' and she just couldn't seem to get her concentration going in the right direction. About 10:45 she decided that she needed a mental break. She thought, I'll go for a quick walk in the park. She did this quite often and it always helped her get centered again. The park was only a 10-minute walk, so she decided to take an early lunch and head out. She tapped Jonathan on the shoulder on the way out and said she was taking an early lunch and would be back by Noon. If anyone needed her, they could reach her on her cell. He nodded as she headed out the door.

She took the 10-minute walk to the park where there was a wonderful, wooded section that was filled with great trails. She had done a particular trail so many times she knew exactly what to expect, and she knew she wouldn't get too messy before going back to work. But she knew she had to watch her time so she wouldn't be late getting back. Then she could plan the afternoon meeting while everyone was at lunch.

Cleo got to the trail entrance and started down the path. She knew this trail so well that she didn't really even need to pay attention to where she was going. As she started down the path, her mind wandered back to the morning and everything that had happened. The woods were quiet. Since it was before lunch, there was no one out, since most people came to the park for their lunch break. She was pleased that she had the trail to herself. As she walked, she listened to the birds in the trees and the gurgle of the stream just off to the right. She was relaxing a little more even though her mind was still racing with so many thoughts. It was usual for her to have an active mind and that was normal, although not really peaceful. She thought to herself, *I wish there was someone who could really help me gather my thoughts and bring me a little peace.*

Then she heard a strange noise to her right. It was a sound that she didn't recognize at all, and she was startled. As she turned to see what the sound was, she got her cell phone out of her back pocket – just in case.

She glanced down at her phone as she pulled it out of her pocket and noticed that the time was 11:11.

BACCHUS

As she lifted her gaze to see what the noise was, she froze in disbelief. In front of her, standing next to a large oak tree was a black panther. Her mind went in a thousand directions. As her mind raced, she thought, there are no panthers around here, what is going on, am I losing my mind? The panther was standing perfectly still. His body was long and sleek, and his fur was pitch black, smooth and shiny. His strong front legs were lean and muscular, and his large paws were turned slightly inward. His head was large and round except for his nose and jaw which protruded slightly. His strong brow led down the bridge of his nose to form the "Y" of his nostrils and then connected directly to his mouth, slightly opened. He had long whiskers on his face and chin that didn't move at all, as if he was just frozen in time. His ears stood straight at the top of his head, rounded at the top and actively listening. His eyes were a piercing gold with deep black pupils. They looked like two stones of purest topaz set into a magnificent black background. He did not blink.

Cleo couldn't move. She stood on the path frozen in fear.

The panther didn't move either, but seemed to be looking straight through her.

Then, as if out of nowhere, Cleo heard a voice. It was a very strong and powerful voice but seemed to only be in her head. Although powerful, the voice was very calming. It said, "Hello Cleo. I am Bacchus." She could not explain nor rationalize to herself what was happening, but she knew the voice was coming from the panther standing in front of her. Then, as if almost compulsively, she thought back, 'Hello Bacchus.'

The panther blinked slowly and continued, "Please don't be afraid. I come in love to help you. You called for help and said you are looking for peace. I am your animal guide, and I will take you on a quest to find that peace, if you choose to come."

Cleo took a deep breath, now even more confused. But as she exhaled, an unexplainable calm flowed over her, and she felt the presence of the most loving, warm essence. It drew her to Bacchus like a magnet and her little inner voice said, *this is safe.*

Bacchus confirmed, "Yes Cleo, this is safe."

As Cleo breathed again, she felt even calmer and was being drawn even stronger to Bacchus. What is happening to me? she thought. How can this be real? What should I do?

Bacchus said, "You have the choice to do whatever you want. And I will not judge you for any decision you make, because it will be the correct one, no matter what it is. However, if you would like to come with me, I know it will awaken inner strength that will lead you further in your life." As Bacchus breathed, Cleo could smell his sweet breath and it seemed to lure her even closer to him. She was drawn to his power and knew that she must take this quest with him. It was just choiceless.

OK Bacchus, she thought. I might be crazy, but I'll take this adventure with you. At that, Bacchus turned gracefully toward the oak tree. The tree had a great trunk, standing nearly 100 feet tall and so large that three men standing arm-in-arm could not reach around the full circumference of it. Cleo was surprised that she had never noticed this mighty oak before. In the center of the trunk was a hole. The edges around the hole were old and worn and there were bumps and knots all around the opening. As Bacchus moved closer to the tree, Cleo noticed that the hole was actually shaped like a heart. Hmmm, that's interesting, she thought. Bacchus said, "The heart is the center of all beings". Cleo then realized that Bacchus could "hear" every thought she had. He must have a sixth sense of hearing, she thought.

Bacchus reached the tree in a few elegant strides and beckoned Cleo to him. She moved slowly but with great anticipation until she was just behind Bacchus. He turned just his head and looked at Cleo saying, "Take hold of my tail". Instinctively, she reached out and gently took hold of his tail. There was an electrical feeling when she touched him, something she had never known before. But it made her feel warm and comfortable and tingly all over. Then, before she could think, Bacchus jumped into the heart opening of the tree. Hanging on, Cleo was pulled in behind him. There was an amazing swirl of energy and they both seemed to evaporate into the tree, becoming one with the old Oak. She instinctively shut her eyes.

As they emerged on the other side, Cleo opened her eyes. They weren't inside the tree at all! They were standing in the most amazing woods Cleo had ever seen. And the feeling she had was much different than when she walked in the woods. It was so beautiful. The woods were vast and she could not see any end to it. There were trees of every kind, plants she had never seen before and the smell of fresh flowers was everywhere. Some of the trees were large and tall and seemed to reach the sky. They had all kinds of funny shapes in their trunks and looked like they had a face! Some had big eyes while others had giant mouths that hung open. Some had huge roots that looked like legs and spread all over the ground. Then there were small trees that only stood as tall as she was, with short little branches and spindly little leaves. Some were full of a thousand shades of green as the leaves covered almost the whole tree. And all of the trees emitted such a peaceful vibration that Cleo could feel in her belly. It was a sense of something she could not describe. Bacchus said, "Trees are amazing beings. And yes, they are beings, and they have a soul and a heart. You can see their aura if you look, and you can feel their love if you open your heart. They are healers and teachers. They have knowledge of millions of years and hold the story of life in their branches and roots. Respect them for their wisdom and thank them for the gifts they bring." Cleo looked around and in a reverent voice said "Thank you, trees."

Through the canopy that the trees provided, there was a light shining through so brightly that Cleo had to squint her eyes to see it. It looked like the sun, but a thousand times stronger. She thought, what is that light? I've never seen anything so bright and beautiful. Bacchus said, "That is *the light*. It is All That Is. It permeates the woods and everything in it. It is everywhere. It has been called many things through the ages. It has been here forever and will be here forever. It is the source of all things. The creator of all beings and it lives in everyone and everything. It is pure, unconditional love at its essence. Can you feel the energy in your heart? It is there and has always been there. For everyone. Close your eyes and breathe deeply and feel it in your body." Cleo closed her eyes and took a deep breath. She felt a surge in her body that touched every part of her. It started at the top of her head, and it flowed down her spine, through her heart, her core, her legs and down to her feet. She could feel herself connecting to the ground, so stable and strong. She was so moved that a tear of joy flowed down from her eye. When the tear hit the ground, a beautiful plant sprang up. It had full leaves that were bright green, soft with a point at the end. Then a stalk grew out of the leaves. On the stalk, magnificent flowers appeared in full bloom. The flowers were tiny hearts and there were dozens hanging from each stalk, one after the other. They were bright pink with a little white tail, reminding Cleo of her tear. She stood in amazement of this beautiful 'bleeding heart' flower, but also couldn't believe that it just appeared in a matter of seconds. How is that even possible, she wondered. Bacchus said, "Here, everything is possible."

Cleo stood for a moment in complete wonder of this amazing place. She knew this was different. She could feel it in her whole body. Bacchus watched her with loving eyes, allowing her to take in the beauty and fascination of this new adventure. As Cleo stood so still, she noticed something unusual. She did not see or hear any animals at all. There is always some kind of animal in the woods, she thought. Birds, squirrels, rabbits … something! But there was nothing! Bacchus said, "Nothing yet…."

ARIEL THE ANT

Bacchus looked over at Cleo and asked, "Are you ready for your life-changing adventure to begin?" Cleo felt as though she was in a dream, something so profound that she could not yet grasp the magical world she had just entered. She thought, I guess I'm ready. This is so bizarre! Then she remembered her world of work. She had so much to do today to prepare for the meeting in the afternoon, and the thousand things she had to do for the office move. She said to Bacchus, "I'm ready, but I have to get back really quickly. I can't be late and I must have already been here for … well I don't know how long. But I can't stay long. I need to get back to work."

Bacchus smiled slightly, his whiskers moved up and down as his face changed to a loving look. "You don't need to worry about time. There is no time here. Everything happens in the moment and there is nothing other than right now, in this moment. Please know that I am aware of your duties and you can get back to them in time. For now, this is your moment, Cleo. Claim it."

And so, she did. Bacchus turned to begin a slow walk down an open path that just appeared before Cleo's eyes. She followed him as he moved slowly onward.

They followed the path around another tree. The path seemed to just appear before their footsteps needed it to be there. As they came to a small clearing, Bacchus stopped. Cleo did so as well. Bacchus looked to his right, finding what he was seeking. He walked over to a small hill.

He approached the hill with what seemed to Cleo to be reverence. She did not understand. It was a mound of dirt with lots of little sticks around it and woven into it. It was as tall as her waist and she could not imagine what this dirt mound was. Bacchus stretched out his front legs and seemed to be bowing at the dirt mound.

An ant appeared at the top of the mound. It was much larger than any ant Cleo had ever seen. But otherwise, it looked like the ants she knew from her walk in the woods. The ant's antenna moved in circles, taking in the energy and vibrations of the new visitors. It clearly knew they were there. It moved its small head while the body remained perfectly still. It seemed to have a pink glow all around it.

Bacchus continued his reverent pose and spoke. "Greetings Ariel. It is our great honor and privilege to see you." And with that, he bowed even further. Instinctively, Cleo also bowed her head.

Ariel then returned the bow, saying, "Greetings Bacchus. It is so wonderful to see you again. And greetings Cleo. It is my great honor to meet you."

Bacchus rose and turned to Cleo. "Cleo, this is Ariel. She is the queen ant of our forest. She oversees the entire forest and is our Nature Mother. She has a deep relationship with all animals and plants and she watches over them." Cleo immediately felt a sense of calm and could feel the energy coming from Ariel. She said, "I am so pleased to meet you as well Ariel."

Ariel said, "Cleo, I understand you are on a great adventure and I am here to help you on your journey of discovery. You see, ants can bring much wisdom and support to you. We are here to show you how teamwork and perseverance can help with your upcoming tasks."

Then, other ants came out from the top of the dirt mound. There were only a few at first. Then streams of ants poured out. They formed long lines that traveled down the mound to the forest floor. What started as hundreds turned to thousands. They seemed to be everywhere! Cleo took a step back as the ants formed a circle around her, Bacchus, and the ant mound. They all seemed to be busy but moving in perfect precision with each other.

CLEO'S FABULOUS ADVENTURES: THE REALM OF THE WOODS

Ariel said, "Ants are the perfect example of teamwork. Although we are thousands, each has its duty and it carries out that duty with all purpose and diligence. Although we are small, we can carry 10 times our weight. We work together as a colony. We work diligently, slowly and purposefully. Together, we can move mountains. And that is what we want to show you."

And with that, the ants began to form in groups and moved to different parts of the forest floor. One group was gathering food for the colony, another group was mending the torn parts of the ant mound. The third group was bringing dirt and sticks to expand the current mound. All were working in perfect harmony with each other and supporting each other when needed. It was a symphony of power, patience, and strength.

Ariel said, "I know that you have just been tasked with quite a large project for your work. It may seem daunting right now, but know that you can call on us to inspire and teach you how to use your team to move mountains as well."

Cleo was surprised that Ariel knew about her upcoming project! How was that possible? As if this whole thing wasn't unbelievable anyway, what else did Ariel and Bacchus know about her? She suddenly felt very vulnerable.

Hesitantly, Cleo said "Yes, I just found out about it this morning," wondering if that would prompt Ariel to reveal how she knew about it. "There is so much work to be done and I don't have the time to cover everything that will need to be addressed. I can see a lot of overtime and weekend work to make this office move happen when it needs to. I am feeling overwhelmed."

Ariel continued. "The key is that you don't have to do all the work yourself. You can inspire your team to work as a cohesive unit and each person will have their tasks to complete, just like my ants do. But you must *trust* that they can, and will do what is needed. Give them your confidence and support and they will move heaven and earth. For you, Cleo, are *their* 'queen' and they respect and revere you. But you must give to them all that they need. With planning, patience, and willpower, you will see the project through to a successful end. Of this, we are all sure."

Cleo nodded to Ariel and said "Thank you, Ariel. I'm not sure about being a queen for anyone though. But I do the best I can." Ariel said, "That's fine, Cleo. You will learn to see your true worth. In fact, you already know how to network with other humans, like my ants do. Isn't that right?" "I suppose so," said Cleo. "Networking with other people is a great way to advance my career. I can draw on others to learn and find new opportunities." Areal nodded. "Yes, you can. But can I offer to you that networking is more important when the goal is to help others. When you mean to serve with no agenda, you are sending a different message out to the world. That is a message of love and service. Then, that is what you attract back. Others will be inspired to help you and it will just flow."

Cleo felt a new sense of purpose and strength as she listened to Ariel's words. But, she thought, can I really depend on my team to do all of that? I have never thought of myself as their *'queen'* and some of them would think I am extremely vain if I did think of myself that way. I'm just a manager with limited personal resources. And as those thoughts swirled in her mind, she began to lose the confidence she had just felt for that brief moment. Doubt, fear, and anxiety were coming back in full force.

Bacchus could sense the emotions that were running through Cleo's body but chose to remain silent about them for the time being. There would be plenty of opportunity to show Cleo that she really had nothing to fear.

Ariel smiled at Cleo, also feeling her anxiety. "Cleo," she said, "just remember that you have so much support from us. You have a strong connection to nature already. We see you walking through the woods to connect back to something greater. Always remember that you can call on nature to help you, inspire you, and ground you. Of this there is no doubt. And never forget, we are all here for you always, in every moment. You only need to ask for our help and we will be there."

And with that, Ariel turned to Bacchus. "Bacchus, thank you for the opportunity to share our wisdom and love. I am sure that you and Cleo will learn great lessons from our natural world, and we commend you for your guidance of Cleo. Until we meet again, love and blessings." Bacchus gave a final bow as Ariel turned and descended into the dirt mound.

BARACHIEL THE BUTTERFLY

Bacchus turned slowly to Cleo, his gold eyes sparkling in the sun that was shining down through the forest canopy. Cleo looked at Bacchus, captivated by his eyes. It was mesmerizing to stare at him, his golden eyes swimming in a pool of deep black fur. It was as if he could see right through her, down into her soul. It was intimidating and comforting all at the same time. Bacchus said, "Well Cleo, what did you think of Ariel?" Cleo thought for a moment, then said, "she was very wise and commanding in a loving sort of way. I felt very encouraged by what she said, but I don't know how to call on her when I feel like I need help. She said I could call on her, but how do I do that?"

Bacchus twitched his whiskers into a subtle smile. "It is quite easy, you see. I will teach you how." He gracefully sat down and invited Cleo to come sit beside him. His long soft tail wrapped around his body as a new sense of calm seemed to emanate from his entire being. He closed his eyes as he spoke. "Sit quietly for a moment and close your eyes. Take three deep breaths, and as you breathe in, feel yourself move from your mind into your heart. You can place your hands over your heart to help you know that you are moving your thoughts there. Breathe from the core of your body and feel your chest expand and contract. With each breath, relax, and let go of any tightness in your body. Feel your shoulders soften, your brow release and feel any tension wash out of your body. Then use your inner senses to see, hear and feel Ariel. Everyone has their own way of connecting. Some will see with their inner eye, some will hear through their inner voice and some will feel in their solar plexus. Whatever feels right to you is right. Then use your inner sense to invite Ariel to come. See her, hear her, and feel her presence. Then ask your question of her or just ask for her guidance. Sit quietly and wait for her to answer. You may see her speak to you, you may hear her talk to you, or you may just feel into the answer that she sends, but she will send you information. The first thing that comes to you is her message to you. Trust yourself and be open and receive her wisdom."

Cleo sat quietly with her eyes closed and followed Bacchus' words. It was amazing to feel so grounded and calm. A small smile rose on her face. This feels *really* good, she thought. Bacchus said, "Yes, it does feel good. And you can do this anytime you want. It only takes five minutes, but the rewards are incredible."

As Bacchus rose, Cleo opened her eyes and stood up. "Are you ready to continue our journey?" he asked. Cleo responded, "Yes, I am." Bacchus turned back to the path that they had followed to Ariel's mound and began to walk. Cleo followed. The path meandered through the woods for a short time and then opened into a large field. The field was covered in flowers. All kinds of flowers. The colors and smells were breathtaking. There were flowers that Cleo knew well and others she had never seen before. Some were as tall as she was and seemed to be dancing in the breeze that blew their incredible fragrance to her. Some were bushes that were covered in blooms and some spread across the ground like a carpet. There was every color of the rainbow before her, and she could not see the end of this magical flower garden. There was a soft song that seemed to be coming from nowhere, but it felt right to hear it as a background to this fabulous garden. Bacchus continued forward through the field as the path seemed to just appear before them. Up ahead, Cleo saw a small bench. It was just big enough for two and was woven in vines and flowers. They walked to the bench and Bacchus nodded for Cleo to sit.

Then, as if out of nowhere, thousands of butterflies began to appear! They were all different colors and sizes, and they flew from flower to flower, lighting for only a moment, then fluttering on to the next. The whole world was alive with movement everywhere as the butterflies seemed to take all the space available. It was incredible!

Cleo sat for a moment to take it all in. As she looked around at the unbelievable moving landscape, a monarch butterfly flew to her and landed on her hand. His colors were incredibly vibrant. His wings were all shades of orange, with an outline of black. It started with a deep orange at the front edge and moved into lighter shades of orange and yellow toward the back. There were the most delicate black lines in his wings that formed little sections of colors and spots. His body was deep black with the tiniest white spots everywhere. He had two antennae on top of his head that moved in all directions as he sat quietly on Cleo's hand. As she looked closer, he smiled at her.

"Oh my!" Cleo said, a little louder than she intended. Bacchus laughed a low, deep chuckle and said, "Cleo, this is Barachiel. He is bringing you blessings and good fortune."

"Hello Cleo!" said Barachiel. In a soft, quick, lilty voice, he continued. "I am so pleased to meet you and share this beautiful place with you. We are so blessed to have you here with us. We love that you have come to play among the flowers and butterflies!" Cleo smiled a big smile and laughed. This is so amazing, she thought.

Bacchus said, "Yes, butterflies are amazing. They love to have fun. They help us remember to play and enjoy our adventures. And to appreciate all that is beautiful in the world". Cleo nodded in agreement. Bacchus continued. "Cleo, did you know that your amazing journey is a lot like the butterfly? Right now, you are in a cocoon. Safe and warm but transforming into something completely different. You are learning a new way of being and soon you will be ready to leave the cocoon and spread your wings and fly. You don't know how yet, and you don't have to know. It will come to you at the right time, and you will remember that you have always been the butterfly. You will know when you are ready to soar."

"Yes!!!" said Barachiel. "I didn't know what was happening to me only a few short days ago. But I changed from a caterpillar into this most magnificent form! As a caterpillar, I could only see things from the ground, and it was very limited. But when I transformed into a butterfly, I could go anywhere I wanted and see things from a whole new perspective. And I discovered that there are so many different and beautiful flowers to choose from! I only had to see what was available to be able to soar!" And as Barachiel was speaking, hundreds of rose petals began falling from the sky and scattered all around Cleo. "See!" Barachiel continued. "Look at the rose petals everywhere! They smell so good! It's like honey-sweet, but fruity and spicy too! And they are so beautiful! Just like you, Cleo."

Cleo stopped smiling and reached her free hand up to her forehead to feel the scar. "Oh, I'm not beautiful," she said. Barachiel didn't seem to hear her, but Bacchus looked over with a small smile and thought, 'Oh Cleo, you have no idea how beautiful you really are. But you will see'.

Barachiel continued speaking to Cleo, "So Cleo you must always remember to call to Butterfly spirit when you need a reminder to have more fun and joy in your life! When you want to stop and smell the roses! Or when you are ready for your next big change! We are all here for you always, in every moment. You only need to ask for our help and we will be there." And then Barachiel nodded his little head to Cleo and Bacchus and flew away to join the other butterflies.

Bacchus turned to leave and motioned for Cleo to join him. She got up from the bench and began to make her way along with Bacchus. She had so many emotions flowing through her. She was so happy and peaceful when Barachiel was there with the beautiful flowers, the intoxicating smells, and the mystery music. And then she so quickly went to that place of self-doubt and self-pity. She felt like she didn't deserve anything this wonderful.

Bacchus continued down the new path as Cleo followed. They walked silently for a while. As they came around the next bend in the path, a lovely stream appeared before them. There were large rocks spread all around where the water ebbed and flowed through them and over them. The rocks were smooth and flat and large enough to sit on, out of the water. The gurgle of the stream was so peaceful and beautiful. It had a music of its own as it meandered along its way. The water was completely clear and carried subtle colors that seemed to change as the water moved from shallow to deep. There was a small pool at the base of one of the rock clusters, a deep blue color. Bacchus slowly moved to one of the rocks by the pool. It was the perfect place to sit and rest and enjoy the solitude of the stream. His body moved so fluidly as his shoulders eased up and down and his tail balanced his every step. He seemed to glide on to the rock effortlessly. Then he turned and looked at Cleo and nodded his head for her to come and join him on the rock. She took a short hop and almost landed right in the middle of the stream. But she caught herself and jumped over to the rock with Bacchus. They stood there for a moment and watched and listened to the water gently flowing over the rocks. Bacchus said, "Cleo, why did you tell Barachiel that you were not beautiful?" Cleo was again surprised that Bacchus had heard her when it seemed that Barachiel had not. She was embarrassed to speak. And she reached up again to feel the scar on her forehead. She sighed and said "Because, I'm not beautiful. Look at this ugly scar on my face. I know that everyone sees it even though I try and hide it. It so huge. I hate it." Bacchus asked, "Do you remember how you got the scar?" Cleo said "I was in a car accident many years ago. It was awful. My parents were driving and my little brother and me were in the back seat. We were hit head on by a drunk driver." Then she paused and looked down with tears in her eyes. Bacchus said, "I know that was devastating for you and your brother. Your parents died in that crash. You and your brother were injured. It was a lot for you to get through." Cleo looked up at Bacchus. She was surprised that he knew what happened. How is it possible that he knows all of this about me, she thought. "Cleo, it's time for your first lesson about life. There is a record of everything that has ever happened to you and to everyone else. It's called the Akashic Records and it has been around forever. It records all your thoughts, your actions, and the events of your lifetimes. It's like the largest library you have ever seen. I can access the records and see what has happened to you in your life. But you can access the records as well. They are available to you any time you want to see them."

Cleo had no idea what Bacchus was talking about, but clearly, he knew all about her somehow. This wasn't making any sense.

Bacchus said "Don't worry that you don't understand this now. You have so much to learn. For now, I want to just talk about your scar. Why do you think that it's ugly?" "Oh my gosh!" Cleo shouted. "Just look at it! It's gross and huge and covers my whole forehead! I know it's the only thing people see when they look at me. I don't have a beautiful face like other people do. I wish I was more like the pretty people." Bacchus said "Cleo, the first lesson for your journey is to know self-love. It is the most important lesson you will learn because everything else flows from that. It is not about being conceited; it is about truly loving yourself for who you are. You are perfect. You could be nothing other than perfect. You will learn to see that outer beauty and inner beauty are the same thing and when you can see that beauty inside and outside of you, you will feel your transformation begin. You went through a great trauma and parts of that haven't healed in you yet. And you still feel that trauma each time you see the scar. Or when you are angry and scared, like you were this morning when you were almost hit by that car." Cleo flashed back to the morning near-death accident and felt queasy. Bacchus continued, "I would like for you to do something for me." Cleo looked over at him with some apprehension, wondering what was coming next. "I want you to lean over and look at yourself in the pool of water." Ugh, she thought. Why do I need to do that?! I know what I look like. Bacchus said, "Please do this. Lean over and tell me what you see." Cleo took a deep breath and leaned over the pool. She saw her reflection just like she thought she would. The scar seemed even bigger in the reflection, and she could feel her gut cringe as she looked at herself. "I'm ugly", she said. "Can I stop now?"

Bacchus nodded his head in agreement. Then he asked, "How do you think I see you, Cleo?" She looked at Bacchus and slowly rolled her eyes. "I don't know," she said. Bacchus said "I see your eyes. I see a beautiful soul reflected in your big brown eyes. I see your warm bronze skin and your big smile. I see your aura. You are perfect, and I can only see you that way. Because that is the truth of you." Cleo shrugged off the comments like she did all compliments, because she knew better. "You're just saying that to make me feel better," she said. "No, I am saying that because it is the only truth that can be so. Please do something else for me now." Jeez, she thought. What now?

"Close your eyes and take your 3 deep breaths." With a sigh, Cleo did as Bacchus asked. "Now, feel my connection to you. Feel the love I have for you. Feel it in your heart. Feel the unconditional love. There is *nothing* that you could do or look like that would change my love for you. You are perfect." Cleo breathed in again and noticed that her heart seemed a little lighter. She took another breath and felt her chest expand and thought about Bacchus and what he said. The self-doubt wasn't gone, but it was less intense. "Now, imagine that I am your eyes. What you see is what I see." Cleo did. "Now, look at your reflection again. See it as I would see you." Cleo opened her eyes and looked into the pool. She smiled slightly and for a brief moment, she did see herself as Bacchus saw her. She saw her eyes seem to transform her face as there was a new light coming from them. She saw a subtle glow all around her. The scar was still there, but it wasn't in her focus. She saw love.

Bacchus was so pleased. His whiskers twitched as he grew a smile across his face. Then he said, "Now, can you say the words 'I love you' to yourself, as you see yourself through my eyes." Cleo opened her mouth, but those words would not come out. She closed her mouth and hung her head. "I can't," she sighed. "It's all right Cleo. You took a step and that's all you need to do. This is a 'one-step-at-a-time' journey and just be proud that you took your first step. Try not to judge yourself. All will come in time. I promise."

CHAMUEL THE COYOTE

Bacchus rose from the rock and crossed the stream. Cleo followed; this time surer of foot so that she didn't step into the water. They walked silently through the woods. There were no sounds and no animals. Only the trees that lined the path and some occasional foliage. As they continued on, the landscape began to change. The trees became sparser until there were no trees at all. The green foliage changed into grass and before them, a prairie emerged. The land was flat, covered in various types of grasses and you could see for miles. There was a small breeze that blew the grasses back and forth, swaying to the sounds of the wind. And there were sections of the landscape where very little grass even grew and it was instead desert-like dirt and rocks. As they continued, Cleo began to see little mounds of dirt with what looked like little heads sticking up out of the top of the mounds. Then she started to hear chatter from the little heads! It sounded like little squeaks, short bursts and high-pitched. Then it became louder as the squeaks turned to more of a louder call, almost like a hawk. "What on earth are those?" Cleo asked and laughed. Bacchus said, "Those are prairie dogs. They are funny, aren't they?" "Yes, they are so cute!" Cleo replied. As they continued to walk, the prairie dogs would come out of their mound, watch for a moment, then dive back into the ground. There must have been hundreds of them!

Cleo laughed as she watched them scurry from mound to mound, squawking and chattering back and forth to each other. It was fun to see them running around, their big eyes always looking around for what might be looking for them! Cleo and Bacchus laughed as they moved along, watching the little guys everywhere. And then in an instant, all of the prairie dogs dove into their mounds. In the blink of an eye, the landscape was completely void of their little bodies and chatter. Cleo looked over at Bacchus and said, "Do you think we scared them off?" Bacchus chuckled and said, "No, I don't think it was us. I think it was *him*." Cleo looked around and saw what Bacchus was talking about. A coyote was coming across the prairie.

He had a sleek body, a slender muzzle, and a long bushy tail. His yellow eyes were piercing, and his pointed ears stood straight up on the top of his head. His fur was a subtle combination of all shades of browns, tans, and a few black spots. He had a black spot at the tip of his tail. He blended so well with the landscape that he seemed to have been born from the ground itself. The coyote was trotting toward Bacchus and Cleo. His gait was smooth but determined. He was stunning.

Bacchus waited until the coyote was only a few feet from them. Then he said, "Hello Chamuel. It is so good to see you again after so long. Thank you for coming." Chamuel said, "Hello Bacchus. It is good to see you too, my friend. I am pleased to be here with you and Cleo. It is a special privilege to be a part of the awakening journey. I am happy to support in whatever way I can." Bacchus turned to Cleo and said "Cleo, this is Chamuel." Cleo nodded toward Chamuel and said, "It's so nice to meet you."

Chamuel had a faint aura of pink all around him and Cleo felt the strongest vibration of unconditional love. The prairie dogs that had disappeared so quickly were now coming back out of their mounds to see Chamuel. Their chatter was fast and loud, telling the others that it was OK to come out. Since it was Chamuel, the prairie dogs felt safe to show themselves. They even seemed to be reverent.

Chamuel looked toward Cleo after gazing around at the prairie dogs. "They are such amazing animals, aren't they? And like coyotes, they are truly wise and attentive, but they know how to have fun as well. I love spending time with them. But I am not here for them today, Cleo, I am here for you." When Chamuel said that, the prairie dogs began to disperse and go about their business. Chamuel laughed and looked back to Bacchus and Cleo. "Shall we walk?" he said. Bacchus and Cleo nodded at the same time, and they began to walk with Chamuel. Cleo was in the middle, Bacchus to her left and Chamuel to her right. She suddenly felt very tall. As they walked, Chamuel asked, "Cleo, what do you think of this amazing journey you are on?" Cleo thought for a minute and then said, "It's all quite a lot to take in, to be honest. There is so much I don't understand but I have met some amazing animals and I'm beginning to at least get the hang of that. Bacchus assures me that I will understand more and more." Chamuel nodded in agreement. "Indeed, you will Cleo. Indeed, you will. I think it's time for your next lesson. Bacchus has talked some about this, but I will help make it real to you. We are all born into a place of unconditional love. That is the 'default' you have in your heart. It comes from the unconditional love of All That Is. As we grow up, we are influenced by thousands of years of ancestral history as well as the influence of the people and places where we grew up. And sometimes, that influence causes us to forget about that unconditional love. But it's always there, and you can always recall it if you feel from your heart. That is where it lives, your heart. That is where your power is. But things happen to us along our path that cause us grief, trauma, and sadness. And that is a very different frequency than love. We build barriers around our heart to protect us, thinking that if we push down the grief and sadness so we don't have to feel it anymore, it will go away. But that's not what happens. When you push those feelings away, they are still stored in your body. And that's not a good thing."

Cleo started thinking as Chamuel was talking. She thought about the immense grief she had when her parents died. It was so painful and sudden. But she had gotten through that, she thought. Or had she? And as she thought about all of that, tears began to well up in her eyes.

Chamuel said, "It's OK to be sad, Cleo. Grief is something we all go through at times in our life. It can be a very strong emotion, but it can also be a great transformer. It's good to feel the emotion, even just be in that grief for a while. Honor what you are feeling. It's important. Just don't stay there for too long. Because if you do, that's when you get stuck. Do you feel like you are stuck Cleo?" "Well, I didn't think so. But maybe I am. How would I know?" she asked. Chamuel replied, "If you are stuck, the emotion will come back again and again. Something will happen to trigger that feeling or thought and you will begin to feel that same emotion again in your body. Did you feel that emotion this morning when you were almost hit by that car?" Cleo was quiet and thought about what Chamuel said. Did she feel that emotion? Wasn't that just being scared and angry? "Well, I did feel something this morning and yes, it did feel a lot like the sadness and anger I felt when my parents were killed."

"That's good, Cleo. Understanding and honoring your feelings is really important," said Chamuel. "Your lesson is to know how to deal with those feelings so you can get back to your heart and your power. Would you like for me to help you do that?"

Bacchus could sense the emotions that Cleo was feeling. She was confused and hesitant about this whole thing, and wondered what she should do next. So, Bacchus said, "Cleo, you have the free will to choose to do whatever you want. I told you that at the start of this journey. And what you choose to do will be the right thing. If you feel you are not ready, then we will wait until you are more comfortable." Cleo took a deep breath and said, "I think I would like to understand more and see if I am ready to follow your guidance." Bacchus looked at Chamuel and said, "OK, Chamuel. Let's explain what Cleo can do to work through the emotions and then she can decide if she is ready to move forward."

Chamuel said, "I think that is a good path forward. Cleo, let me tell you a way to address your emotions and see if it feels right to you. The first step is to acknowledge it from a different perspective. When you are in an emotion, it's hard to see things clearly. Your mind and your body are immersed in the emotion, and it may seem you can't see a way out. If you take a step back, as best you can, and look at *yourself* feeling the emotion, you begin to get a higher perspective. It's like if you were another person, looking at yourself. In other words, when you are in the emotion, you are an actor on the stage, playing a part in a drama. You embody the role of sadness, and you are deeply in that emotion. But if you see yourself as someone in the audience watching the play, then you will understand that it is just a play, and you can choose to follow that actor or not. As you choose the role of the observer, you can then separate yourself from the emotion. And that's when you can call in your power. When you are ready to release that emotion, here is what you can do. You can see the emotion as energy, and you can change that energy into something that supports you in a positive way. Close your eyes and do your breathing. Then see that emotion as a big ball of energy. Because in reality, that's really what it is. Then, pull that energy to your heart. Acknowledge that it's there and thank it for what it showed to you and the lessons it taught you. Then imagine the energy becoming an incredible ball of light. It is so bright that you can barely look at it. Then imagine that the ball of light has become unconditional love. You have transformed the emotion into love through the power in your heart. And as you see that and feel that, release it out to the Universe and send that love to the world. It will stay with you in your heart, and it will be released to others who also need that love. You can do this with any emotion that feels dense and not supportive of your happiness. And when you release that emotion, your body will release it as well. And the triggers will dissipate. The more you practice, the better you get. And remember, there could be layers of emotions wrapped up in what feels like just one emotion, so you may have to do this several times to work through all of the emotions. And as new traumas come into your life, you can use this to ease the pain of them before they get too big to deal with."

Cleo thought about this for a long time. Then she said, "I'm not sure I understand everything you just said. I understand the part about being an actor in a play versus being in the audience. I think I can practice that. But I don't think I understand the ball of energy and changing that into love and releasing it to the Universe. It sounds a little woo woo to me." "Yes, I can certainly see that" chuckled Chamuel. "You still have a lot to learn about your power. Let's leave it at that for now. If you can become the observer in your life story, that's a great start. The rest will come in time when it is supposed to." "Thank you for trying Chamuel," said Cleo. "I'm sure it is great advice, and I will try and remember what you said."

"The other best advice I can give you is to laugh! Life should be fun and not taken too seriously so remember that laughter can be great medicine," said Chamuel. "Think about the prairie dogs when you need a smile. We are all here for you always, in every moment. You only need to ask for our help and we will be there." Chamuel turned to Bacchus and gave him a low bow. "Thank you, Bacchus, for including me in your journey with Cleo. I hope I have been able to bring you love. Until we meet again, I wish you joy and peace." And then he turned and loped back to the prairie dogs to have a little fun.

DANIEL THE DEER

Bacchus turned to Cleo and said, "Cleo, how are you feeling? You have already seen so much, and we are only just beginning. Are you seeing things in a new light? Are you ready to keep going?" Cleo smiled and said, "Yes, I have certainly seen a lot of new things. All of which I thought were impossible. So, I guess I am more aware of things that I never knew even existed before. That's kinda cool. But Bacchus, I really think I need to get back. It must be so late at this point, and I can't afford to lose my job." Bacchus looked at Cleo, his golden eyes glowing with love and said, "Please don't worry. As I said, time does not exist here like it does in your world. We have all the time in the world, and you won't be late at all. It will be as if you were never even gone." "OK" she said, still a little skeptical but willing to play along. "Then I guess I am ready to keep going."

Bacchus nodded in agreement and turned toward the path. Cleo followed. They walked for a while through the prairie until the landscape began to change again. More green plants started growing out of the ground and there were trees in the distance. The path under their feet began to be covered with leaves. As they moved closer to the trees, the aura of the new forest was different than before. This forest had an airy feeling, like there was a lot of foliage but it seemed more open. The tree canopy was less dense, and lots more sunshine was able to come through. The sun gave the feeling of a more friendly, warm place and Cleo really liked the feeling of these woods. It reminded her more of what she was used to when she would walk at home. This is really nice, she thought.

"Yes, you can feel the difference here," Bacchus said. "This place is aligned with your heart chakra so you should be able to feel more love and compassion." "What is a heart chakra?" Cleo asked. Bacchus looked up and told Cleo to look up as well. Above them was the most beautiful, radiant rainbow! It crossed the entire sky, and you could not see the start or the end of it. Cleo gasped in excitement! "Oh my gosh, look how beautiful!" she said.

Bacchus smiled. "Cleo, did you know that you have a rainbow inside of you? It's your energy centers and it is a very important part of every human. And just like the colors of the rainbow, each energy center has a color as well. There are 7 main chakras in your body. A chakra is an energy center. And their colors are the same as the colors of the rainbow.

The first chakra is the Base Chakra, and it is at the bottom of your spine. Its color is red, like the first band of the rainbow. The Base Chakra is the energy of survival, stability, and health. It is the element of Earth.

The second chakra is the Sacral Chakra, and it is right below your navel. Its color is orange, like the second band of the rainbow. The Sacral Chakra is the energy of passion, pleasure, and sexuality. It is the element of water.

The third chakra is the Solar Plexus Chakra, and it is right in your gut. Its color is yellow, like the third band of the rainbow. The Solar Plexus Chakra is the energy of strength, willpower, and determination. It is the element of fire.

The fourth chakra is the Heart Chakra, and it is right in the middle of your chest. Its color is green, like the fourth band of the rainbow. The Heart Chakra is the energy of compassion, love, and relationships. It is the element of air.

The fifth chakra is the Throat Chakra, and it is in your throat. Its color is blue, like the fifth band of the rainbow. The Throat Chakra is the energy of communication, creativity, and inner hearing. It is the element of sound.

The sixth chakra is the 3rd Eye Chakra, and it is between your eyebrows. Its color is indigo, like the sixth band of the rainbow. The

3rd Eye Chakra is the energy of imagination, vision, and intuition. It is the element of light.

The seventh chakra is the Crown Chakra, and it is at the top of your head. Its color is violet, like the last band of the rainbow. The Crown Chakra is the energy of awareness, wisdom, consciousness, and spiritual connection. It is the element of thought.

These chakras, or energy centers, are all connected through the spine, where energy flows to and through each one. Just imagine that the energy that comes from Mother Earth starts in your base chakra and flows up through the sacral and solar plexus chakras to the heart chakra. The energy from All That Is flows into your crown chakra and down through the 3rd eye and throat chakras to the heart chakra. So, you see, the heart chakra is the power of you. It is where the energy combines into pure love. And that is why I asked you to go from your head to your heart when you need to call to the animal spirits for assistance. Because the heart is your power."

"Wow, that's amazing!" said Cleo. "I knew about rainbows, of course, but I had no idea that I had a rainbow inside of me! So that's why these woods feel different? Because they are aligned with my heart?" "Yes," said Bacchus. "And did you know that your heart has its own brain? It is more sensitive than the brain in your head and it will know things faster. It holds memories of your life journey. And when your head brain is not aligned with your heart brain, you feel stressed and confused. Not really connected. But when you pause, take a deep breath, and go from your head to your heart, you align the two brains and they become cohesive. And then you *really* feel all of your power."

As Bacchus and Cleo were talking, they heard footsteps coming toward them. They stopped and turned to see what was coming. Through the trees, they saw a deer. He had large antlers that stood on the top of his head. His body was strong and lean, and you could see his ribs under his fur. He was the most beautiful shade of brown with white fur peeking through on his legs. His face was brown with big brown eyes, and there was a small circle of white fur right above his black nose. He was so regal. He slowly made his way to Bacchus and Cleo, as he seemed to glide down the path. When he reached Bacchus, he stepped forward with his right leg ever so slightly and bowed his head, his antlers following until they almost touched the ground. "Hello Bacchus" he said. "I have not seen you in a long time and that has made me sad." Then he rose again, standing tall and proud.

"Hello Daniel," Bacchus replied. "Indeed, it has been a long time since our paths have crossed. I am pleased and honored to see you again." Daniel grew a faint smile at hearing Bacchus' words. "And this must be Cleo," Daniel said. "It is my great honor to meet you, Cleo." And he bowed again, this time toward her. "Thank you, Daniel" Cleo said. "It is an honor to meet you as well."

Daniel continued. "I understand that you are learning about the heart chakra. That's good, because it is so important and so powerful. The heart is your center for compassion and love. And that is not only love for other people and other beings, but also for yourself." When Daniel said that, Cleo cringed inside. All of this talk about love for myself makes me anxious, she thought. And then her hand instinctively reached up to touch her scar. "I know it can be difficult to love ourselves," said Daniel. "But Cleo, did you know that you are a divine being? The energy that creates all life is a part of you. It is a part of everyone and everything. I know you appreciate the beauty in the world, and I know that you love your brother very much. How can you not see that same beauty in you? You are a divine soul. You are Universal Consciousness. You are the creator of your reality and therefore, you can create anything and everything you want. So, you must be beautiful, because you are divine. Feel that love in your heart, Cleo, and embrace the magic that is you." Daniel's words were so soothing. The resonance of his voice was like hearing beautiful music and there was such peace around him. And as he spoke, Cleo's heart opened just a little. The anxiety eased just a little. And compassion grew, just a little.

"Tell me what you like about yourself, Cleo. What is your magic?" asked Daniel.

Cleo thought for a moment, trying to come up with something that she actually liked about herself. "Well, I guess I'm a good big sister. My brother depends on me a lot since our parents aren't here anymore, and I do a lot to take care of him. I am paying for his college now and I always make sure he has what he needs." "Yes, that is something you do very well. Why do you do that?" Daniel asked. "Because he is my brother, and he doesn't have anyone else." said Cleo. "Tell me what emotion you are feeling as you say that and where do you feel it in your body?" asked Daniel.

Cleo thought for a minute. What was the emotion she was feeling? Obligation? Duty? Compassion? Resentment? "Well, I guess I mostly feel compassion for him, for everything he has been through. What the world has done to him. But sometimes it feels like a lot, like it is overwhelming for me. I sometimes feel obligated to help him and sometimes resent having to sacrifice things I want so that he has what he needs. If I'm being totally honest." "And when you feel those dense emotions, the obligation, the resentment, where do you feel those in your body?" Daniel asked. "Oh, I definitely feel them right in the center of my gut!" Cleo said. "And is that the same place you feel anxious when you think about loving yourself?" Daniel asked. Cleo stopped and took a breath. "Yes, that's the same place," she sighed.

"That's great!" Daniel shouted. "Knowing where you feel things is a really important part of coming to terms with those feelings. Your body is like your antenna. When you can tune in to what you are feeling and where you are feeling it, you can begin to be in the audience again. You can see yourself from a different place and you can acknowledge those feelings. It is important that you do that without judgment. What you feel is right. There is no judgment, ever."

Bacchus was quiet but had a subtle smile on his face. Cleo was beginning to really feel the things she might have not been willing to acknowledge. He was so happy to see her really think about her feelings honestly. He knew her power was growing.

"Now Cleo," Daniel said, "remember what Chamuel said about those feelings? They are energy. Those feelings are energy that you are carrying in your chakras. And when you choose, you can change that energy into any feeling you want. That is when you become the master. That is when you create your reality. That is when you come into your real power. I know you were confused about what Chamuel said to release feelings and convert them back to love. Would you like to try a slightly different version of that work with me, right now?"

Cleo felt open to work with Daniel. His energy was so loving and compassionate. And so, she agreed that she would try.

"OK, great," said Daniel. "let's sit down. When you can feel the energy of Mother Earth, it is grounding." Cleo sat down, cross-legged on the ground. "Now, close your eyes. Take three deep breaths and feel the energy of Mother Earth rise from the ground through your chakras. Pretend you are growing roots deep into Mother Earth. Feel the emotion in your body. Create a picture in your mind of what that emotion feels like or visualize a time when you felt that emotion. Can you see it and feel it?" Daniel asked. Cleo nodded.

"OK. Now hold out your hand, palm facing up, in front of you. Move that picture and feeling into the palm of your hand. See it there. Acknowledge it, without judgment, and thank it for the gifts and wisdom that it brought to you. Now, imagine the brightest light you can, streaming down from above, shining directly into your palm. Feel that light grow even brighter and feel it surround your whole body. As you see that light shining on the picture you hold in your palm, begin to see the picture start to dissolve into that light. It slowly breaks apart into small pieces and becomes absorbed by the light. Now lift your palm higher and see that picture completely disappear into the light. When it is gone, you can lower your hand." After a minute, Cleo lowered her hand. "Now repeat these words with me. I am safe. I am love. There is only love." Cleo repeated the words that Daniel said. She could feel something different. It was peace. It was harmony. It was a sense of calm that she had not had in a long time.

It was love.

"You can open your eyes when you are ready," Daniel said. Cleo opened her eyes and smiled at Daniel. "Wow," she said. "That felt really good. I can understand a little more about what Chamuel was talking about. I feel very calm. Thank you, Daniel, for helping me through that."

"You are welcome," Daniel said. "Deer Spirit will always help you find compassion for yourself and others. It will help you create peace in yourself. You are poised for an exciting adventure, Cleo. There will be many paths that you travel, and they will all lead to important things. Trust yourself, Cleo, and you will never go wrong. Bacchus will show you how to do that, using your intuition. We are all here for you always, in every moment. You only need to ask for our help and we will be there."

Daniel nodded to Cleo, his antlers following the nod of his head. He turned to Bacchus and said, "Bacchus, thank you for allowing me to be part of this great adventure. I wish you and Cleo great success on your journey, and I hope to see you again soon."

Bacchus nodded to Daniel. "Thank you, Daniel, for your wisdom and teachings. Deer spirit is very special. You are loved." Daniel turned and began to make his way back down the path that brought him there. His white tail flicked back and forth as he left.

EL MORYA THE EMU

Cleo felt better than she had for a long time. It was so calming to be in these woods. She didn't want to leave. "I really like Daniel," Cleo said to Bacchus. "He is so wise and loving. I learned a lot from you and Daniel in these woods. This has been my favorite part of our adventure so far." Bacchus was so pleased to see Cleo in this light, almost glowing. She is seeing her power for the first time, he thought. Now it is time to awaken that power.

"I can see how much that meant to you Cleo. It certainly makes me happy. Your aura is expanding, and it is now a wonderful shade of green." said Bacchus. "What do you mean Bacchus? What is an aura?" asked Cleo. "Your aura is part of your energy field. The more joy you have, the larger your aura becomes. And because that joy is coming from your heart, the color is green. Remember the colors of the chakras? The heart chakra is green. And because it is energy, it can be infinitely large. Not only can your aura surround you and expand out to the width of your arms, it can go well beyond what you can even see. It can expand out to encompass the whole earth. And it can expand into space, the Universe. You are connected energetically to everything. And because of that, you can send the love you are feeling right now to anyone or anywhere. Imagine sending that love to your brother. He will feel it, even if he doesn't know exactly what it is or where it came from."

Cleo laughed. "Bacchus, you are beginning to sound a little woo woo again." Bacchus laughed. His laugh came from the very core of his belly, and it was the first time Cleo saw him really let go. He was usually so stoic and reserved. She liked to see him like this. And it just made her laugh even harder. It reminded her of when she and her brother would laugh so hard that they both fell to the floor, holding their bellies. She instinctively put her hands on her belly to contain the glee. Bacchus said, "I bet you can feel that joy and laughter in your belly – your sacral chakra. That's where you feel pleasure. Child-like pleasure like you had with your brother. Remember that feeling Cleo and where you feel it."

"We have a long way to go to get to our next destination, so we should begin," said Bacchus. He turned toward the path and Cleo followed. She noticed she was skipping.

They walked for what seemed to be hours. Through the woods, the path continued to open before them. As they moved on, the landscape began to change again. They entered a grassy woodland. There were trees, but they were quite different from the forest. These trees were spread out so there was plenty of room between each one. They had several branches from the base of the trunk, but they were smaller branches. There were no leaves on the lower branches so you could see through them. At the top, the branches expanded into a large, wide canopy. They looked like an umbrella. The leaves were vibrant green and merged together to form a beautiful arch. They dotted the landscape for as far as Cleo could see. On the ground, there was scrub brush and grasses. The ground had a tint of yellow, light green and tan and was covered in short, stubby grass. The bushes in between were sparse, but the colors matched those of the trees. As they approached, Cleo could only think that this looked like a beautiful painting. The air was dry, also unlike the forest. It was arid and warm. Cleo thought how nice it felt on her skin.

The sky was an amazing blue with a few clouds striated across it. There was a wonderful melody of birds chirping and singing. Their songs blended into a symphony of sounds, and it was impossible to tell how many different songs made up the melody. And it smelled so earthy, rich, and vibrant. It had the smell of what Cleo could only describe as *wild*.

Then, in the distance, they heard a low-pitched drumming sound. Cleo could not remember hearing anything like this. As the sound grew louder, it became more like deep rolling grunts and thumping. It was guttural and growing louder. Then they heard the stomp of very strong and rhythmic footsteps. As Bacchus and Cleo looked toward the sound, they saw an emu coming towards them. He was very tall and erect. His body was covered in grayish-brown feathers that were shaggy and long. His legs were long and bare of feathers, so that you could see the strong muscles that supported this large bird. At the top of his long neck, his head stood tall, looking toward where they stood. There were only very small feathers covering his head and his beak was short and pointy. His yellow eyes had large black pupils and there were round holes for his ears. As the emu reached Bacchus and Cleo, he stopped, and the grunts stopped as well. Bacchus looked up to the emu and said, "Hello El Morya. How grand to see you looking so well!" El Morya lowered his head slightly and grunted, "Hello Bacchus. I am honored with your presence again. It is wonderful to see you." El Morya turned to Cleo and introduced himself. "And hello Cleo. My name is El Morya. I am pleased to help you along your journey." Cleo was amazed at this incredible bird and smiled a big smile back to him. "Hello El Morya. I am pleased to meet you, and thank you for your help."

Bacchus turned to Cleo and said, "Cleo, El Morya is a wonderful teacher. In fact, he is a spiritual force-field. He is here to reveal your inner teacher and your connection with the earth." Cleo smiled again.

El Morya said, "Thank you Bacchus. What a kind thing to say. Cleo, I am a teacher, that is true. But I am here to show you that you have an inner teacher within you. It knows everything about you and loves every part of you. It never has judgment for you, and it will guide you in opening up to new ideas and possibilities. I think you have already seen things on this journey that are new possibilities for you."

"Yes, that's for sure!" Cleo said.

"And you already know how to ask for the help from your animal guides, right? By breathing deeply and feeling your heart energy. Well, that's the same way you can reach your inner teacher. Let me tell you a little about life on this earth as we explore your inner teacher more. Everyone on earth has a state of being. It is the core of who you are, and it cannot be changed. That state of being is unconditional love. It is who you are always, even if you choose to forget that at times. Like Bacchus said, you are made of energy, and that energy is the same energy as All That Is. It is divine energy, that can never be destroyed. You are a soul in human form, having a fabulous adventure on earth. You are also a higher soul, your higher self, that has never lost the connection to All That Is. So, your higher soul can see things and know things that your human mind and human body won't know in this lifetime. But always remember that you have an unbreakable connection with your higher self. And that is your inner teacher. You always have access to it, and it is always guiding you along your path."

El Morya continued, "There are some constant laws of the Universe that have always existed and will always exist. The greatest of these is that everything is created in unconditional love. It is all perfect because it comes from All That Is. The other constant law is that everything is a mirror for you. What you have inside you and what you put out to the Universe is what you get back. It can work no other way. So, whether you are consciously creating or unconsciously creating, you are always creating. And so is everyone else. And you are always learning new things about yourself. So you see, everything that happens, happens *for* you, not *to* you. It allows you to see things you like and things you don't like so that you choose how you want to live. Maybe you have in the past said something like, 'I shouldn't have done that.' But in fact, you should have, because it showed you something that you can now choose to keep or release. It's a constant process of making choices. And you are always doing it. Each individual has the choice to create what reality they want to live in. It is the frequency that you connect with. And you can change your frequency any time you want. So, you can choose to live in the frequency of lack and fear, or you can choose to live in the frequency of love. And because love is your natural state of being, it is the easier choice, whether it seems that way or not."

Cleo thought for a moment about what El Morya was saying. It didn't all make sense, but it was very intriguing. "This is all very new to me." said Cleo. "And I'm not sure I completely understand it all. If I am creating my own reality all of the time, then how can you explain the car crash that killed my parents and injured me and my brother. I wouldn't want that to happen, so how could I have created it?"

"Yes, that's an excellent question and shows you are beginning to understand. As I said, you are creating unconsciously as well as consciously. And your unconscious mind is your sub-conscious. And like everyone else, you began to develop your sub-conscious when you were just a child. You are born with no beliefs and therefore no lack, no fear, no limitations. But thousands of years of human group consciousness has existed and formed on earth. That begins to become part of your sub-conscious. It is usually feelings of limitation and lack and very much the feeling of fear. As you grow up, you also begin to take on the beliefs of your family and your community. Since your parents fed you and clothed you from birth, you associated that survival with them and their beliefs. And so, you imprinted those beliefs into your sub-conscious. There is nothing wrong with that. It is the path of the human species. And your sub-conscious mind is there to help protect you. So, when you are presented with things that you don't know or understand, your sub-conscious will tell you to reject it, to fight it, because it is protecting you from the unknown. As you grow up, you develop more and more beliefs. And these beliefs are part of what you are sending out to the Universe as a frequency. And that is then what you get back."

Cleo said, "Yes, I do know about the sub-conscious and I understand how my beliefs are created and how they impact my life. So that makes sense to me. But I still don't understand how I could have created the car accident."

"OK," El Morya said. "Let's do some exploring. Tell me about some of the beliefs you have about yourself." "Well," Cleo said, "The world can be a tough place sometimes and I have to push and fight for what I want. There are people who seem to have everything they want, but I am not one of them." "That's good Cleo. You are feeling some of your beliefs. Why do you feel that you are not someone who can have anything they want?" asked El Morya. "I guess I feel like I am not worthy of having things I want," said Cleo. "Again, that's a great observation," said El Morya. "That is a common feeling for most humans. Remember what I said about the Universal laws? If that is your belief, and there is nothing wrong with it, then that is the frequency you are in and therefore that is what comes back to you. It is where your focus is. And what you focus on is what you get. And that focus draws things to you that you may not consciously want. But as you attract those things, you can now look at them from a different perspective. You can 'observe it from the audience' now and you can decide whether you want to keep that belief or whether you want something else. This adventure on earth is all about seeing the duality – the black and white, the right and wrong, the have and not have. And your sub-conscious likes to be in duality. But now that you see things as they are, you can choose to change that belief at any time. You can change anything and everything, according to you. Because it is your reality. And when you change your beliefs on the inside, you begin to project something different. You raise your frequency and the world changes around you. And that, Cleo, is using your inner teacher! Call on your higher self when you need that clarity. And then you can release it and let your higher self-work out the details. Remember your higher self can see things you can't, and so it can guide you to the next thing, down your path of discovery."

"Sounds like most of us are kinda screwed up," Cleo said. "On the contrary Cleo." said El Morya. "Everyone's path is perfect for them and what they are here to experience. And there are so many things to experience! You are all on a pilgrimage. And everyone's pilgrimage is different, but none of them are ever wrong. It's important to understand that. Because everyone's path is perfect for them, it means you don't need to judge them or try to change them. They are all just learning lessons and doing the best they can. And everyone, including you, can only choose to do their best in the moment. That is the path to self-discovery. And it is magnificent." El Morya shook and fluffed his feathers. "Our connection to the earth and nature is also such a large part of that journey. The earth has a soul just like you. And it has cycles that are energy you can feel. You can use that energy to ground you and make you feel safe. Your base chakra is very connected to the earth. You can feel the earth energy there. Use that energy when you feel unsafe; when you feel you don't have enough. Gaia, or Mother Earth, can always help you remember the abundance that is here for you everywhere. Abundance that is here for everyone."

As El Morya said that, Cleo did that cringe thing again inside. She didn't feel abundant. She was always struggling to get to the next paycheck, to afford the things she wanted while taking care of her brother. It was an adventure alright, just not a very joyous one. Bacchus noted what Cleo was thinking. He would ensure that they look at that when the time was right. But for now, it was time to move on.

Bacchus looked over to El Morya and said, "El Morya, your wisdom is appreciated and honored. Cleo and I have a lot to discuss about your visit. Thank you for sharing your insights. Until we meet again, my friend, I wish you love." El Morya stood proud and erect. "I am always honored to show the way Bacchus." Then El Morya turned to Cleo. "Cleo, always feel free to call Emu Spirit when you have questions about what we talked about. We are all here for you always, in every moment. You only need to ask for our help and we will be there." As El Morya turned to leave, Cleo thanked him for his wisdom.

Bacchus said, "Well Cleo, let's move on." And with that, they turned to follow the path to their next destination.

FAIRY THE FOX

Cleo caught up to Bacchus and walked beside him along the path. She looked over to admire how smoothly Bacchus moved. His shoulders would rise and fall with his footsteps and his movement was so fluid he almost looked like he didn't even touch the ground. His black fur was reflecting the sun and it illuminated all of the shades of black that were there. Cleo thought how amazing he was. Without a word, Bacchus smiled slightly at Cleo's silent compliment. As they walked away from the grassy woodland, the warmth, and the arid feel, they began to see a different type of woodland. This new part of the landscape had a variety of different trees, but sparse enough to allow the sunlight in. As they continued on, they came upon a large stream that was followed by an open meadow. The stream was so wide and deep however, that they could not cross it. Bacchus said, "We need to get to the meadow on the other side of this stream." Cleo shrugged, saying "It's too deep for me to cross, Bacchus." He nodded back to Cleo. Then he turned around and seemed to be "saying" something to the trees behind him. As she watched, the trees began to move. First at the top, swaying like they were in a growing windstorm. Then the trunks began to sway as the wind grew stronger. The trees all moved with the same rhythm and in the same direction. Then ever so slowly, they began to lean toward the ground. It seemed as if the trunks would soon break in half, but instead they became more fluid. As Bacchus nodded before them, the trees laid down fully on the ground. They were so tall that they completely spanned the stream to form the most amazing bridge! "Oh my gosh!" shouted Cleo. Bacchus turned back to Cleo and said, "The trees have offered to help us along our way. Shall we proceed?" Bacchus stepped up on the tree trunks and began to make his way across the stream. Cleo followed in utter amazement. As they reached the other side of the stream and stepped down from the tree bridge, the trees began to move again. In complete rhythm with each other, they rose up and returned to their standing place in the woodland.

Cleo shouted, "Bacchus that was incredible! How did they do that?" Bacchus smiled and said, "It's magic. In our world, anything is possible if you ask, see it, and allow it to happen." Bacchus then turned back to see the trees now on the other side of the stream. He bowed deeply and thanked the trees for their help. The trees bowed back one last time before resuming their uprightness. As Bacchus turned back to the meadow, he began to move forward along the new path. The meadow was brimming with flowers, bushes, and grasses of all kinds. The colors of the flowers were like a rainbow spread over the ground. There was something that was fluttering around the flowers. It looked like it could be butterflies or hummingbirds, but it was too hard to see from their distance. As they moved closer, Cleo could not believe her eyes, again. They were fairies. Thousands of them, flying among the flowers. Cleo could hear them laughing and singing and it was the most beautiful sound. They seemed to be playing hide and seek from each other and then would burst out in laughter as they were seen. Then some would just disappear altogether for a few moments, only to reappear on the next flower. It was the most magical thing that Cleo had ever seen. Then out of the corner of her eye, she saw a flash of something that she couldn't make out what it was. Like the fairies, it seemed to be there for a moment and then just disappear. She concentrated to try and see it again. Another flash. This time she could make out a hint of red before it was gone again. Bacchus laughed. "Fairy, you can come out" he said. It appeared behind them. Cleo jumped in surprise! Both Cleo and Bacchus turned around to see a small red fox standing now in front of them. She had big, pointed ears that stood atop her head and had a pointed nose. Her chin and chest were covered in thick white fur that went all the way down to her front legs. It was such a contrast to the red fur that covered her shoulders, back and belly. Her front legs were covered in black fur and made it look like she had on long gloves. Her tail was thick and covered with various shades of red, brown, and black fur. And there was a beautiful white tip at the end. She wore a mischievous smile.

Bacchus laughed again and said, "Hello Fairy! I thought for a minute you had decided not to join us!" Fairy laughed and said, "Hello Bacchus. I was just having a little fun. You know I would not disappoint you." Bacchus said, "Yes, I know. You are here to teach Cleo some valuable lessons, aren't you." "Indeed, I am," said Fairy. "Cleo, it's nice to see you. I hope you are ready to have some fun!" Cleo laughed at Fairy and her crazy antics. "Yes, that would be grand!" she said. "May I ask first, where you got your name? I see all of these fairies around the flowers and your name is Fairy. Is that a coincidence?"

"Hahahaha," Fairy laughed. "How funny you say that because that's exactly what we are going to talk about! Coincidences! But to answer your question, it is not a coincidence that my name is Fairy. I live among the fairy world, and we have so much fun together that they all started calling *me* Fairy, so it just stuck." Cleo laughed again. "I see," she said, chuckling.

Fairy said, "Cleo, have you ever been thinking of someone and then they text you?" "Yes! I have had that happen several times," Cleo answered. "That's a funny coincidence." Fairy smiled and said, "Good! But I am here to offer you another explanation of why that happens. Instead of coincidence, I call that intuition. It may seem the same, but it's actually very different. You have an inner voice inside you that tells you things. It can come in several ways though. You might see something with your *inner* eye or hear something in your *inner* ear or get a feeling in your gut. All of those are your intuition. Most people have one or two of those as their main way to get intuitive messages, but they are all available to you. The animals use intuition all the time. It is a natural part of the way we live. And after all, we are all animals. So, let's teach you to use your intuition too." Fairy wagged her tail. "Remember the chakras that Bacchus told you about? Well, your intuition is directly related to them. If you "see" something in your inner eye, that's your 3rd eye chakra. If you "hear" something with your inner ear, that's your throat chakra. And if you feel it in your gut, that's your solar plexus chakra. And do you remember what those chakras really are?" asked Fairy. Cleo smiled and said, "They are energy centers." "Indeed they are!" agreed Fairy. "And energy can travel through space! So really, when you got the text from your friend that you were thinking of, you were actually connecting your energy with them. And that is no coincidence!"

"OK Cleo, I am thinking of a number between one and ten. What number am I thinking?" Fairy asked. Cleo thought for a minute and then said, "Uh, I don't know. Eight?" "No!" Fairy laughed. "But you were just guessing, weren't you? Did you see the number eight in your 3rd eye?" "No, I guess not," said Cleo. "That's OK Cleo. I did that to prove a point. Intuition doesn't come from the mind. It's in your body. And intuition must be developed. Just like any other muscle in your body. The more you use it, the better you get at recognizing it and listening to it. But sometimes intuition kicks in strongly, especially if there is danger. Think back to this morning, Cleo, when you were in the car about to turn. And that other car came flying by! You hesitated for just a second, but that was long enough for you to be able to stop and avoid that speeding car. That was your intuition kicking in strongly to keep you safe."

"Oh my gosh!" shouted Cleo. "I don't even remember hesitating! But I'm sure glad I did. I guess I do have intuition! I just didn't know it!" "And then, didn't you feel something this morning when you were getting ready? Didn't you feel like something major would happen today?" asked Fairy. "Yes!" said Cleo. "It was just a little voice in my head that said something big was coming." "And you were right!" laughed Fairy. "Only you couldn't even guess how big! That shows you Cleo that your intuition is quite strong. Now how can you develop it even further and be able to use it consciously? Because when you master that, new power will unfold for you." "I don't know," said Cleo. "But I think it would be super exciting to be able to do that!"

"Well, first of all," said Fairy, "you have made a great start by recognizing that it is intuition and that you already use it. But you can also develop it by being still. Remember the breathing that your other guides have talked about? Being still and quiet will allow you to see, hear and feel things – your intuition. It's the most important thing you can do to develop intuition. When you can calm your conscious mind and listen and feel what's in your body and heart, you will get intuitive messages." "But how will I know it is my intuition and not just my mind making it up?" asked Cleo. Fairy shook his head in agreement. "That's a great question and a great observation Cleo," said Fairy. "Intuition is always a clear message. It is usually very positive and can always be felt in your body. If your mind is conjuring it, it may come with doubt, fear, or confusion. And you won't have a distinct feeling in your body. Also, when you begin to understand your own form of intuition, you will learn to distinguish and trust it even more. You can also journal about your intuitive experiences. You can be a scientist of your intuitive abilities. Write down the intuitive messages you receive and then just observe. You don't have to act on your intuition right away. Just watch over the next days and weeks and see if that intuitive message rings true. Then remember what that felt like in your body. If it was a true intuitive message, it will still be there after a few days. Then, review your journal often. Make notes about what happened to your intuitive feelings. As you do that, you will hone your skills to an incredible level. And even though foxes don't write, we have an incredible memory and so we can do that same thing through our memory. Remember, foxes have incredible intuitive abilities. Use us as your inspiration and guide."

Bacchus was watching Cleo discover her abilities and smiled at her excitement to learn more. She is recognizing more of the ways that her power is available to her, he thought.

"Now, let's talk about one more kind of intuition," said Fairy. "That is the intuition of just pure *knowing*. When there is absolutely no doubt about the message and feeling that you are getting, and you can't explain how you know, *you just know*. That is a very strong kind of intuition, and it can be very powerful. And it will also develop more over time as you recognize what it is. Finally, you can also use mantras to help you develop your intuitive powers. Mantras are great for a lot of reasons but are really good in helping you focus. And what you focus on is what you get. So, when you are taking a walk in the woods, say a mantra to yourself, like 'I see, hear and feel; my intuition is real'. If you do that long enough, it will put you in a kind of trance, a walking meditation. And it will begin to train your sub-conscious which will then instill new beliefs. It doesn't happen overnight though, so trust yourself that each day, it will get stronger and more powerful. And then it just becomes part of who you are, and you won't even have to think about it because it just is."

"And Cleo," Fairy concluded, "Promise me that above all else, you will have fun with it! This adventure is meant to be fun! Play with your intuition. Practice doing something silly like taking a deck of cards and trying to guess the suit or the number on the card before you draw it. And then laugh when you get it right and laugh when you get it wrong. Discovering your power doesn't have to be serious all of the time. Remember joy is one of the highest frequencies there is. And it is the greatest feeling ever! So, choose joy as much as you can and watch your life really change! We are all here for you always, in every moment. You only need to ask for our help and we will be there." "Thank you, Fairy!" said Cleo. "I did have joy talking to you and learning. It was great fun!" Fairy turned to Bacchus and winked. She's really getting it, she thought. Bacchus nodded in agreement. "Thank you, Fairy," Bacchus said. "You are always such a wise teacher. I look forward to seeing you again soon." "Me too, my friend," said Fairy. And then, she just disappeared in a red flash.

Bacchus laughed at Fairy's quick exit. "She is so fast and cunning; I couldn't even see her leave!" laughed Cleo. They both had a delightful laugh. Then the fairies that were still playing among the flowers looked over to Cleo and came to surround her. They darted in and out and around and brought more laughter to Bacchus and Cleo. As they circled Cleo, they grabbed her hands and beckoned her to come with them. She laughed and followed along. They drew her to the edge of the large stream and Bacchus followed. When they reached the stream, the fairies all called out to Cleo, "We love you, Cleo! Come back and play with us anytime!" And then they gathered together and flew off into the sky. Bacchus said, "Cleo, will you look into the stream. Can you see the joy in your heart? Look at your eyes." Cleo was beaming. She looked down and saw something a little different than before. She had a light in her eyes that she couldn't explain, but it was beautiful. "And now Cleo, can you say, 'I love you' to those bright, beautiful eyes." She looked down and saw her reflection looking back. Then she murmured a very quiet, 'I love you' to herself. It wasn't bold and she felt like maybe she didn't even mean it, but she had been able to say it for the first time. And then she smiled.

GABRIEL THE GOPHER

Bacchus let Cleo just be there for a few minutes, but he didn't say a word. Inside he was beaming for Cleo and what she had just been able to do. But this was her moment to savor and so he let her do just that. After a few minutes, Bacchus turned and began walking by the edge of the stream, on to their next destination. Cleo stood and then followed Bacchus. Was she standing just a little taller than before?

They moved in silence for a while. The ground was moist and fertile under their feet and made a squishing sound as they walked. The grass became taller, and it looked like a luxurious green carpet. There were daisies mixed in with the grass and the colors were in sharp contrast to each other. The green of the grass offset by the bright white petals of the daisies with their yellow center. It was beautiful. As they continued forward, they started seeing mounds of dirt spread out over the ground. These mounds were not as large as the one they saw with Ariel and the ants, and there were more of them. They could hear a faint clicking sound. Then they heard a low whistle. Bacchus moved slowly over to one of the mounds closest to them and whistled back. How strange to see a panther whistle! thought Cleo. Then a little head popped out of the mound! It was so furry and cute. It wore a light shade of brown fur and had big black eyes. But the most amazing part of its face was the teeth! There were two long protruding front teeth that were dirty and yellowish. And its nose was wiggling back and forth, clearly smelling who had come. Bacchus laid down on the ground so that his eyes were at the same height as the creature emerging from the mound. He whistled again and then said, "Hello Gabriel. And how is the life of my favorite gopher these days?" he asked. Gabriel was so excited to see Bacchus that she jumped out of the mound and landed right in front of him. "Bacchus!" she cried with excitement. "I didn't expect you so soon! I would have been out and about to greet you!" Her little body was small, if not a bit plump, and her legs were short. She stood up on her hind legs, her front legs hanging down to her belly. She had short claws that were colored black, and they stood out next to her brown fur. Her short little tail was whipping back and forth with all of the excitement. "Life is magnificent!" Gabriel exclaimed. "I could not be happier to see you and Cleo! Hello Cleo!" "Hello Gabriel." Cleo answered back.

Gabriel continued, "Allow me to set the right mood." And then Gabriel closed her eyes. The sky began to change, and the sun drifted away and was replaced by a large, radiant moon. As it became darker, the entire mood did indeed change. Gabriel opened her eyes and said, "Ah, that's much better! I prefer the twilight and I love the moon energy. I guess living underground most of the time makes me prefer the darkness." she laughed. "Wow, that was incredible!" shouted Cleo. "I'm still amazed at the things that can happen in these woods!"

"Yes, I'm sure it can seem impossible!" said Gabriel. "But really nothing is impossible. Cleo, I am so honored to be able to spend some time with you. I know that you have already learned so much on your adventure and I think we can learn a lot together too. Shall we start by talking about masculine and feminine?" Cleo blushed slightly and said, "I think I know the difference between masculine and feminine." Gabriel laughed. "Yes, I am most sure that you do! But I am talking about energy, not sexes. You see, it's important to understand the harmony and balance in the Universe. And one of the most important balances is masculine and feminine energy. For your spiritual bodies to be in balance, you need to have both of those energies. The masculine energy is important for logic, robustness, being direct and firm. The feminine energy is important for creativity, nurturing, fluidity, and refinement. These energies complement each other and help everyone be more balanced. You need all of these traits in your life, and you need to call upon them in different circumstances. I know that *you* know this all too well in your job. Don't you have to use different aspects of each of these energies depending on what is needed at the time?" "Oh, yes of course," said Cleo. "Sometimes I have to be very firm about things when I am doing planning and forecasting. Then I may need to be more compassionate and creative if one of my co-workers needs some encouragement or support." "Yes, that's exactly right!" said Gabriel. "And you can call on animal spirits to help you engage those energies. For example, Lion Spirit is a good representation of masculine energy. And of course, Gopher Spirit is a good representation of feminine energy!" "And how is that?" Cleo asked. "Because gophers have a strong connection to the Earth and fertility." "Oh, I see," said Cleo. "And do you know what else gophers can do?" asked Gabriel. "Oh, I'm sure there is a lot!" Cleo quickly responded.

"Hahahaha," laughed Gabriel. "Yes, that's true. I could have been more to the point. Which as it is, is exactly my point! Let me try and explain. Cleo, tell me about a time when you wanted to say something to someone or to a group and you found yourself only telling part of your heart. You didn't say what you fully wanted to say." "I don't think we have enough time for me to tell you all of the times *that* has happened!" Cleo laughed but was beginning to see the seriousness of the question. "What about this morning, with your boss?" asked Gabriel. "Oh yes, that's true. Instead of explaining to her that the deadline she just gave me was extremely challenging, I just choked it down, like I always do with her, and agreed that we would find a way." "And do you know why you did that Cleo?" asked Gabriel. "Hmmm." Cleo mused. "Well, I didn't want to be too difficult and then she would get angry with me and maybe I would be in jeopardy of losing my job." "OK, that's perfect," said Gabriel. "Now, look at that from the audience. Don't judge it as good or bad, just observe it. Now, think back to your school time. Were there also times when you didn't say what you wanted to say?" "Yes, I can think of several times when that happened. Like the time everyone was talking about the new kid that came from a different country and they were laughing and making fun of him. I didn't think that was nice, but I didn't say anything." "Again, that's perfect. Now again, look at that from the audience. No judgment. Why didn't you say anything?" asked Gabriel. "Well…... I guess it was more important for me to fit in with the crowd. If I had said something about how mean I thought they were being, then they would have made fun of me too." "That's very insightful," said Gabriel. "Let's keep going. Now think back to when you and your brother were young. Did that also happen when you were with your parents and your brother?" "Yes, it happened a lot," said Cleo. "OK. Tell me about one of those times," said Gabriel. "Well, I remember one time when we were all talking about my brother and me going to camp. I didn't really want to go because it was something I had never done before, and I was scared of what might happen. My mom and dad said I was just being silly. Nothing bad would happen, they said. Then my brother said I was being so stupid! How could anyone be scared of going to camp! Then he called me a scaredy-cat and said I was so lame." Cleo felt her gut clench and she had to catch her breath for a minute.

Bacchus could feel Cleo's emotions very strongly. Even though this would be a difficult lesson for her, she was feeling the emotion of the scene she remembered and that was very brave of her. He silently sent her love and support.

"Cleo, I am sooo proud of you!" said Gabriel. "Remember that you are just in the audience though. You can look at that time now as a witness instead of a participant, and you can acknowledge what happened. And you can see how that shaped who you became through the years. You see, when you feel emotions you don't want to feel, sometimes you ignore them or forget them. They stay in your body. But your body and your soul want to release them. So it will send you triggers through your life to remind you of that feeling so that when you are ready, you can see them from a different perspective. Then you can choose to release them forever, when the time is right for you. And I think the time is right for you to release those old emotions once and for all. To do that, you will also be acknowledging your own self-worth. And that is powerful. Would you like to release those old emotions now?" asked Gabriel. "Yes, I really would," said Cleo.

Gabriel and Bacchus guided Cleo using the release method that she had learned from Daniel. She acknowledged all of those times when she was unable to speak what was on her mind. She looked at them without judgment and she thanked them for helping her become who she is today. And they also added releasing judgment of the others that were involved in the situations over the years. They were only doing the best they could at the time. And more importantly, they were Cleo's mirror. And seeing them in that way, she was able to ease the emotions she had towards them, as well as herself. After the meditation, she felt tremendously better. Like a weight she had been dragging around for what seemed her whole life was finally lifted and removed. It was very freeing, and she felt "lighter," even if she didn't understand exactly what that feeling was.

Gabriel was so proud of what Cleo had just done. "Cleo, you took a really big step just now. And I am honored and thankful that you felt safe enough with me and Bacchus to work through that. Remember you may have to do that several times before you release all of those old emotions, but know that you have seen more of your power in doing that. And you are a stronger person for it. Use that when you are faced with a situation where you need to speak your truth. Know that you have the power to say what you need to, while still being respectful of others. You are learning to speak with integrity. And when you speak with integrity, you don't have to worry about what other people think of you. Because you will know that you are following your heart. And if someone else doesn't appreciate that in you, stand in the power of your convictions. You can't change others, nor should you try. They are on a journey as well and maybe they are learning a lesson from you. Draw on your masculine energy to stand your ground and speak with courage. Draw on your feminine energy to be compassionate to the others that may not agree with you. And then you can remain balanced and true to yourself. And that is something that no one can take away from you." "Thank you, Gabriel. I think that is one of the most important lessons I have learned yet. Your kindness and wisdom is very much appreciated." "You are so welcome Cleo. That brings me a lot of joy. Remember your power, Cleo. We are all here for you always, in every moment. You only need to ask for our help and we will be there."

Then Gabriel closed her eyes. In a few minutes, the moon became larger and more brilliant. "You'll need to see down the path to your next stop," said Gabriel. "And I need to return to the earth! Love and blessings to you both and enjoy your adventure, Cleo!" Gabriel turned and jumped back into her mound, a little tuft of air and dirt rose as she descended back to her home. And then Cleo and Bacchus heard a faint whistle. And they both chuckled.

HANIEL THE HAWK

B acchus and Cleo turned to find a new path laid out before them. In the glow of the moon, it was easy to see which way to proceed. The two looked very different in the moonlight. Bacchus had a glow around him that was radiating from his black fur, and it seemed like he was absorbing the moonlight and then shining it back out to the world. Cleo's complexion took on a deeper shade of bronze and her hair took a similar glow as Bacchus'. They walked for only a short time. The landscape quickly became filled with trees and there was a distinct line between the meadow where Gabriel was, and the woods they were about to enter. In the moonlight, the trees took on an almost ethereal feel. Most of them were tall and skinny, lots of evergreen trees with a few oak and sweet gum mixed in. There was a night symphony playing that included insects, frogs and crickets and an occasional hoot from the nearby owl. Once Bacchus was well into this forest, he stopped. He was completely still, not a muscle twitching. Cleo followed his lead. Then they heard it. It was a screaming, loud cry that sounded like "kree-eeee-ay." It came three times before the hawk flew down and landed on a low branch in one of the sweet gum trees. In the moonlight, it was hard to see it clearly. Bacchus looked up and said, "Hello Haniel. I can barely see you in the moonlight!" "Yes," she screeched. "I love the power and pull of the moon. It really helps me restore my intuition. But I, too, need the sun and daylight. Please bear with me for a moment." Haniel launched from the tree limb back into the night sky. She became a vision in form. Her wings spread out to an amazing width, and the colors of her white and brown feathers merged together to become a gorgeous picture. She flapped her wings only twice before she became airborne. And then it was completely silent as she glided up into the heavens. She disappeared for a while. Then the sky began to grow brighter. Bacchus and Cleo looked up to see Haniel clutching the sun in her claws and dragging it across the sky. When it was just in the right place, she released it and traveled back down to the earth. "That's going to sting for a while!" she said, hopping up and down to cool off her feet. "It's a cool thing to be able to do, but look what it does to our feet! They are always yellow, like the sun!"

Haniel flew down to a lower branch so that she could see Bacchus and Cleo more clearly. And now they could see her as well. Her coloring was exquisite! Her feathers were a myriad of white and brown, interwoven to form a tapestry of a regal coat. Her beak was sharp and curved and her eyes were almost transparent. And she had huge claws at the base of those yellow feet. "Bacchus, it is my honor to see you again. You are looking very well," said Haniel. "The honor is all mine," said Bacchus. "And thank you for bringing us the sun." Cleo just stood there, stunned. "Cleo, it is my honor to meet you as well," continued Haniel. "I have been looking forward to this for some time." Cleo tried to regain her composure as she greeted Haniel.

Haniel nodded back to Cleo and said, "I am so pleased to know that you have been learning about your intuition! Trusting your inner guidance is a skill worth developing. It will serve you well, as I know it already has today. If you will allow me, I would like to show you a different perspective of that." "That sounds great. I am curious to learn all that I can," said Cleo. "Then it will be my honor," said Haniel. "Look around you now. Where you are. What do you see?" she asked. "I see trees of all kinds, leaves and small plants on the ground. And a lot of those sweet gum balls!" said Cleo. "Yes, that is what you can see from your perspective," said Haniel. "Now, will you close your eyes for me?" Cleo closed her eyes. "I will take you on a flight so that you can see it from a much broader perspective. Will you allow me to be your eyes?" Cleo nodded in agreement. "OK, here we go!"

As Haniel launched from her tree, Cleo could see the world through Haniel's eyes. Haniel flew through the trees, sometimes barely missing a branch, and Cleo felt as though she was flying with Haniel.

It was exhilarating! She held her breath as Haniel soared up into the sky. The flight was so smooth, Cleo felt like she was floating. As Haniel looked down, Cleo could see for miles. She saw the woods become a green form of treetops. She could not see the trunks any longer, just the green tops. Then she saw the separation of the woods and the meadow where Gabriel and the other gophers lived. She could see distinctly, the mounds of the gophers. And she could see the gophers that were out of their holes. She saw the stream that they could not cross without the help of the trees. The color was a rich, deep blue at its deepest point. Now she could see the depths of the water and how it changed. The stream was so long, she could not see the end of it. As they circled back, she could see Bacchus on the ground! And even at their height, she could see him quite clearly.

Haniel then took a turn and rose even higher in the sky. As she ascended, Cleo now saw yet another view of the landscape. As Haniel reached 100 feet, the world became even smaller. Cleo felt like she was looking down from a 10-story building. From this height, the trees looked like bushes, the stream looked like a trickle of water and Cleo could no longer see the details of the animals on the ground. She almost had to catch herself, because it felt so real, being that high up.

Haniel flew back down through the trees to her original branch and lightly touched down. When Cleo could see they were back where they started, she opened her eyes. "WOW!" she screamed. "That was the most amazing thing ever!"

Haniel nodded in agreement. As Cleo regained her balance, she laughed. Haniel smiled. "Cleo," said Haniel, "did you know, that is the height I fly when I am hunting prey. I make large circles in the sky, looking for my next meal. My eyesight is about eight times better than yours, and when I see my catch, I dive down at 120 miles per hour! I even have a third eyelid that I can use to protect my eyes when I am diving. It's fascinating how we both have a third eye, isn't it Cleo?" Haniel laughed and Bacchus joined in as well.

Haniel continued, "Do you see what I mean when I say different perspective? What looked like such a small space to you from here is actually vast. And it only takes a different perspective to see that. And when you look at things from a different perspective, it is easier to let go of the small stuff that doesn't really matter. All of the prickly details that no one really cares about. What is it they say in your world, don't sweat the small stuff. That's when you can really feel the joy. And Cleo, there is nothing better than joy. You are ready to fly higher than you ever have before. And I hope you can remember our flight as you continue your adventure." "I don't think I could ever forget that!" Cleo said.

Haniel said, "Do you remember when El Morya was talking about your higher self? Well, now you can imagine what your higher self sees when it is looking at you. It doesn't see the small space that you all live in most of the time. It sees the broader view of your whole life. It sees your potential. It sees you as a part of a vast larger whole. And that's how it can help you navigate through things that you can't see from your perspective. So, when El Morya said to release things to your higher self and allow it to guide you, now you can see what he meant. And that circles back to the intuition we were talking about earlier. See how you can trust your intuition to help guide you, because it is coming from the higher self, the higher perspective. Your intuition knows things that your physical senses don't know and will never be able to know."

"Yes, I can definitely see that now," said Cleo. "It is much clearer. But I still don't really understand it." Haniel said, "There are some things your mind will never understand. Because it is controlled by your ego, and your ego doesn't want you to experience things like the higher self. That can only come from a feeling, a knowing. Trust your inner senses and your heart, and you will understand, from a different perspective. From a higher perspective. And then you will begin to understand your soul purpose."

Cleo smiled and said, "Sometimes I wish I knew what my soul purpose was. It just seems that I keep doing the same thing over and over again every day. I mean, I like my job and all, but sometimes it just feels like it's not enough. And I certainly can't say that I have joy every day in doing what I do." Haniel said, "Your search is just beginning. Trust Bacchus to help guide you. Think of him as your higher self. He can also see things from a higher perspective, and I think he still has a lot to teach you."

Bacchus looked over to Haniel and a very subtle smile rose on his face. "Thank you, Haniel, for taking Cleo on her flight adventure. I am sure she will remember that always. And thank you for your words of wisdom. What you have shared with Cleo is of vital importance." "You are both most welcome," said Haniel. "Remember Cleo, we are all here for you always, in every moment. You only need to ask for our help and we will be there." Haniel then looked back to the sky and took flight. In only an instant, she looked like a small black spec in the sky. She cried 'kree-eeee-ay' three more times, and then she was gone.

Cleo looked back at Bacchus and said, "So, Bacchus. Can you show me my soul purpose? I would really love to know what it is." "Patience, Cleo. We have much more yet to learn." Then he turned toward the path that was opening up before them and began the journey to the next destination.

ISRAFEL THE IGUANA

B acchus and Cleo walked to the edge of the forest. As they emerged, they entered into a lush tropical rainforest. The temperature rose dramatically as they entered into this hot, moist place. It was vibrant with all shades of green and there was a light rain falling. The tree canopy was amazing. It was thick with giant trees whose canopies were so large that they mostly blocked out the sun. There were thick, long vines that hung from almost every tree. Under the large trees was an endless variety of vines, ferns, small trees, and palms. They walked across earth that was covered in wet leaves and decaying material. It had a pungent smell of earthy, moist soil that hung in the air. But instead of smelling like decay, it actually smelled of new life. The flowers spread through the ferns and palms and with the background of green, their colors popped everywhere. There was yellow, purple, pink, orange, and red. And they were all so unique in shape and size. The sound saturated the rainforest with a cacophony of insects, frogs, birds, and rain. And even though the place was heavy with sound, it was a soothing rhythm of life. It reminded Cleo of her trip to Central America years ago.

Bacchus took a deep breath to soak in the magnificence of this beautiful place. The path then emerged through the thick green foliage to beckon them on. Cleo and Bacchus followed the path as it wound through the rainforest. After a few minutes, Bacchus stopped. Cleo stopped as well. There was a weird, glowing light in the trees above them. Cleo could not imagine what this was! They remained still as the light began to move. It worked its way down through the trees and on to the rainforest floor. It was like a glowing orb, floating to earth. Then the light faded enough for them to see what was in this glowing ball. It was an iguana! It was over seven feet long and almost as large as Bacchus himself. He was a fabulous blend of scales and colors, and his tail was as long as his body. His face had a long snout, razor-sharp teeth, and a big red tongue. There were bumps and scales all over his face and his jaw expanded into something much larger below. He had a huge flap of skin under his chin that dragged the ground. It was green at the base of his neck and then morphed into a yellowish gold. He had scales along his spine that stood straight up and formed a point at the end of each one. His legs were chubby and covered in green-orange scales and his toes were long and distinct, with large claws at the end of each one. Cleo thought, you could not make up anything like this in your wildest imagination!

Bacchus laughed at Cleo's silent commentary and then greeted the iguana. "My, my, Israfel! I don't think I have ever seen you quite so vibrant as today! The glow was a nice touch," laughed Bacchus. Israfel laughed a hearty laugh and said, "Well, Bacchus, you just have to own it! What good is it to have such a crazy body and not show it off!" They all laughed at Israfel's comment. "And you must be Cleo," he said. "Yes, this is me," said Cleo. "What a pleasure to meet you Israfel!" "Oh, Cleo," said Israfel. "It's not a pleasure, it is pure joy! And today, we are going to choose joy."

Israfel slowly climbed up on a grouping of rocks. For such a large reptile, he moved with grace and ease. He looked Cleo straight in the eyes and said, "What is your joy, Cleo? What makes you smile so big you can't contain yourself?" "I really love singing and dancing," said Cleo. "My favorite songs always get me going!" "Yes!" said Israfel. "Music is so important. And do you know why? It's because music has a frequency that resonates with us. It aligns to our energy centers and amplifies them." Israfel looked up and turned his head slightly. As he nodded, music started playing, out of nowhere. This wasn't the music of the rainforest that they heard earlier. It was upbeat, lively and had a strong base line underneath. It permeated the rainforest as it grew louder. "Now that's what I'm talking about!" said Israfel. Cleo felt a lift in her spirit, and she could not help but start tapping her feet. Israfel was bobbing his head and then let loose into a dance. His body was swerving back and forth, and his tail was thumping the rocks, loudly. He had a huge grin on his face and the flap under his chin was swaying side to side. He looked outrageous! Cleo laughed from deep in her belly and started dancing as well. She could not have stopped herself if she wanted, and she didn't want to. Her arms were spread wide and moving in all directions. Her hips were swaying to the beat, and she started moving her feet to match the rhythm. She was humming to the song, even though she didn't really know this tune at all. It just all came so naturally. Bacchus started laughing at both of them. "If that's not the picture of joy, I don't know what is!" he said.

As the music faded, Israfel and Cleo laughed, feeling a wonderful sense of joy. "I love that!" shouted Cleo. "Me too," said Israfel. "What a way to start the day!" Then Israfel climbed down from the rocks and stood next to Cleo. "Cleo, can I please ask you to scratch me right behind the ears?" Cleo laughed again and said, "Sure." She reached over to give him a scratch. As she did, a big layer of skin fell away from Israfel's body. "OH!" shouted Cleo. "I'm so sorry! Did I do that?" Israfel let out a wonderful sigh and said, "Yes! Thank you! That's been itching for some time, and I could never get to it! I didn't mean to alarm you, Cleo. That's just me shedding another layer of skin. Don't worry, it doesn't hurt. Without shedding that skin, I can't grow. It feels so nice to release that old skin, you have no idea. Would you mind, again?" And Israfel lowered his head so that Cleo could scratch the top of his back. More skin peeled away. "Ah, that's magnificent!" sighed Israfel. "Cleo, *you* don't have outside skin that needs to shed. Your wonderful body knows how to shed skin all of the time, so it happens gradually. But you do have inside skin that needs to shed and your body won't naturally do that. That has to come from you. And like you helped me shed my outer skin, I am happy to help you shed your inner skin." Cleo was on such a high from the music and dancing that she heartily agreed.

"Nice!" said Israfel. "You were so gracious to share what brings you joy. I could see that in your eyes as you were dancing. It was quite wonderful. Would you also share with me what makes you anxious and unhappy?" Cleo began to feel the joy melt away into something less pleasant. "Ugh. I was having so much fun! And now I have to think about the other stuff?" she asked. "Well," said Israfel, "you don't have to lose your joy when you are thinking about shedding your inner skin. Look at me! I love to get rid of the old stuff. It's itchy and uncomfortable. But I still have joy as I am shedding the old layer. You can do that too. In fact, it's really better when you can do that. You can always opt for joy in any moment. It is a choice." "I'm not sure I see that," said Cleo. "How can I feel joy when I am feeling anxious?" "Just remember the audience, Cleo," said Israfel. "You can see yourself feeling anxious, but you don't have to dive down into the abyss. You can notice the feeling from outside. Then you can have joy in knowing that the feeling is actually serving to help you grow. And there is always joy in growth. It's like understanding that there is a time for responsibility and there is a time to relax and play. Both of them are very important. And so it is with your feelings. There is a time to work through feelings that you don't need any longer and a time to be happy about the journey."

"OK, I can understand that," said Cleo. "I guess I'm anxious and unhappy most when I look in the mirror. This ugly, stupid scar is always there, and I know people stare and think how gross my face is." "Yes, I can feel that in you," said Israfel. "And you have mentioned this already on your journey. Now, can you take a step back and look at you, thinking about that scar, from the audience? You can acknowledge where you feel that feeling in your body but try and broaden your perspective. Remember what Haniel showed you." Cleo closed her eyes and remembered the flight she took with Haniel. "Now," said Israfel, "can you notice why Cleo is feeling ugly? Take a flight up and review from the higher perspective." Cleo thought about this. She began to remember comments that some of her classmates said after the accident. Things like, 'Oh Cleo. I'm so sorry that happened to your face! You must be devastated.' And comments like 'Are you going to have plastic surgery to fix that?'. But then she also began to remember the other comments from her close friends. Comments like, 'Cleo, you have been through so much and I feel for what you are going through. If I can help you, please let me know.' And she also remembered that they didn't say anything about the wound on her head. In fact, they didn't even seem to see it. They were only looking into her eyes. And as she remembered those comments, she felt like she shed a layer of skin. Bacchus smiled.

"You see Cleo," said Israfel, "everyone has their own journey to experience. And sometimes that negativity can seem like it is directed *at* you. You can blame others for not being kind. But they are really your mirror. And you drew them to you so that you could experience different feelings. So you could see things from a different perspective. And as you see the things you don't like, you can choose something else. It's not really the scar at all. It is how you feel about what the others said. And remember what Chamuel said about honoring your emotions and how some of them get trapped in your body when you don't acknowledge them? Well, perhaps, when you look in the mirror and see that scar, your body is triggering you to remember those feelings of rejection, and that can cause you to feel less love for yourself. But now that you are just in the audience seeing Cleo feel those things, you can choose to release them, and you can choose something else. Your inner beauty shines through to your outer beauty. And Cleo, you have both."

Cleo thought for a moment. She did see herself from a higher perspective. She did see herself absorbing those negative comments. She felt those emotions. And she was making the decision to choose something different. And a little bit of that joy returned.

Israfel continued, "I can also be your mirror, Cleo. I mean, look at me. If *I* had scars, which I do, you couldn't see them through this glorious body of mine! I may look crazy ugly to some people, but really, I am the most beautiful thing I could ever think of. And the greatest part of this wonderful adventure is that it doesn't really matter to me what others think. It only matters what *I* think because this is my reality and my world. And nothing brings me more joy than **me**!"

Cleo couldn't help but laugh.

"So, sing your songs, dance like there is no one looking, and enjoy every precious moment of this outrageous adventure! It is all meant to be fun, after all, so don't take things too seriously. Keep your focus on what you love. That is the key to joy. And remember Cleo, we are all here for you always, in every moment. You only need to ask for our help and we will be there."

Israfel turned to Bacchus and with a big smile he said, "Keep it real, Bacchus!" Then he climbed up the tree and was again immersed in the golden glow.

Cleo looked over at Bacchus and said, "That was really funny. He is quite a unique character." Bacchus laughed in agreement. Then he said, "Cleo, tell me how this compares to the rainforest that you visited in Central America. The trip you were thinking about earlier." "Oh! It looks a lot like that place. That trip was so cool. Except the travel was awful! We had to fly there, of course, and had to make a connection at the airport. It was horrible! The plane was late, so we missed the connection. We had to wait for hours in the airport with NOTHING to do but stare at the walls. Then the flight down was crowded, and air turbulence was so bad that people started getting really scared and upset. It was all pretty miserable." "Hmmm," said Bacchus. "Cleo, can you take a step back again, and this time look at what you just told me about your trip." "What?" said Cleo. "I just told you how horrible the traveling was to get there." Bacchus nodded. "And yet," he said, "the trip itself was really grand, right?" "Oh yes," said Cleo. "It was one of the most amazing places I have ever been!" Bacchus nodded again and said, "So can you explain why the part of the trip you spoke about most was the most unpleasant part?" "Oh, wow," said Cleo. "Did I really just do that! I did, didn't I? Why would I do that?! It was the most beautiful place ever and I didn't say one thing about how great it was. I just complained about how bad the traveling was. What's wrong with me?" Bacchus smiled and said, "That's mostly centuries of human conditioning. You humans seem to always remember the bad stuff over the good stuff. I bet you see that when you talk to your brother or your friends." Cleo nodded. "It's OK. Don't feel badly about it. Try not to judge yourself or your friends. When people are not in a good place mentally, they like to complain. It's the energy around them and inside of them. And that energy draws the same energy from other people. So when one complains, usually the others complain as well. It's the frequency they are in. And you can guess that it is not the same frequency of joy." "Yes, I can definitely see that," said Cleo. Bacchus continued, "it is so important to stay conscious of what you are thinking and saying Cleo. It's so easy to get caught up in what everyone else is doing and saying, that you forget you have a choice. Remember what Israfel said. Joy is a choice you can make at any time. Just think about it Cleo. No judgment, just observe. And when you see yourself doing something that may not be for your highest good, shift your frequency to something you like better."

JEREMIEL THE JAGUAR

Bacchus stopped speaking and just stood totally still for a moment. Then he looked at Cleo and said, "Cleo, I need to leave you for just a few minutes. I won't be long. Remember that you are completely safe. Are you OK if I leave for just a moment?" "Is something wrong?" asked Cleo. "Oh no," said Bacchus. "In fact, I think you will really like what's coming." Cleo nodded and said, "OK, that's fine." With that, Bacchus nodded quickly and then sprang forward through the rainforest. Cleo had never seen him run before. He was so graceful and fast. He disappeared in an instant. When he was out of sight, Cleo thought about this crazy thing she was doing and started to worry again about missing the important stuff at work. But before she could get too caught up in the worry, a large path began to open through the rainforest. It was as if a bulldozer had come in and cleared everything away. She stopped breathing for a minute and just watched the path unfold. Then, in the distance, she saw two shapes, moving at lightning speed, coming her way. She stood totally still, in utter amazement. As the shapes got closer, she began to make out two figures running beside each other. One was black and she could tell that must be Bacchus. The other was a little larger and was a pale yellow, tan color. Then she could see Bacchus more clearly, running beside a jaguar. They must have been coming towards her at over 50 miles an hour. It was awe inspiring the way they moved! The jaguar was ahead of Bacchus, but only by a small amount. As they reached Cleo, they stopped dead still. Both of them were panting hard but laughing as well. If they were racing, the jaguar clearly won.

After taking a few minutes to breathe and calm down, they both laughed a hearty laugh. Cleo started laughing just looking at them. Bacchus took a final deep breath and then said, "Cleo, this is Jeremiel." Jeremiel was grinning ear to ear. "Hello Cleo!" he exclaimed. "What on earth are you two doing?!" asked Cleo. Bacchus explained. "Well, Jeremiel is a very good friend, and a little competitive. So, when we are able to see each other, we have to see whether he is still faster than I am. And it seems he still is. He is like a brother to me even though he is a jaguar, and I am a panther. But I can still climb trees faster than he can!" laughed Bacchus.

They were so similar, Cleo smiled at them both. Jeremiel was larger than Bacchus and his body was stockier. Bacchus was very muscular but slender. Jeremiel had a broader forehead, and his jaw was wider. His legs were also stockier than Bacchus. His color was tan and yellow except for his chest, which was white. And he had black spots all over his body. "So, Jeremiel," asked Cleo, "do you win every time you and Bacchus race?" "Oh yes," said Jeremiel. "But we have so much fun with it. And it's good to get the blood pumping. He is a good inspiration and helps me push myself to be better; both physically and mentally. But I do try and show him a little mercy. If you set your intention and focus on what you really want, you can stay with it until it's done. And I love to focus on winning, with a good heart." Cleo said, "Oh I dated a guy once that was super competitive. But I don't think he really had a good heart. We fought a lot and he always had to be right. It got so bad, that I started hating him for acting so stupid all the time."

Jeremiel said, "That's interesting Cleo. Can you tell me more about it?" Cleo sighed. "Well, it started out nice, I guess. It was fun to have someone that would push me and challenge me. We did sports and stuff together, but he would always have to win in the end. So I guess I started resenting him for that. It seemed like it was more important for him to win than to just have fun." "And did you tell him how you felt about that Cleo?" asked Jeremiel. "No, I suppose I didn't," she answered. "I would just get mad. And then he started judging everything I did. He'd say it was wrong or it wasn't good enough or I was stupid. And then he would tell me how I should have done it, how he would have done it." Jeremiel smiled at Cleo and said, "Cleo, you have explained the relationship quite well and I have a good picture of what went on between the two of you. Thank you for that. Now, can you begin to see those same scenes from the audience? Remember that you can still feel the emotions, but you don't have to be dragged into them again. Look at yourself in those scenes. Tell me what you see." Cleo closed her eyes and watched herself as she reviewed those experiences. "Wow," she said. "I really wasn't being kind to myself at all, was I? I wasn't wrong all the time, but I just let him talk to me like that. I'm mad that I let him do that to me!" Jeremiel nodded. "But now you know about speaking your truth, like Gabriel taught you. You can tell someone how you feel in a kind and compassionate way. But remember, it is up to them to take or leave what you say. And it's OK either way. All relationships are really mirrors for you. And it's good to ask what you are learning from your relationships. And clearly you learned a lot from that one." "Yes," said Cleo. "Just not soon enough!"

Jeremiel continued. "I would offer, Cleo, that you are learning it now. And the timing is perfect. Because now you have the tools to see it and understand it for what it is. And now may I offer something else for you to think about." "Certainly," said Cleo. "Thank you," said Jeremiel. "Let's talk about forgiveness. It is a powerful act and can be very liberating. It only takes an intention to forgive someone else for something you feel they did to you, to start the process. Forgiveness is about letting go of fear and anger and choosing love instead. And that opens your heart. Gabriel talked about this as well in a different way. Remember when she said that everyone is on their own journey as well. Did you fully understand what she meant?" Cleo shrugged and said, "I think I understand. Like we are all living our lives as best we can." Jeremiel nodded and said, "Yes that's true. And there is a bit more to it. Everyone is creating their own reality in every second. And they are doing that by what they are thinking, what their beliefs are and where they place their focus. You've talked about this with some of the others on your journey today. You see, they are all souls that have incarnated into human bodies on the earth to discover and expand. Just like you. Your soul is energy, and it can never be destroyed. It can only take different forms. And most of the souls that are now incarnate on the earth have been through earth before in other forms and other bodies, in other lifetimes. It is an opportunity for a soul to feel emotions and experience them as they move to change their consciousness. Most people don't know this or believe this because they have not shifted to a different frequency. They are still living in a 3rd dimension reality. And that's fine. Each person has the choice of free will and that is a Universal law that can never be broken. So like you have seen, they are all actors playing a role on the stage of life in their incarnation. And their purpose was defined and agreed to before they actually incarnated into this life. They may not remember that, and they don't have to, but they decided their soul purpose. And they are all powerful. Because they are divine. They are literally an extension of All That Is. And All That Is is divine. It only creates from unconditional love. It can be no other way. So, everyone is actually as divine and as powerful as All That Is. And when you look at others in that way, you can see a different perspective of their behavior. They are learning lessons, just like you. And they act the way they are so that they can learn those lessons and explore those emotions. It is not wrong or right. It just is. It is consciousness expanding. When you can see others in that light, it is easier to understand and forgive them, because they are not doing anything *to you*. You are in total control of your reality. And they are in total control of theirs."

Cleo looked at Jeremiel. She was trying to process everything he just said. And it was a lot to process! Then she said, "Well I didn't understand all of that. But I'm trying to." Jeremiel smiled and said, "Yes, I know it's a lot to digest. And I recommend that you don't try and understand all of it with your mind. Not just yet. Feel it in your heart first. When you feel that unconditional love fully, then you can better process it with your mind. It's really about being in the present moment. That's what is real. And it is changing every second. Just imagine that the past doesn't exist. All there is, is the present. You are not bound by what you think happened in the past. You are free to choose whatever you want right now, in this new moment. And when you forgive others in that light, you free yourself from judgment of them and you regain your own power. But more importantly, Cleo, you can also forgive yourself. And that is the other key to your power. You humans are so hard on yourself for the past choices you have made. But when you can see those as opportunities for learning and healing instead of judging yourself for doing something you think is wrong, you can walk back to love. Love for yourself. Because you are divine, you are perfect. All That Is does not make mistakes. So see yourself as the divine being that you are. And know that everything has happened at the perfect time with the perfect people. They are your mirrors. Remember that everyone is your mirror. They could be there for different reasons, but they are your mirror. They are there because you needed them to be there for your adventure. Think about what you learned from your boyfriend. Look at it from the audience and see if you can tell me why you think he was a mirror for you."

Cleo thought for a minute. Then she said, "Well, he was very competitive and sometimes very harsh. If I am honest with myself, I have those qualities too. Like at work, I can be really driven to get things done and I compare my work with the people that I work with. I can see how I judge them for not doing the things I think they should. I can see how I think I am doing more work and better work than them. And I can be harsh when they don't complete things when they should. Wow, that's really eye opening." Jeremiel said, "That is very honest and insightful Cleo. Now you see things from that higher perspective – from the perspective that Haniel showed you. And you can choose to be different with them and with yourself. Humans have been conditioned into a consciousness of competition, lack and fear. It is a global consciousness that has been around for thousands of years. So be compassionate with them and with yourself. It will take some time to change that consciousness.

But each time you choose love over fear, you change that frequency. And you show others that there is another choice they can make as well. And just by being who you are and choosing love, they can see that fear and lack doesn't have to be the only answer. Then they can use their free will to choose it or not. But it is not for you to judge that or try and convince them. They are learning and growing in their own reality, and they have that choice. Always. Just as you do."

Cleo smiled and said, "I really do like the way that feels. And I can see how looking at things from that perspective makes forgiving people a lot easier." "And forgiving yourself," said Jeremiel. "Yes, and forgiving myself," said Cleo. "Good," said Jeremiel. "One last thing to consider Cleo. When you can see why people do the things they do, and why you do the things you do, you can begin to see that there is no need for blame. Everyone is doing their best to fulfill their soul contract. And when there is no blame, there is no need for forgiveness." "Yes, I can totally see that!" Cleo exclaimed.

Bacchus was watching Cleo through this exchange with Jeremiel. He smiled to himself. This was a powerful lesson and one that she will need to go to her heart and process. I think I know the perfect next step, he thought.

Then Bacchus said, "Jeremiel, that was powerful. You are indeed the transformer you claim to be. We are honored that you have shared this wisdom with Cleo. You are my brother and I thank you for your enlightenment. Until we meet again, I wish you strength and speed." Jeremiel smiled back at Bacchus and lowered his head in a bow. He said, "Bacchus, thank you for letting me be part of the journey." Then Jeremiel turned back to Cleo. "Cleo, we are all here for you always, in every moment. You only need to ask for our help and we will be there." "Thank you, Jeremiel," said Cleo. Jeremiel then turned back to the path and sauntered off, looking back one last time with a smile, before he was gone.

KALANI THE KOALA

Bacchus turned to Cleo and said, "Cleo, that was quite a lesson. I think we need a bit of a break after that. And I know the perfect place. Shall we move on?" Cleo nodded. "Yes, it certainly was an intense lesson," she said. "I think I could use a break." Bacchus turned slowly and began to make his way down the path. Cleo followed. The rainforest began to change after a short time. They were still in woodlands, but the trees and the landscape here were very distinct. There were tall trees scattered throughout this woodland and they all had very distinctive leaves. They were long and slender and tapered to a point. They had a bluish-green hue and appeared to be very leathery. The bark was blue-grey and revealed yellow patches where some of the bark had peeled away in strips. The trunks of these trees were bare at the base and the limbs spread out to form a wide canopy with lots of branches. And they were quite tall. The smell of this new woodlands was minty, with a touch of honey and citrus. Underneath the trees there were grasses and sparse shrubs. It was a very pleasant temperature, and the air was quite dry. As they moved forward into the woodlands, they heard loud snoring, up in one of the trees. Cleo looked up to see what it could be. When she saw it, she cast a big grin on her face. "It's a koala bear!" Cleo shouted. Bacchus laughed. Their voices woke the koala and she let out a short grunt. She opened her eyes and saw Bacchus and Cleo standing below. "Ah! Greetings my friends!" she said. "Give me a minute to come down."

The koala gripped the trunk of the tree with her mighty claws and began to descend, slowly. You could see the great strength in her arms and legs as she moved her way down the tree. When she reached the ground, she sat on her haunches and smiled. "I don't come down from the trees very often. What a different perspective!" Bacchus laughed. "We've been talking about perspective all day," he said. "Cleo, I would like you to meet Kalani." Cleo was so thrilled. "Hello Kalani. I have never met a koala bear before!" she said. Bacchus said, "Well, Cleo, koalas are not actually bears. They are marsupials."

"Oh, I'm so sorry!" said Cleo. "I meant no offense!" "Oh, that's quite all right" said Kalani. "We get that a lot. Not to worry though."

Kalani was the cutest animal yet! She had a round head with big fluffy ears on top. She had a great big black nose that was flat against her face. She had soft, brown eyes, and her fur was very thick and gray except for the white fur on her chest, arms, and ears. She was quite stout, and she didn't have a tail. Her hands were amazing. She had two thumbs and her fingers all had long razor-sharp claws at the end.

"Kalani, you are looking well," said Bacchus. "Yes, thank you," said Kalani. "The eucalyptus are especially good right now." Bacchus continued, "We've had quite a day already and I thought it would be nice to have some peaceful, relaxation time with you." "Oh Bacchus, that's great. You know there is nothing I love more than some relaxation," Kalani laughed. "Nothing better to restore your mental and emotional clarity I always say. Shall we sit for a while and chat?" she asked. "Thank you," said Cleo. "I would really like that."

They sat in a circle of three and began to take in the wonder and beauty of the woodlands. "Nature is such a peaceful place to be," said Kalani. "Cleo, I know how much you love and appreciate being in nature." "Yes, I really do," said Cleo. Kalani continued, "We koalas really love these woodlands. It's pretty quiet most of the time and if we aren't eating or sleeping, then we are meditating, becoming one with this nature. We like to think of time gone by and our ancestors. It brings us peace. Cleo, do you meditate?" asked Kalani. "No," said Cleo. "I am so busy all the time and I'm not sure I would know how to meditate even if I had time to do it." "Well," said Kalani, "there are many forms of meditation. In fact, when you take your walk in the woods at home, that is a form of meditation. Or if you are engaged in something you really love, like reading, gardening or listening to music, that is also different forms of meditation. So, you see, you do practice meditation after all!" Cleo said, "Wow, I had no idea I was meditating when I am doing those things. That's not what I always understood meditation to be. I thought meditation was what the monks do, sitting cross-legged and chanting and stuff."

Kalani continued, "What the monks do is also meditation. If you want, I can teach you this ancient practice. And it is indeed a *practice*." said Kalani. "You don't need to be intimidated by meditation. It's really quite easy to do and it doesn't have to take long. Although the more you do it, I think you will find that you want to stay there longer. It's the peace that it brings you that makes it something you want to do more and more of. Let me describe the steps to you and then we can practice, since you have all of the time in the world."

"First, find a comfortable seating position, like you are now. If you can sit up, it will help the energy flow better, but try not to be rigid. It's all about being relaxed and letting your body just be. Then close your eyes. Take three of the deepest breaths that you can. As you exhale, let your body just melt a little more each time. And as you breathe, set an intention of gratitude. Find something that you are grateful for and concentrate on that. Then put your hands to your heart and feel yourself going there. Put your focus on your heart chakra. And basically, that's it! See, not so hard."

"I didn't know it could be that simple," said Cleo. "If that's it, then why are there so many books and videos about how to meditate?" she asked. Kalani said, "What you will find with meditation, as in most things, is that there are many ways to do it, depending on your intention. And there are some really deep meditations that you can do for accessing your spirit guides, healing your body, or becoming more conscious. Let's just call those more advanced than what we want today, which is just a little peace and quiet. I want to show you that you can meditate any time, even for just a few minutes. It will bring you back to you, and it will help to center you if you are worried or anxious. You learned about the chakras, right? The energy centers in your body?" "Yes, I did! My rainbow inside of me," laughed Cleo. "Oh, that's good! I hadn't thought about the rainbow in a long time," said Kalani. "You can use your chakras as you meditate if you want something to concentrate on. You can feel the energy of Gaia rise through your base chakra up to the crown chakra, or you can visualize All That Is light energy coming into your crown chakra and flowing down to your base chakra. There is really no way to get it wrong. Just find what works for you and do that."

"OK," said Kalani. "Want to try it?" "Yes, I do," said Cleo.

"Close your eyes, Cleo," said Kalani. "Now, take a deep breath from your solar plexus up into your chest. Feel the rise of your body. Try to do that to the count of four. When you can't breathe in anymore, hold your breath for the count of seven, then exhale slowly to the count of eight. Feel your whole body just relax as you exhale. Maybe even wiggle around a little bit and feel your muscles let go." Cleo took a deep breath and held it like Kalani said. As she exhaled, she could feel her body start to relax. She did wiggle around a bit too. "Now," said Kalani, "do that again two more times." As Cleo exhaled her second breath, she noticed that her shoulders were still a little tense. By the third exhale, she felt like she was pretty relaxed. Kalani continued to guide her. "Find the gratitude Cleo. Something you are thankful for and something that makes you happy. Maybe a baby koala. And then put your hands to your heart and feel that feeling there." Cleo instantly thought of a baby koala and smiled. She put her hands to her heart and thought about the baby koala. It was really nice for a few seconds, then her mind started to wander, and she began to think about other things. Her job, her brother and her bills started to enter her consciousness. "Oh boy," said Cleo. "I can't seem to stop thinking about other things. All kinds of thoughts are going through my head."

"That's OK Cleo," said Kalani. "Just acknowledge those thoughts and ask them to move on. As you practice more, your conscious mind will begin to see that there is no fear or danger, and it will begin to let go more and more. You can use your teachings about being in the audience. Step away from your mind and just see yourself from outside, from the audience." Cleo did that. Since she had done that already today, it was easier for her to understand and do. And as she did that, the random thoughts weren't quite so loud. Cleo continued to meditate for a while. It was a new thing for sure to get comfortable with, but it did actually feel really good.

"OK, Cleo. Now let's try something else. From where you are now, start to notice your body. We will do a scan of your body to see if there are any places where you are still holding tension. Start with your feet. Concentrate on your feet and feel if there are any parts that are still constricted. If you find places that are tense, consciously release the tension. Now move to your ankles. Feel your ankles and any places where you may have tension. Now move to your calves. Again, if you feel any resistance, just relax into it. Notice, without judgment. Now feel your thighs. Feel for any tension and just relax it. If you begin to notice any emotions, just acknowledge them, without judgment. And remember your breath. Breathe through the relaxation. Now move to your base chakra and sacral chakra. You may find more emotions as you notice these areas as they are very powerful parts of your body. Let go and breathe. Now feel your heart, your chest, your back. If you are holding any restrictions, let them go. Feel your arms, your wrists and your hands. You can turn your hands over in an open position as a sign of receiving. Next, feel your shoulders and neck. This is where a lot of people hold most of their tension. If you feel any constrictions, release them and feel a deeper relaxation. Finally, move to your face. Are you tensing your lips, your cheeks or your brow. If so, just release the tension and let go. Once you have scanned your whole body, you should notice a deeper sense of calm and peace. Now, just breathe easily and notice any emotions or feelings you might be having. Let them come and send them love."

Kalani and Bacchus let Cleo just be there for a few minutes. They stayed very quiet. Then Kalani said, "OK, Cleo. I think you are getting the hang of meditation. It works best if you can set aside a few minutes at the same time every day and do what we just did. Your conscious mind will begin to get used to you going from your head to your heart and will stop sending you those random thoughts. Then as you practice more, you can reach out to your guides or be still and listen for messages. But for now, just being at peace is a lovely thing."

Cleo opened her eyes and felt so relaxed and peaceful. "Thank you, Kalani," she said. "And I can call on koala spirit when I need to remember what you have taught me?" she asked. "Of course, Cleo!" said Kalani. "We are all here for you always, in every moment. You only need to ask for our help and we will be there." They all stood up and Kalani turned to Bacchus. "Thank you, Bacchus, for coming and spending some peaceful time with me. It is always my joy to help bring peace and relaxation." Bacchus nodded. "And it was our pleasure." he said to Kalani. "Until our paths cross again, I wish you peace and lots of eucalyptus leaves." Kalani laughed and made her way back to her eucalyptus tree. She started her slow climb up and halfway there, she turned and looked down to Cleo and Bacchus for one last smile. Then she reached a crook in the tree and curled up for a lovely nap.

Bacchus turned to Cleo. "I hope you are feeling relaxed and refreshed now, Cleo." he said. She nodded in agreement and said, "Yes, Bacchus. This was really helpful. I do feel refreshed and ready to move on to our next destination." "Then let us proceed." said Bacchus.

LAKSHMI THE LION

Bacchus and Cleo headed out of the woodlands onto a new path. As they walked, Cleo asked, "Bacchus, Kalani mentioned that you can reach out to your guides during meditation. What did she mean by that?" Bacchus answered, "All humans have guides that help them along their journey. We talked about your higher self, remember, when we were with El Morya? Well, that is one of your guides. But you have many others. All of the animals that we have met have an animal spirit that can guide you. The animals we have met have already taught you how to invoke those guides by being still and listening. But there are so many others! There are ancestral guides. Those people that have lived before you, whether you are related to them or not. There are angel guides from the Angelic Realm, there are extra dimensional guides who reside in other parts of the galaxies, there are dragons and unicorns and you already met the fairies. All of them can be your guides. Most humans have a stronger connection to some than others and so you will resonate more with them, but they are all there and available to you when you ask. You can also consider me as your guide." Cleo was a little skeptical about all of this. She was willing to acknowledge the higher self and the animal spirit guides and even Bacchus and the fairies, but angels, aliens and unicorns were beyond what she was willing to concede. "OK Bacchus, you are getting into the woo woo territory again," Cleo laughed. Bacchus smiled. "Not to woo-woo worry Cleo. There is more than enough time to explore any of the guides you would like to meet." Cleo chuckled to herself.

Fewer and fewer trees lined the path as they continued walking. The temperature began to rise and it was getting quite hot. It felt dry and arid. The trees that began to emerge were covered in thorns. They were small with leathery looking leaves, but the leaves were interwoven with the thorns that ran up and down every branch. Some of the trees were taller with more clustered leaves but they also had thorns on the branches. These thorns were shorter and closer to the branch and were spread out further. There were grasses and scrub brush on the ground. As they came closer to the thorny trees, Cleo could see the most colorful birds perched in between the thorns. There were hundreds of them! Cleo asked Bacchus what they were. Bacchus said, "Those are Fischer's lovebirds." They were the most beautiful birds that Cleo could remember seeing. Even though they were only about 6 inches tall, they made up for their small stature with an array of the most vibrant colors! Their beaks were scarlet red and the feathers on their head went from red around their beak to a tangerine-colored face that was laced with yellow hues. They had a bright white ring around each eye. Their chest feathers were yellow while their body feathers were bright green and their wings were a deep jade. The birds were making quite the noise! Their calls were high-pitched and twittering and they seemed to be endlessly calling back and forth to each other. Bacchus laughed. "They can be quite loud and bold for such a small bird. Seems they have quite the courage." Cleo laughed and agreed. They were loud but strikingly beautiful.

As they continued into the thorn forest, they eventually came upon an opening with fewer trees and more scrubby grass. As they entered the clearing, Bacchus stopped. Cleo followed his lead. They stood in the open clearing for a few minutes and Cleo could sense something was coming. Bacchus smiled. She is using her intuition, he thought. That's a good sign.

Then from the thorn forest, they saw a female lion approach them. She was regal and graceful and seemed to glide along the path. Behind her were four lion cubs. They were darting in and out of the path and even though they stayed close together, they would wander here and there through the scrub brush. The cubs were laughing and jumping and talking to each other. When they saw Bacchus and Cleo though, they stopped instantly. The mother lion looked back at them and smiled. She turned to Bacchus and in a soft sweet growl said, "Bacchus, I am so pleased you both got here.

I hope you don't mind but I need to keep my cubs close." Bacchus nodded in acknowledgement and said, "Hello Lakshmi. I completely understand. We are happy to see the new additions to the pride. Cleo, this is Lakshmi." Cleo smiled at seeing the lion and her cubs and said, "Hello Lakshmi. It is so nice to meet you. Your cubs are so sweet and cute." Lakshmi laughed. "Thank you, Cleo. It is my honor to meet you. Yes, the cubs are wonderful if not a handful sometimes. But I am grateful to be able to raise them. I feel I have great fortune to have four and to be able to protect them and nourish them. Sometimes it can be a dangerous place." Lakshmi turned back to the cubs and told them to settle down and rest while she spoke to Bacchus and Cleo. The cubs all laid down together and seemed content to rest for a while. Lakshmi turned back to Cleo. "Cleo," she said. "I hope that if it is your choice to raise a family one day, that you will be blessed with all of the children that you want." Cleo smiled and said, "I'm not sure if I will even get married, much less raise a family. But thank you for your kind words." Lakshmi nodded and continued.

"Cleo, you have already been through some great adventures today. I can sense your auric field getting stronger. You are learning to follow your heart and that is a great thing in and of itself. As you have more adventures today, you will no doubt learn even more lessons, some perhaps more difficult than others. How do you feel so far?" Cleo thought for a minute. Then she said, "Yes, some of the lessons have already been difficult, but all of it has been fabulous. Bacchus is a great guide and all of the animals have taught me so much. I don't understand everything, but I do feel different." Bacchus smiled. Lakshmi said," Yes, you are changing every second. Your cocoon is now open and you are finding your butterfly wings. I want you to know that what you are undertaking takes courage and determination. The lion spirit can always support you when you need to draw on your courage. In fact, I think you have needed to do that several times already today, before your journey started. Like this morning when you almost had your car accident or in the office when you found out about the changes to your business. Those types of events in your life require your courage as well as your compassion. Do you feel like you had the courage you needed to address those events?" Cleo could feel her peace from the meditation session with Kalani begin dissolving away. The images of the morning events played through her head at lightning speed and she surrendered to Lakshmi that perhaps she didn't have all of the courage that she needed. Lakshmi said, "Thank you for being honest with me and with yourself. That is a lesson that a lot of humans have not yet learned. So, you should be proud of yourself for acknowledging that. Would you be willing to talk with me about how you felt when you found out the business that you manage is being sold?" "Yes, of course," said Cleo. "Good," replied Lakshmi. "What are you feeling about the situation?"

"Well," said Cleo. "It makes me very uncomfortable to have so much responsibility placed on me to deliver everything in such a short timeframe." "I'm sure it does." said Lakshmi. "But is that what brings you fear?" "No, I guess not," said Cleo. "I am more afraid that I will lose my job. It happens a lot in my world you know. New owners come in and don't recognize what people can do and they think they can do it better with their people. Or they are trying to control costs for the new company and end up firing people to save money." "And why does that make you afraid Cleo?" asked Lakshmi. "Because," said Cleo, "I can barely afford things now. If I lose my job, I don't know what I would do or how I would support myself. And my brother is depending on me for money and schooling as well. I haven't been able to save much money so I don't really have much to fall back on." "I understand," said Lakshmi. "I'm sure it can be an uncomfortable place to be. Let's step out for a minute and look at that from the audience. You know how to do that, right Cleo?" "Oh yes. I've done that several times today." "Good," said Lakshmi. "Now can you see that from a higher perspective. Can you see that if you look at that from fear, you will be sending out the fear frequency to the world around you and that is what will come back to you. You will see fear in your mirror so that's what will be returned to you. You see, the Universe, All That Is, wants to give you what you are inside. It's that Universal law that cannot be changed. Now, see yourself on the stage, from your audience seat, as something different. Can you see yourself as the successful manager that you know you are. Can you see yourself as successful, regardless of what happens with your business? Can you see yourself as abundant?" Cleo thought for a moment and her stomach started getting tighter. "I have to admit," said Cleo, "that's a picture I can't really see."

"I understand," said Lakshmi. "Let's look back a bit, shall we? Were you feeling the same way before you got the job you have now?" "Yes." said Cleo. "I knew I had to find something that would support me and also have enough to help my brother. I was really lucky to find the job I got." Lakshmi smiled. "I would offer Cleo, that perhaps luck had nothing to do with it. You had an intention and you made that intention a reality. And you did that even before you knew what you know now. Realize how much more strength you have to draw on. You understand the Universal laws. What you put out is what you get back. So, you can change the fear and choose to release that. Use your courage and knowledge to replace the fear with your intention of a new job, of more prosperity, of more abundance. And do that from your heart space. Feel how good it feels to get that new job, have money in your bank account. If you can't feel good about that, then find something you do feel good about and think about that as you set your intention. The emotion is the important part. The emotion generates the frequency. The frequency changes the energy. Then the energy transforms into what you intend into your reality. Remember, you are creating all of the time, whether you are doing it consciously or unconsciously, so isn't it better to bring your courage and see yourself as you want to be, instead of being a victim to fear. Fear is not real. It is your subconscious mind trying to protect you. So, you can see that for what it is and move past it. Remember your power, Cleo. You are stronger than you think. You are a part of Universal love and consciousness, so your power is greater than you can even imagine right now. Hold the vision of what you want, not what you are afraid of. Feel the emotion behind what you want. That is the key."

Cleo thought about what Lakshmi said. She understood more about seeing what you want and feeling that from her heart. But she still had fear of the unknown and what might happen. "Lakshmi, I can understand what you are saying. But sometimes it's hard to release the fear," said Cleo. "Yes, I know that is true for most humans. So, look at it from the lion's perspective. We understand how powerful we are and that if we live in fear, our very existence could be in question. So, we draw our courage and strength from the earth, from inside of us, and we act from there. We know our power to be great and we rely on that power to survive and thrive. You can do that same thing, Cleo. See your power, take back your power, stand in your power." Cleo was beginning to feel Lakshmi's words and felt a growing energy in her body. She was breathing deeper, standing taller and felt a surge of power flow through her that she had not known before, or at least not ever acknowledged. "I can feel it!" shouted Cleo. As Cleo shouted, the cubs all jumped up and wondered what was happening! Lakshmi looked over at the cubs and laughed. "They can feel your power as well Cleo," said Lakshmi. "See how they jumped up! They can feel the energy moving through you and around you. I think you have spread your butterfly wings just a bit further." Bacchus felt the energy too. He was so pleased to see Cleo take back her power. This has been a very important lesson, he thought.

Bacchus spoke, "Lakshmi, I think your courage is one of the most powerful lessons. Finding and holding your courage is so important. Thank you for sharing your wisdom with us." Lakshmi smiled and said, "It is my honor and great privilege to remind us of the power within. To bring prosperity through courage is a fine lesson indeed." Cleo smiled and said, "Thank you Lakshmi for your words. I do feel more empowered and I can see a new way to look at my situation and what may come. I am grateful for your kindness in sharing that with me." Lakshmi smiled and said, "We are all here for you always, in every moment. You only need to ask for our help and we will be there." Then Lakshmi turned and gathered up the cubs that were coming to life again. She nodded to them to follow her as they walked back toward the thorn forest. Her graceful strength carried her forward as the cubs started playing and running in and out of the path, but never too far from mama. Lakshmi turned one last time back to Bacchus and Cleo and gave a slight bow of her head. Then she headed into the forest with the cubs close behind.

MICHAEL THE MONGOOSE

Cleo was feeling pretty good about herself as she and Bacchus turned back to once more follow the opening path before them. Bacchus was so pleased about Cleo's continued growth and said, "Cleo, we have a very special place to go now. Shall we move on?" Cleo nodded.

From the thorn forest, the path opened into a wide field. It was so quiet and peaceful and Cleo did not see any wildlife at all. That seems strange, she thought. "Sometimes it's nice to just be still and have a little quiet," said Bacchus. Cleo laughed to herself as she remembered that Bacchus seemed to read her mind. They moved through the field in quiet strength. The path then emerged into an open forest. It was light and though there were trees, they were spread apart to reveal an openness and allowed the sun to shine through. They began to hear a lovely sound of birds singing in the trees and the chatter of animals that were just out of sight. It was cooler than the thorn forest, but it was not cold.

As they went deeper into this new forest, they began to hear a very high-pitched chittering, squeaky noise. It was not a sound that Cleo could recognize. It was everywhere around them. There were short grunts interspersed with the squeaks. What could this be coming from? thought Cleo. Bacchus turned with a small chuckle to see a mongoose heading toward them. He was small but quite fast as he approached. Cleo had never seen a mongoose before. She didn't know quite what to make of this creature and she could not even be sure what it was. Bacchus turned to Cleo with a smile and said, "It's a mongoose, Cleo". "Oh!" Cleo exclaimed. The mongoose approached them. He stopped when he was just a few feet from them and sat up on his back legs as he held his front paws up to his chest. He was not very big and they both had to look down to see him. He had short legs and a pointed nose. His ears were small but furry and he had a long furry tail. He was the most unusual color, almost blue. His fur was mixed with grey and blue shades and he glowed as he stood in front of them. It was really quite astounding.

Bacchus made a very deep bow to the mongoose, a reverent pose. He arose and with a soft voice said, "Hello Michael. It is my great honor to see you again. I am humbled and grateful for your time." Micheal smiled and greeted Bacchus with a short grunt. "Bacchus, I am the honored one. To be part of Cleo's journey is truly a fabulous thing." Bacchus nodded and turned to Cleo. "Cleo, this is Michael." Cleo made a slight bow and said, "Hello Micheal. It is good to meet you." Bacchus continued, "Cleo, we are half way through our journey and it is time for you to meet one of your most important guides. Michael is very special in our world. And soon you will understand why." Cleo felt a sense of awe and humility at hearing Bacchus' words. "Bacchus, thank you for that introduction!" said Michael. As he spoke, his blue glow seemed to get stronger. "You know that I am always here to serve however I can."

Michael turned to Cleo and had a big grin on his little face. "Cleo," he said, "you were just with Lakshmi, right?" "Yes!" said Cleo. "She is a great teacher. We spoke about courage and vision and making things happen in a good way." "Yes, she is a great teacher and a great mother. She does such a good job of protecting her cubs." said Michael. "And they were so cute!" laughed Cleo. "Well, did you know that she and I have a lot in common?" asked Michael. Cleo looked a bit surprised. "No, I didn't know that," she said. As she said that, she wondered about what these two very different animals could have in common with each other. They were so different in every way. Bacchus had a small chuckle at hearing what Cleo was thinking. Micheal continued, "We are both known for our great courage and bravery. And when we need to defend ourselves, we do so with absolute courage. We may be very different in size and shape, but sometimes what you can't see is even more important than what you can see. In both of our cases though, we defend with courage, honesty and openness. But because of my size and form, I am super-fast! Did you know that I can out jump and out maneuver a King Cobra snake? They are the ones that are poisonous you know." Cleo was captivated by what Michael was saying. She had no idea that such a small creature could or would stand up to a King Cobra! "Oh my gosh!" shouted Cleo. "Eww, I hate snakes anyway. Why would you even want to be around one?!"

Michael laughed and chattered, "They taste good! But that's not really the point. The point is that we know our strengths and have the courage to use them. And that's what you are learning Cleo. First, that you have strength and power that you never knew you had and that you can use that power anytime you need or want to draw on it. But the other thing is that we use our intuition and our guides to help us and protect us. It's not something you can see on the outside. For example, did you know that I am immune to the venom of the King Cobra? Something that can kill you in 30 minutes has no effect on me. You see I have DNA, a genetic mutation really, that doesn't recognize the venom's toxins, so it can't harm me. You can't see that in me because it is deep in my DNA, but it's there, trust me. It protects me if I get bitten, which is rare, by the way," Michael laughed. "It's kinda like how your guardian angel protects you. You can't see it, but it's always there."

Cleo looked over at Bacchus with a mischievous grin. "Oh, yes, Bacchus was just talking about angels a little while ago." "Yes," said Michael, "and I understand that you may not be a believer yet. But no woo woo worry Cleo. You will come to know the angels in time. And you may discover that they can be some of your strongest and most trust-worthy guides. Like for me, I am named after one of the most powerful Archangels there is, Michael. I call on him when I am about to engage with a King Cobra and he surrounds me with his protective glow." As Michael spoke, his fur seemed to glow even more strongly. "But how do you know he is there?" asked Cleo. "It is a *knowing*," said Michael. "You've learned about your intuition, right?

Well, the knowing intuition can be the strongest kind. Imagine it like how you know the sun will rise in the morning. You have no doubt at all and sometimes you even take it for granted that it is there. It's the same kind of feeling. You just know. And when I call to Michael, I just *know* he is there."

"So," asked Cleo, "if I wanted to understand more about angels, how would I do that? I don't really know anything about them." Michael smiled. At least she is interested in finding out more, he thought. Bacchus smiled as well. Michael said, "The first step is to believe, to *know*, that they are there. Everyone has a guardian angel, so let's start there. Your guardian angel is with you before you even incarnate into the world and they follow you through your different lifetimes. In fact, some people have more than one. Your guardian angel is fascinated with you and it wants nothing more than to have a relationship with you. It is dedicated to you. It knows nothing but unconditional love and that's how it always loves you, unconditionally. Angels are not incarnate and they aren't male or female. But they will appear to you in whatever form brings you most comfort. They will always speak in your language so you know they are authentic when they send you messages. I know your guardian angel. And it certainly wants to know you." "That's so cool," said Cleo. "Can you show it to me?" Michael grunted and smiled. He said, "I can help you see it for yourself, Cleo. You don't need me at all, but I am happy to guide you." Cleo thought about the doubts she had when she spoke to Bacchus about angels. Then she thought about all of the lessons she had been given, the strength that she now recognized as hers and the amazing world that had unfolded before her eyes. She laughed to herself and thought, how can I not do this? I believe everything else. Bacchus lowered his head slightly so Cleo would not see his smile.

"OK Michael," said Cleo. "I would be honored if you could show me how to see my guardian angel." Michael jumped up and did a small flip of his body and then settled back down again. He laughed and said, "Sorry, I needed to get my energy flowing just a bit! OK Cleo, let's begin. You know how to start your meditation practice. It's the same thing. Take your deep breaths and relax your body. Let go of your thinking thoughts and just be still." Cleo followed his direction. Michael continued, "Now, imagine or feel that you are in a beautiful garden. There are fabulous, colorful flowers everywhere. The fragrance of the flowers is sweet and pleasing. Stay in the garden for a while and just enjoy it. Feel how happy it makes you. Feel the gratitude you have to be in such a beautiful place." Cleo thought about the garden, the colors, the smells. She felt very happy and peaceful. "Now," continued Michael, "we will ask your guardian angel to come. *Know* that it is there with you in the garden. Ask the angel to reveal itself to you. Say that you are so happy and grateful that your angel has come to meet you and spend time with you. Feel it as if you have already met your angel. Open and allow that unconditional love to fill your heart chakra with angelic glow." Michael then stayed very quiet while Cleo meditated.

In her mind, she could see the garden, but just barely. She could really smell the flowers though and she could really feel the peace in her heart. She was trying to feel the presence of her angel, knowing it was there. She thought, I am so happy and grateful that my angel is with me now in the garden. Thank you, angel, for coming to reveal yourself to me. Then she waited. Nothing happened. She was still in the garden, but there was no angel. She thought harder and harder but nothing happened. Michael could see what she was doing and feel that she was about to get frustrated. So, he quietly said, "Cleo, just let go. Surrender to the garden and where you are. Your angel is there. You just need to allow it to come to you, not force it." Cleo took a deep breath and a big exhale and surrendered. She stopped trying to force the angel there and just saw herself standing in the beautiful garden. In her mind, she stayed there for a while. As she relaxed further, she began to feel a presence around her. It was something she had never felt before in quite that way. Michael continued to lead her further. "Cleo, your angel could be anywhere around you. In front, behind, on your left or right side. Feel the warmth of the essence of your angel. You will know where it is." Cleo was now only thinking about her guardian angel. All other thoughts had completely cleared her head. She could feel it. She could feel her angel at her right shoulder. It was becoming much stronger, although she didn't see anything. Michael said quietly, "Thank your angel for coming Cleo. It is there with you now. You feel it. Ask its name. See if you get an answer." Cleo asked the angel for its name. She waited for an answer. She could feel the presence get stronger, but there was nothing else coming through. So, she just stayed still and enjoyed the warm feeling that was at her shoulder. Then a thought popped in her head. It had come quickly but was very clear when it came. Ezrael. Cleo smiled and said it out loud. "Ezreal" she said. Michael smiled and nodded toward Cleo. He said, "Cleo, you have now met your guardian angel."

Cleo felt a warm glow in her heart and had a huge smile on her face. She opened her eyes and looked at Bacchus and Michael. She quietly said, "My guardian angel is real. His name is Ezrael. I know he is there." Michael smiled even bigger and said, "Yes, Cleo, he is there. And he has always been there and always will be. He is your new best friend. Spend some time with him. Get to know him. Ask him questions. Talk to him. It will be a lifetime of discovery. Always something new to learn and feel. Call on him when you need support, have a question or just need a love hug." Cleo felt so elated. Her heart was about to burst it felt so full. This is the most amazing thing ever, she thought. Bacchus looked at her and said, "Cleo, this is one of the most important lessons you will have today. And one of the most joyous. Bask in the love that Ezrael has for you. It is the purest kind of love and it will never leave you." Cleo nodded as tears of joy ran down her face.

Michael said, "Cleo, what a great thing for you and Ezrael to meet. And he can introduce you to the Archangels as well. There are lots of them to meet and call on. And they are always there for you. They are multi-dimensional you see, so they can be everywhere at once, helping to guide you as well as all of the other humans. So, not so woo woo after all." He and Bacchus laughed.

"Thank you, Michael," said Cleo. "This has been amazing!" Michael smiled and said, "It was my honor, Cleo. Always remember that you are stronger than you think and there is so much support for you. Look for us in your heart. We are all here for you always, in every moment. You only need to ask for our help and we will be there." Michael looked over at Bacchus and said, "Bacchus my dear friend. You and Cleo are now halfway through your journey. The rest will be unlike anything you have ever imagined. Embrace the new adventures that await you both. Our butterfly is spreading her wings even further now. It is time to fly!" Bacchus nodded quietly. "And so, my dear friends, I must leave you now," said Michael. "But know that I go with you as you journey forward. My protection is always around you. You are safe." As Michael turned to leave, his glow became so brilliantly blue that Bacchus and Cleo could hardly look at him. Then he seemed to just dissolve into the ether.

NETZACH THE NUMBAT

Cleo took a deep breath and looked over at Bacchus. "That was so amazing Bacchus!" she said. "I can still feel Ezrael right beside me. I think I am really going to love having a guardian angel." Bacchus smiled. "Yes, it is one of your greatest awakenings. Your relationship with Ezrael will be so important for the rest of your life. Cherish that love and watch it bloom. Now, we have a very special animal to meet. Shall we begin? You can ask Ezrael to come along as well." Cleo smiled and said, "Yes, let's go."

Bacchus turned to a new path that was forming in front of them. Cleo followed, with Ezrael by her side. They walked in silence for some time. It was peaceful. As the path continued to unfold, they followed it to a fence. It was very tall and it reached so far that they could not see the end of it. But you could see through it. Cleo was confused. Why would there be a fence in the middle of nowhere? she thought. Bacchus said, "Our next animal friend needs protection from the wild. You will understand." Then Bacchus asked Cleo to grab his tail. She did. He closed his eyes and nodded for Cleo to follow him. They walked toward the fence and with no hesitation, Bacchus walked right through it, as if it was not even there. Cleo of course did the same. They emerged on the other side and Cleo had a small chuckle. She was laughing because nothing really surprised her any longer. She really could do anything.

Inside the fence, there were trees and bushy grasses and scrub brush. The trees had bare trunks with short green leaves at the top. They were sparse enough to have plenty of room to walk between them. There were beautiful flowers of purple, pink and red that dotted the landscape around them. Among the bushes and grasses were lots of old fallen trees. The limbs and stumps were spread everywhere and were all different lengths and sizes. The landscape colors were a mix of dark greens and browns. The trio of Bacchus, Cleo and Ezrael continued making their way around the fallen tree limbs until they reached quite a large branch that stretched across the path.

Bacchus stopped. "Let's wait here," he said. Cleo sat down on the end of the fallen branch to wait with Bacchus. The limb was hollow and open at the end. Cleo's legs were in front of the opening. They sat for only a short time when Cleo felt something behind her legs. She looked down just as this little creature emerged from inside the fallen branch. She jumped up in surprise but making sure she didn't step on it.

Bacchus laughed as the numbat emerged and turned toward them. She was just a little thing, about 10 inches long. Her shape and coloring were so unique. She had a rather pointed nose covered in brown thin fur and each of her eyes were surrounded in a white fur band. She had short front legs but large claws on each foot. The fur on her back was a lighter shade of brown and as it crested her shoulders, it became a series of white and brown stripes. The stripes went all the way to her tail, getting darker and darker with each stripe. Her tail was wispy and almost as long as her body. She ducked slightly as Cleo jumped up and then let out a small, squeaky laugh. She made some soft clicking sounds and then said, "Hello Bacchus! Hello Cleo! I'm so happy you made it! Any trouble with the fence?" Bacchus shook his head and said, "No trouble Netzach. We are so pleased you are in good health! Cleo, this is Netzach. She is a numbat." Cleo looked down and bowed her head slightly. "Hello Netzach. I have never had the pleasure of seeing a numbat before."

Netzach smiled back and said, "It is my pleasure to be seen!" Cleo laughed and said, "May I ask what the purpose of the fence is?" Netzach sighed and said, "Well Cleo, numbats are an endangered species. There are only about a thousand of us left on the whole earth. The predators that we have were too great in number for us to defend ourselves. So, the Universe graciously enclosed us in this wonderful sanctuary so that we could repopulate. And it's working." "Oh goodness!" said Cleo. "I'm sorry to hear that there are so few of you. But I'm glad you have the opportunity to thrive once again. I have a special place in my heart for animals and it makes me sad when they are threatened with extinction." "Thank you," said Netzach. "It takes endurance and patience to rebuild an entire species, but we will not be distracted from our goal of repopulating. And this sanctuary has everything we need. You see, we only eat termites. Thousands of them a day! And there are enough old limbs and stumps to attract the termites we need to live on." And then Netzach stuck out her skinny tongue and made a sound, mm-hmm, yummy. Her tongue was almost as long as her whole body! They all laughed in delight.

Netzach said, "Even though we are a bit shy, we are organized and super productive. I think that could describe you as well Cleo. You always have a lot to do at work, but you are able to get things done in an organized way. Much like Ariel said at the beginning of your journey. And now you are seeing that power even more clearly. Your ability to rally your team and motivate them is a strength that will serve you well in all areas." Cleo smiled at the compliment. "Thank you Netzach. It is something that I wasn't really aware of until this journey. I mean, I do that every day but I didn't realize that as a strength." "Actually," said Netzach, "it is a very important strength. And just as important as things like your intuition. You can use that strength when you are looking for a new job, or even, looking at doing something completely different. Following your joy is the main thing. You love animals and nature. Maybe your joy, your purpose, is to help animals. Have you ever thought about that?"

Cleo felt a small spark in her heart. "Oh, that would be so great." she said. "I would really love to do something like that. But I've never had enough money to do that kind of work and I don't have time to volunteer right now." Netzach said, "If that is your joy, Cleo, then start small. If you prioritize your joy, it will open doors for you. Focus on what is essential. That's the joy of following your heart. Everything else comes from that. When you know what you want and you make the start, the Universe, the spirit animals and the angels will always lead you on the right path. Maybe the numbat will inspire you to help the endangered species on your Earth. There are a lot of animals that could use your help. You could help Mother Earth, Gaia, herself. There are so many ways you can contribute to a new Earth."

Netzach continued, "I know you are used to doing things in a big way, Cleo. And that's always grand. But remember that you are contributing every day by just enjoying nature and being happy there. Everyone contributes in their own way and everyone's contribution is as important as everyone else's. Did you know that just one person living their joy, even in the seemingly smallest way, can have huge ripple effects across the Universe. Yes, not just Earth, but the whole Universe. It is *that* important. There is no higher calling than living your joy, Cleo. Have the patience to follow your passion. Live every moment in your highest joy and you will never want for anything."

Bacchus smiled as he felt the joy rising in Cleo's heart. Not only has she found her strength, he thought, she is now also finding her joy. He said, "Netzach, we are grateful for your time and wisdom. And we are so pleased to see the new sanctuary and how it is helping you repopulate. We wish you great success." "Thank you, Bacchus," said Netzach. "With your love and support, I'm sure we will rise again to great numbers. And although we are small, every living creature deserves to live their life to the fullest. And we will do so as well, as long as the termites hold out!" she laughed. Cleo and Bacchus laughed with her. Then Cleo said, "Netzach, I am confident that you will be successful in your goal. I hope I can come back here one day and see many thousands of numbats. That would bring me great joy." "Thank you, Cleo," said Netzach. "That would bring me great joy as well. But until then, always remember that we are all here for you always, in every moment. You only need to ask for our help and we will be there." Netzach made a soft clicking sound and walked back in to the fallen log.

ORION THE OWL

Bacchus and Cleo turned to leave the sanctuary. They headed down the path they came from. Cleo talked as they walked. "It's so sad about the numbats and what happened to them. I think it is such a horrible thing when we lose a whole species of animals. I want to do something to help, Bacchus." Bacchus smiled and said, "Then you shall Cleo. Like Netzach said, start small. You never know what the end result will be. Just keep that joy alive in your heart. It will lead you to what you will do next." They walked for a while until they came upon the fence. Cleo reached out to grab Bacchus' tail. He turned to her and said, "You don't need to do that." Then Bacchus proceeded to walk through the fence just as he had done before. He turned back to Cleo and said, "Believe." Cleo nodded and closed her eyes as she moved toward the fence. "I believe," she whispered as she walked through the fence with Ezrael.

Bacchus and Cleo continued down the path. As they walked, it began to get darker. They approached some woods that were dense with tall trees. As they entered this new forest, it became even darker. There was a very distinct feeling about these woods. It felt mystical and magical. Cleo began to feel tingly inside but she was not afraid. And it was completely silent. The only noise was the sound of Cleo's footsteps. Bacchus walked so quietly you could not hear him at all. They wandered through the woods as the path seemed to disappear into the forest floor of pine needles and leaves. It was now very dark except for the millions of stars that shown above. They were so bright, they lit up the forest so Cleo could see. Bacchus and Cleo then emerged into a large clearing. It was a perfect circle surrounded by the forest. There was one lone tree in the exact center of the circle. It was very large. Its branches were thick and illuminated by the stars. The base was larger than Cleo could reach around and there were lots of branches that seemed to be reaching for the night sky. Bacchus silently walked to the tree and sat down. Cleo followed. "Wow Bacchus," she said. "This is fabulous! Look at all of the stars. I don't think I have ever seen them so clearly. And there are so many of them!" Bacchus said, "Yes, they are amazing. Why don't we lay down here by the tree and just look at them." Cleo was happy to take a short rest and so she laid down on the ground beside Bacchus. "Can you feel her?" asked Bacchus. "What do you mean?" answered Cleo. "Gaia. That's what we call mother earth. She is real. She has consciousness and she has been around for billions of years. Your earth is the physical manifestation of Gaia's consciousness. It is made of the mineral, vegetable and animal kingdoms. And all of them are assisted by Gaia and her nature spirits from birth to death. When you are close to the earth, you can feel her presence. It is a nurturing feeling and very grounding." Cleo closed her eyes and felt the cool ground beneath her. It was very solid and supportive. She felt the energy of the earth in her whole body. That tingly feeling was getting stronger. She took a calming deep breath and said, "Ahhh. Yes, I can feel that. I can feel Gaia. I feel so connected."

Bacchus smiled and said, "Now look at the stars. You are connected to them as well Cleo. Remember, you are All That Is, so you are connected to everything in the Universe." Cleo looked up at the night sky. As she was pondering what Bacchus just said, she saw something amazing happen. Three stars that were in a row began to glow even brighter. They seemed to be pulsing with light. Then each of the stars formed a stream of light that began to descend to the ground. The three light streams met in the sky and combined to form one large stream. It came down directly toward them and lit up the whole top of the tree. Then it vanished as quickly as it came. Cleo held her breath. She and Bacchus both looked up at the tree where the light had touched. There was a form on the tree limb that was white and fluffy. Bacchus stood up and said, "Hello Orion." Cleo stood and squinched her eyes to see who Bacchus was talking to. As the form became clearer, she could see it was a snowy white owl. He perched on the highest branch in the tree and was difficult to see clearly. So, in order to meet his guests, he launched from the tree limb. His wings spread out easily and gracefully into a 4-foot span.

After just two flaps of his wings, he floated through the air, making no sound at all. He circled the tree three times and then landed on the lowest branch. His mighty claws gripped the tree and he folded his wings back to his body.

His feathers were as white as snow. He had a black beak and bright golden eyes with dark black pupils. There were a few black markings on his body and wings that looked like little dots. His black claws were huge and covered in white feathers. In the darkness of the tree, he was glowing. "Helloooo Bacchus" he said. The telltale hoot echoing his words. "I am soooo pleased to see you all. You, Cleo and Ezrael." Bacchus introduced Orion to Cleo. "I am so pleased to meet you Orion," said Cleo. "That was quite an entrance!" "Thank you, Cleo," Orion said. "Nothing short of miraculous if I do say soooo myself." Cleo watched as Orion began to scan the area. He moved his head very slowly and it almost looked like he could move it in a complete circle around his body. It was mesmerizing to watch him move. It was so fluid. "Ah," said Orion. "So many visitors here tonight!" Bacchus smiled. Cleo looked around but saw nothing. It was an empty field with one lone tree. Cleo looked at Bacchus inquisitively for some sort of explanation. Bacchus said, "Orion, Cleo is not seeing the other visitors. Can you help her to understand?" "Ooooooh, of course!" hooted Orion. "Cleo, you are going to discover something amazing. You see, there are quite a few galactic visitors tonight. They came to meet you and observe. They come from different places in the galaxy. When they heard you would be here, they wanted to help."

Cleo looked around again, completely confused. I don't see anything, she thought. "Well, that's because they are in a different frequency than you," said Orion. "You can only see with your human eyes the things that are vibrating in the same frequency as you. In order to see them, you have to change your vibrational frequency." Cleo thought, well I guess he can read my mind just like Bacchus. Then she said,

"What do you mean by galactic visitors, Orion? You mean like from outer space?" Orion hooted in a soft laugh. "Well, I guess *you*, as a human, would see it that way. They are beings from other places in the galaxy. Some from your solar system and some from much farther away. They exist in a different dimension than we are in now. So, they are here, but not visible to you as a human." Cleo turned to Bacchus and said, "Bacchus, can you see them?" Bacchus nodded yes. "I can go between dimensions Cleo," said Bacchus. "So, I can see your 3rd dimension as well as the others. Of course, you can do that as well. It is not forbidden or impossible. It's just a matter of raising your 3rd dimensional vibration to open up to new things." Cleo was puzzled and frustrated. "Bacchus," she said. "This is the MOST woo woo you have ever been! You mean there are little green men here!?" Bacchus laughed. Then he looked to Orion and said, "Orion, perhaps you can draw on your wisdom and mysterious powers to help Cleo understand."

Orion was pleased to be asked. And so he began. "Thank you, Bacchus, I would be most honored. Cleo, as an owl, I have access to ancient wisdom and a connection to all of the magical aspects of life. We are a most mystical animal. We have access to ancient knowledge that is just now coming back to your world. What you would call 'alien' in your human language are actually the beings that came to earth millions of years ago. That was done with the permission of the galactic council. Earth was to become the great experiment. Sometimes the galactic beings were more directly involved, other times they became less visible. But they were always there. Yooooou see, Earth was to become the great experiment with emotions. And Universal Consciousness, the All That Is, wanted to feel and experience every depth of emotion possible. But Universal Consciousness could not feel those emotions because it only existed in unconditional love. So, in order to really see and feel the emotions, Earth became the planet where its inhabitants would be allowed to forget that they were source energy, that they were unconditional love at their core. As the souls came to earth, they went through a process of descension, where they would literally forget that they were source energy, All That Is. That is the only way humans could feel all emotions to the depth they do, because they were allowed to forget. And so, this incredible game of 3rd dimension emotions has been playing out for millennia. Through the thousands of your earth years, human consciousness would ebb and flow, much like Gaia ebbs and flows. The galactic beings were on earth, some trying to help and others trying to control. And at the darkest times, the galactic council would send masters to incarnate on earth to help the humans see what their potential really was. To help them remember their source power. They came to show the humans that there was an enlightened path that was available to anyone who chose it. But free will is a universal law, so the human was left to decide if they would remember their core of unconditional love, or whether they would stay in the game and continue to play. And either way, it was and continues to be the perfect path for them. So, Cleo, you see, there have been galactic beings here from the start. Most of them have been through their own path of ascension and awakening so they better understand what earth humans are experiencing now, and they want to help. It can take years of practice for some humans, and for others it can happen in an instant. That ability to open and allow the other frequencies and dimensions to be seen. But if that is your choice, then you will see and feel the galactic friends and ancestors that you have and understand even more who you are and what your path is."

Cleo was stunned at what Orion had just said. How is this possible that all of this had been around for so long and I don't know anything about it. That's crazy. "So," said Cleo, "you mean I can see these other beings if I just change my frequency? What does that mean and how would I even do that?" Orion continued, "Your consciousness is what molds your energy. And you are already more conscious than most humans. You know that you can change your reality by changing your thoughts and focus. When you are conscious of what your energy can do and just how powerful you are, then you raise your vibration, your frequency. And Cleo, you have already done that. In fact, you have done that many times today. Now it is just a matter of honing your skills. Your animal guides can help you with that as you work on it every day. Ezrael can guide you as well. For now, you will need to trust me that they are all here to help you. As you continue to raise your consciousness and stay in that state for longer and longer periods of time, all will be visible to yooooou."

Orion looked around at the visitors and nodded his head as his eyes slowly blinked. "Cleo," he said, "remember that your body is actually an antenna. It is a miracle really. The miracle of life that happens in your body every split second. Realize how amazing it is. Your body is creating new cells, beating your heart, taking in air to breathe, digesting your food and processing everything your physical senses are perceiving. Yet, you don't have to think about any of that nor do you have to direct any of that to happen. Wouldn't you say that is a miracle?" Cleo laughed softly, realizing what Orion was saying was indeed true. "Wow," she said. "It really is a miracle when you put it that way." Orion nodded his head again. "And Cleo, imagine what else is possible. Everything is possible. Because everything is energy. And energy can take whatever form you want it to. You are the master of all of your energy. And you can co-create miracles all of the time with All That Is. Because you are one and the same. Miracles aren't always super, spectacular things, remember. Humans are so predisposed to expecting everything to be huge and grand. No judgment, humans are evolving. But you can now see that miracles are everywhere. In nature, in your physical world and in your spiritual world. They can be as beautiful and simple as a butterfly emerging from a cocoon to a mongoose who is immune to cobra venom. See all of those things as a miracle, because that's in fact what they are. And when you are ready to manifest miracles in your life, like your next job, starting your own sanctuary for an animal that is facing extinction or paying off your mortgage, then call on me. I can help you manifest any miracle you wish. If you can see it in your mind's eye, it is yours for the receiving. Or when you are ready to see the visitors."

"Thank you, Orion," said Cleo. "This has been a truly magical visit. And even though I can't see the visitors yet, I'm sure they are there. You really are very mystical and very wise. It has been my greatest honor to spend time with you."

"It is I whoooo am honored Cleo." said Orion. "Anyone whoooo is willing to explore this magnificent Universe is a special friend. We are all here for you always, in every moment. You only need to ask for our help and we will be there." Orion slowly turned his head toward Bacchus and said, "Bacchus, you are also a special friend to help Cleo on her adventure. All of us continue to support you on your quest. Be in magic my dear friend." Bacchus bowed his head to Orion. No words were needed. Orion heard Bacchus' thanks. Orion spread his wings to fly. As he lifted off the branch, he winked at Ezrael. Three flaps of those magnificent wings and he was off again. He flew back toward the three stars in the sky and soon disappeared among the blanket of starlight.

PHANUEL THE PRAYING MANTIS

Cleo and Bacchus watched as Orion flew back to the stars. They were quiet for a moment, just looking up at the sky. Then Cleo turned to Bacchus and asked, "Are they all still here?" Bacchus chuckled and said, "They are always here Cleo. Just like Ezrael. You may not be able to see them with your human eyes, but you can feel their energy." "OK," she said. "I still have so much to learn. But it is all so fascinating! So where are we going next, Bacchus?"

"Well, we are actually going to stay here a bit longer. There is someone else who wants to meet you." said Bacchus. "Oh!" exclaimed Cleo. "Is it a little green man?" she laughed. Bacchus laughed as well. "In a manner of speaking." he said. "In fact, he has been here since Orion came, observing." "Well, then I can't see him," said Cleo. "On the contrary." said Bacchus. "He is right in front of you." "I don't see anything Bacchus." said Cleo. "Look closely." said Bacchus. "Walk closer to the tree. He's right in front of you." Cleo took a few steps closer to the tree. She was looking around for anything that was moving. She began to sense something was there, but she couldn't see it. "Be very still Cleo." said Bacchus. "Use your intuition. You will see him." Cleo stood very still and began to relax into the stillness. She knew something was there. She watched the tree. Then she saw it! It was a praying mantis hanging on the side of the tree trunk. How could I have missed that! she thought. Bacchus laughed. "You see Cleo, he really is a little green man."

Cleo looked at this crazy, green insect. And it was staring back at her. But it was frozen in time. There was no movement at all. He was bright green. He was about 6 inches long and he looked like a green stick attached to the tree. His long front legs were reaching up to hold him to the bark. He had two more legs in the middle of his body, also attached to the tree. And two more legs at the bottom of his torso. His body was long and narrow with folded wings at the end. But the most amazing part was his head. It was triangular and had two bulging eyes at the top that formed two ends of the triangle.

There were two small antennae on the top of his head. His mouth formed the bottom of the triangle and he had two small pinchers that wrapped around his mouth. Even in the dark, Cleo could see him very clearly now that she knew where he was. As she stood very still, studying him, his head began to move. But it seemed like it was all in slow motion.

Bacchus walked closer to the tree and looked up at the praying mantis. "Hello Phanuel." he said. "Cleo, this is Phanuel." Cleo was now completely captivated by this little creature and she said, "Hello Phanuel. I'm sorry I didn't know you were here. It is nice to meet you."

Phanuel moved his head a little more and said, "Hello to you all. I have certainly enjoyed watching the goings on so far. Orion is a magical bird. And now I am pleased to have some time with you as well. Ah, time. What a curious thing. It is so linear in your world Cleo. In my world, time is so different." "What do you mean Phanuel?" asked Cleo. "How can time be anything other than linear. Isn't that the nature of time anyway?" Phanuel slowly moved his head a bit more and said, "That is the nature of time in your 3rd dimension earth, yes. You perceive that there is past, present and future. It is that way so you can play out your adventure in your human body. It is quite unique in the Universe and is of great interest to myself and the others. But in the broader Universe and Multiverse, there is only the present moment. It is something that you truly won't remember until you go back to your spirit body. So don't worry about trying to understand it. And that's not really what I want to talk with you about. I would like to talk about truth. The truth of the Universe. Shall we sit down?" Cleo nodded but didn't know how to sit down with a praying mantis. Phanuel said, "Just hold out your hand Cleo and let me climb on. Then you and Bacchus can sit down and you can put me on your knee." Cleo smiled. Everyone can read my mind, she laughed to herself.

Cleo reached out for Phanuel. He moved so slowly! Every motion was deliberate but graceful nonetheless. As Phanuel finally completed the move to Cleo's hand, she backed away from the tree a few steps and sat down. Bacchus did the same. As she moved her hand toward her knee, Phanuel turned his head. Like Orion, it seemed he could move his head almost in a complete circle. Cleo thought there must be something to being magical and being able to move your head like that. Phanuel climbed off her hand and on to her knee. When he stopped there, he folded his front legs twice, at each joint, and he pulled them to his body. Now he really did look like he was praying. Cleo smiled.

"Thank you, Cleo," said Phanuel. "That's much better." Then he looked up toward Cleo's shoulder and said, "Hello Ezrael, my dear friend. I am so pleased you and Cleo have found each other." Then with a slow slight nod of his head in acknowledgement to Ezrael, he turned back to Cleo. "Now, where to begin." Phanuel said. "Cleo, the mantis beings have been around for almost as long as the Universe itself. Far longer than you can even imagine in your earth time perception. We have learned and played and raised our consciousness much like you are doing now, but through so many millennia, that we are now very highly evolved. We can sense the consciousness of every sentient being on planet earth, all at the same time. And we help orchestrate your miracles, as you call them. We lay out the plans for every human so that all events line up exactly when they need to in your earth timelines. So, for example, let's say you wanted to meet the man who will be your next relationship. But he lives in Australia. We put together the series of events over years and years that will ultimately bring you together to meet. Maybe at the sanctuary where Netzach lives. All of it is perfectly orchestrated by us. You see, time is irrelevant to us. As you on earth would say, we can watch grass grow. Patience is something most of the humans still have not adopted. They want everything in the next minute. They live in the future or the past, instead of enjoying each present moment. No judgment, they are still learning the ways of the Universe. But we mantis have so much fun doing this! It's important to have fun, Cleo. That is what you were meant to do here on earth, play. That's the other thing most of you are still learning."

Cleo was mesmerized at Phanuel. This all sounded so incredible, but yet she totally believed everything he was saying. She just *knew* it to be true. "I bet you could tell some amazing stories, Phanuel" she said. "Oh yes." he said. "We are the masters at observing. And we can teach you the art of letting things come to you, Cleo. When you have the knowing, like you just thought about, then you don't have to push or chase things. Good things will come to you when you allow them and you know they will happen. It is, I think, the greatest part of being able to play the human game. Yet so many do not want to understand that. At least not yet. They are still absorbed in just playing the 3D game. But now you know something different Cleo. And that makes you very special and unique. And when you work on your consciousness and are able to hold your higher vibration for longer and longer periods, you will see the miracles that Orion spoke of. Miracles that you cannot even imagine right now. And then you will really understand that consciousness and frequency move energy into form. That's the key Cleo. And then let *us* do our thing to make it manifest." "I would love to understand more Phanuel." said Cleo. "How would I do what you just described?"

Phanuel shifted his head just slightly. The darkness was beginning to move into light and he seemed to be beckoning it forward. He said, "Just as you are now seeing the darkness move to light, Cleo. Earth has been in sleeping darkness for a long time in your earth years. It is now moving into light, into higher consciousness. Gaia's consciousness is rising. And so must yours, to match her frequency. Of course, this will happen over decades, but it is now coming closer. You know how to raise your frequency already. The things you have learned about meditation and the way of the other worlds have shown you how to move into a different frequency. Think of it as a dial on the old radios. You tuned into different frequencies to get different broadcasts. The same is true for your consciousness. So, when you are meditating, you can choose to tune into whatever frequency you wish. But you must do that through your heart chakra. You cannot 'think' it so. Your ego was designed to keep you playing the game, the game of separation from All That Is, so it will not allow you to change your frequency. But you can move beyond your ego into your heart and do that. You can use your throat chakra, your third eye chakra and your crown chakra to open to new dimensions. And once you see what that's like, you will never want to go back to just living in a 3rd dimensional earth. It will be far too dense and confining. Then you will know that you have raised your frequency. And when you do that, you will see things that you cannot see now with your human eyes. You will see the others that are here now. Remember what Kalani said, it is a practice. And you need to practice it every day so that you can train your ego to let go when you are meditating. But please don't think badly of the ego. It is a wonderful thing and it is here to protect you and allow you to play the game. You wanted to play, so you still want to stay in the game. But now, you will see the game from a completely different perspective. And what Haniel showed you is so small compared to what you will see."

As Phanuel finished speaking, the darkness had completely moved to full light. The sun was beaming brightly on them all. Cleo could now see how truly amazing this little green man was. She said, "I think I have a lot to do and a lot to practice, but I really do want to see the others and I really do want to experience other frequencies. And I really do want to manifest these miracles. Thank you so much Phanuel." Phanuel nodded ever so slowly and said, "You will do great things Cleo. You are here to learn and play and be happy. And when you do that, you will help raise the consciousness of the earth. You are that powerful. We are all here for you always, in every moment. You only need to ask for our help and we will be there." Bacchus stood and made a very deep bow toward Phanuel. He said, "Thank you Phanuel for this valuable insight and for your time and attention. Each now moment with you is such a gift." Phanuel nodded back to Bacchus as well. Then he did something that he very rarely does, he raised his wings and he flew back to the tree. And after he landed, he became frozen in time again.

QUAN YIN THE QUAIL

Bacchus turned to Cleo. "Are you ready to move on?" he asked. "Yes, I suppose." answered Cleo. "My mind is still whirling from all of this new info." They both turned to leave the clearing and headed back to the dense forest. In the daylight, it didn't seem quite so mysterious. The path opened in front of them again and they began to make their way out of the forest. The trees became sparse. They started to see more grasses. Then they saw thickets. These were made from blackberry bushes and at times were very dense. There were shorter broad-leafed bushes that had bare ground underneath. They seemed to provide some cover to the ground below. The path was clear and they walked for a while. Then they started hearing a strange call. It was guttural and throaty and repeated the same 3-syllable sound over and over. There was more than one animal making the sound, maybe a small group.

Bacchus stopped at a small clump of grass and looked down. "Hello Quan Yin." he said. A quail emerged from under the grass and looked up at Bacchus. She was camouflaged so well that Cleo almost didn't see her. She had a stocky little body with pointed wings. Her face was black feathers with a white line under her eyes. Her body was covered in brown feathers that were streaked and striped with beige. Her belly was brownish orange. But the cutest part was the plumage that stood up on top of her head. It looked like a big feather that hung forward toward her eyes, but it stood almost straight up. She was surrounded by a small group of other quails and they all looked identical. "Hello Bacchus!" she said in a chirpy voice. "It's so nice to see you again. I have been anxiously awaiting your arrival. And this must be Cleo! It is so nice to meet you!" Then she turned her head just slightly and with a smile said, "Hello Ezrael." Then she turned back to Cleo. "Cleo, we have all been eagerly watching your journey with Bacchus. What a grand adventure you are on! I think this will stretch you to new heights. I can already sense that your compassion and love has grown tremendously. You are surely a gift to your world."

"Oh, thank you Quan Yin," said Cleo. "It is a fabulous adventure, that's for sure!" Quan Yin smiled and said, "I am so pleased to hear that. You will do amazing things when you return to your earth. Be aware that there will be some that won't understand the changes you are going through. They will sense that you are very different and they won't know what to make of it. Let's talk about that for a while." Cleo agreed. She hadn't really thought about what her life would be like when she completed her adventure and went back to her real life. She didn't understand why some people would see her differently. She thought that everyone would be excited to hear about all that she was learning and experiencing. "I would be pleased to talk about it, Quan Yin," she said.

Quan Yin continued. "Cleo, I know that you have had experiences with others in the past where you felt like you were being criticized. Would you agree?" Cleo nodded in agreement. "And when that happened, what did you do?" asked Quan Yin. "Well," said Cleo, "I guess I believed what they were saying and I probably agreed with the criticism. Most of the time I would stay quiet and not really answer, but then I would think about it for weeks. What they said. I would get caught up in the feelings and not really be able to stop thinking about it." "Yes," said Quan Yin. "That is a typical response for most humans. You are all conditioned to believe that your survival depends on having others around you to protect you. So, you are not often courageous enough to stand in the power of who you really are. You don't want to push others away because your basic instinct is to not alienate yourself from others. It's a very old pattern. And there are a lot of people who have not realized the true meaning of compassion. No judgment, that's just where they are in their game. But you are now seeing things differently. You understand that when people criticize others, they are actually criticizing themselves. Judgment is a very strong emotion in your world. It is a way that the ego keeps you in the duality of the 3rd dimension."

Cleo said, "I'm not sure what you mean by duality? Can you explain that?" "Of course," said Quan Yin. "Earth 3rd dimension is a polarized place. Things are right or wrong, black or white, good or bad. Your ego does that because it's part of the game you are all playing on earth. It comes from thousands of years of survival, where you had to judge quickly whether something was a threat to you or not. Of course, those days have long past, but the group consciousness of that still exists. In our world, there is not that level of polarity. We see things in versions of gray, not black and white. Think about when you judge something yourself. Whether that is you, or something outside of you. Tell me about any time that you have judged someone for what you thought they did to you." "Hmmmm," said Cleo. "I guess that happens pretty much every day. Seems I am always judging someone for something. Like this morning. I was judging my boss when she told us she sold the company." "Yes," said Quan Yin. "That's a perfect example. So now that you know how to witness that and see if from the audience, how would you see that differently?" "Oh," said Cleo. "Let me think. I was judging her for not caring for her employees and doing things only for her behalf. That she was doing this to us and then giving us more to do because she made a selfish decision." "OK, that's good." said Quan Yin. "Now look at it from a higher perspective, and from a neutral standpoint." Cleo thought for a minute and said, "She was doing what she thought was right. And I was taking that personally, like it was an attack on me and my co-workers. And she has the right to make decisions for herself and her company. That decision was her reality and was not directed at me. Yes, I can see that now very clearly."

Quan Yin smiled and ruffled her feathers. "You are really seeing the truth now, Cleo. I could not be more pleased. So now can you see this business change as an endeavor that will stretch you but also allow you to expand? Maybe even see this as the opportunity for you to look at what you really love and start to follow a different path. You know, sometimes the Universe sends us opportunities by forcing a change. So, you could see this as a push to act on your dreams."

"Yes," said Cleo. "I can see this in a new light. And really it could be an opportunity for me. And now I have the tools to embrace that and really shine." Cleo felt a warm sense around her, almost like a hug. She felt the presence of Ezrael all around and smiled. Thank you, Ezrael, she thought. Bacchus smiled.

"You have so much to look forward to," said Quan Yin. "Always remember that you are the master of your life and reality. Embrace that with love and compassion. Act on your dreams. And never let others change who you really are because of what they might say or do. Move forward with all diligence. Your quest is just beginning. And remember, we are all here for you always, in every moment. You only need to ask for our help and we will be there."

Quan Yin looked to Bacchus and said, "Bacchus, this has been a grand time! I enjoy our time together. Thank you for allowing me to play with you all." Bacchus nodded. "It is always my pleasure Quan Yin. I bid you peace and love, with our thanks." "Yes," Cleo said. "Thank you for your kind words and insights."

"You are both most welcome," said Quan Yin. "And now my fellow quails and I have a lovely send off for you." Quan Yin beckoned the other quails to come and form a circle with her. They all faced outward from the circle with their tails tightly woven in the center. And then, they all took flight at the same time, going in all directions, like an explosion of energy. Cleo ducked her head quickly in surprise and laughed. Bacchus smiled as he watched them disappear into the sky.

RAGUEL THE RAM

After the amazing exit of the quails, Bacchus turned to Cleo. "Cleo, we have quite a journey ahead of us now. Perhaps we should move on." Cleo nodded, still with a smile and laugh on her lips. Bacchus turned to follow the new path away from the thickets. They walked and talked for a long while, watching the landscape become sparser. There were huge mountains on the horizon. Cleo asked, "Are we going up there?" Bacchus nodded. Cleo sighed.

The path led them to the base of the mountain. As they looked up to take in the awe-inspiring view, they could see the caps of the mountains covered in snow. "I'm not sure I am dressed for this Bacchus," said Cleo. "Don't worry," said Bacchus. "I will always ensure you are safe and warm." As the path led them up the mountain, the rocks formed the perfect staircase. As they ascended the mountain, they could see the landscape that reached for the sky. Snow lined the circular pattern of the mountain. It was a tapestry of rock, snow, rock, snow. Even though their path was quite easy to maneuver, the rest of the mountain landscape was filled with jagged edges and small ledges that were only a few inches wide in some cases. The snow became deeper all around them but their path was clear. It looked so cold, but Cleo could not feel any sense of chill. Bacchus glided up the path as he always did, with stealth and ease, his shoulders moving rhythmically with his body. "This is so beautiful, Bacchus." said Cleo.

Bacchus nodded in agreement. "Not only are the mountains beautiful, Cleo" he said, "they are also very spiritual. Mountains hold ancient wisdom and can reveal your life's purpose. They run along the grid lines of the earth and they hold powerful energy. The grid lines are aligned across the whole of your earth. Many of your ancient temples and pyramids were built along those grid lines. You can feel the energy when you are there. And this is one of those places. Feel the energy, Cleo. It is very powerful."

"I do feel something very different," Cleo said. "Maybe I can find my life purpose while we are here." Bacchus nodded.

They continued to ascend the mountain. It was so quiet. No sounds, no animals. Just a slight breeze blowing across the snow. The path wove a circular pattern around the mountain as they climbed their staircase. Turning a corner, they could see a large animal coming toward them. He was amazingly agile as he walked across the mountain, sure footed, even when there were only a few inches of mountain cliff to traverse. Bacchus looked over and said, "Ah, Raguel! So wonderful to see you in this beautiful, amazing place." Cleo looked up to see a huge ram standing above them. He was an incredible sight. He was much larger than Bacchus with strong legs and a firm body. His horns were incredible. They grew from the center of the top of his head. Very thick at the base, curving upwards and around to a downward spiral as they wrapped around his head. At his chin, they spiraled forward, ending in sharp points near his mouth. His body was layered in thick cream-colored fur, and his face was pure white except for his black nose and eyes. He took on the glow of the bluest sky that stretched out behind him, radiating such a positive energy.

"Hello Bacchus," he said in a booming voice that reverberated across the mountain. "What a lovely day for you and Cleo to come. It is wonderful to see you both. Cleo, it is my honor to meet you." Cleo smiled and said, "Thank you, Raguel. It is my honor to meet you as well." Raguel continued. "I am pleased to show you this wonderful, magical place. Many amazing things have happened on this mountain. In fact, some may say it is life-changing. I hope it will be magical for you as well." Then Raguel looked over Cleo's shoulder and said, "Hello Ezrael. I am pleased you are here to protect our precious Cleo." Then he nodded back as Ezrael thanked him.

"Cleo," Raguel said, "I am demonstrating for you the concept of balance and harmony. Balance is obviously quite a key thing for rams. As we move across the mountain, we draw on Universal balance to sustain our footing and be in harmony with the mountains and the rocky peaks. Of course, that is physical harmony, which is also important for you humans as well. Cleo, do you have balance and harmony in your life?" Cleo smiled and said, "Well I do try and balance my life so that I don't work so much, but I find it hard most of the time. The demands from my job are a lot and now it's even worse." "Yes," said Raguel. "I understand you have quite the challenge before you. And it's good that you acknowledge that you need harmony in your physical world. That is very important. But I am also speaking about the balance and harmony between your physical and spiritual world. As you know already, you are a soul first, living an adventure in a human body. And because you chose to come to your earth to play and have that adventure, you should do just that. Live the life that is offered on earth. It is truly the only place in the Universe where the adventure is as intense and emotional. Enjoy it and do everything you can to learn, play and feel what is available. But also remember that your soul is always connected to your higher self and that is always connected to All That Is. So, it is as important for you to honor your spiritual path as it is to be in harmony with your physical life. When you combine the spiritual with the physical, you will feel a new sense of harmony. And it will help you see the infinity that is all around you."

"So, what would I need to do to have more harmony in my life Raguel?" asked Cleo. "That's a great question. First, don't take your physical life too seriously. Your earth adventure was always supposed to be fun. To feel all of the emotions and have all of the experiences without getting too caught up in the dense stuff. It's important to feel that and honor those emotions, just don't dwell there for too long. And second, set aside your time for meditation and stillness. That is how you reconnect to your higher self and to All That Is. That is your true state, after all. That unconditional love is your default. Connect to it every day. Then you will be open to have guidance show you the way for your physical life. That is the harmony I am speaking of and how you can achieve it. Do you understand?"

"Yes, I do," said Cleo. "So many of the animals on this adventure have shown me ways to do that and it always feels really good. No matter what else is happening in my life, I will set aside time to reconnect. I see why it is so important." "Ah, that's great Cleo." said Raguel. "Then you are ready to charge ahead with your life and your next adventure." "Yes," said Cleo. "I'm just not sure exactly what that is yet. Do you think the mountain can help me understand my purpose? Bacchus said that a lot of people have found their purpose when they are on the mountain." Raguel said, "Yes that's true Cleo. Many people have come here to understand themselves better and find new meaning to their lives. And you can do that too, of course. But I cannot tell you what your purpose is. I can only guide you to feel into it. But I will tell you a secret." "Oh, please do!" said Cleo. Raguel shook some of the snow off his face as he answered Cleo. "Your real purpose is to be happy. That's really it. You may not see it, but when you are happy, you are raising your consciousness and you are shining your light to others. And that's what it's all about. And being in harmony with life helps make you happy. Let go of trying to control things and just let things unfold before you. Listen to your intuition and your guides and you will never go wrong."

"So," asked Cleo, "I should use my intuition to help me find my real purpose?" Raguel nodded in agreement. "Think back, Cleo, to when you were talking to Netzach. He asked you about your joy and you talked about how you love to work with animals. There are hundreds of ways you can do that, you know. If that is your joy, then I can tell you, that if you follow your intuition, your purpose does involve animals in some way. Following your joy will lead you to your purpose."

Raguel then started to make his way down the mountain, closer to Bacchus and Cleo. He moved with such grace and ease that you would never imagine the steep terrain he climbed down was so dangerous. His hooves were split and had a rough bottom, so his grip was incredible. He was almost face-to-face with Cleo when she took a slight step back, seeing him descend. As she moved backward, her heel got caught on a small rock and she began to lose her balance. She started leaning backward, too far. As if in slow motion, she began to fall. Her head was spinning and she could not catch herself. And as she was about to fall, she felt a mighty grip behind her. It was so large and strong that it completely enveloped her. Before she could comprehend what was happening, the force pushed her back up to a standing position. It was Ezrael. Cleo stopped breathing and just stood there, stunned. Then she felt something change inside of her. It started in her gut, spread up through her heart and moved through her entire body. It was not anything that she could put into words. The energy that soared through her body was a thousand times stronger than anything she had ever felt. In that moment, she not only felt what Ezrael had done for her, she could see him. With her human eyes. He was immensely tall, wearing a flowing white robe. His face was almost transparent with a brilliant light shining from his eyes. He had angel wings as large as his body, covered in snow-white feathers with glimmers of gold. He looked at her with eyes so loving that Cleo felt the overwhelming sense of the most unconditional love imaginable. At that moment, she understood what Bacchus had said about seeing herself through the eyes of someone that loves you unconditionally. She took a breath and looked back at Ezrael. She smiled with a radiance that she had never had before. "Ezrael!" she shouted. "I can see you! Thank you for saving my life!" Ezrael smiled back, his eyes still beaming with light. And then he said, "I have always been there for you Cleo. I have watched you and protected you through all of your life times. I am your guardian angel and I will always protect you."

Raguel jumped down to the step that Cleo stood on to make sure she was balanced and secure. Bacchus wrapped his tail around her to make sure she knew he would also always protect her. Cleo had never felt so safe and loved. Bacchus thought to himself, she is now standing in her power. And he smiled.

"Ezrael," said Bacchus. "Thank you for protecting our Cleo." Ezrael nodded.

"Well, that was quite amazing." said Raguel. "Perhaps, Cleo, you could do with a ride back down the mountain." Cleo was still gathering herself and trying to come to terms with what had just happened. She smiled at Raguel and said, "Thanks Raguel. I think that would be a really good idea." Raguel leaned down so that Cleo could climb up on his back. As he stood up, he said, "Grab hold of my fur." Cleo grabbed his fur with both hands. It was so soft and warm. "Ready?" he asked. "Yes," she said. Raguel turned to begin the descent down the mountain. Bacchus and Ezrael followed.

As they made their way down the mountain, Cleo began feeling quite strong and empowered. Sitting on Raguel's back, she felt she was transforming. From cocoon to butterfly, and now beyond. The balance of masculine and feminine energy inside her was settling her into a harmonious place. She felt like a queen, a goddess, as they moved closer to the base of the mountain. Bacchus saw the changes happening within her and felt her strength, saw her glow. He knew now that she would never be the same girl who started this adventure. She was now awakened to the secrets of the Universe.

They reached the base of the mountain. Cleo climbed down from Raguel's back and was happy to be standing on firm ground. Thank you, Gaia, she thought. Raguel turned to Cleo. "That was truly an amazing adventure Cleo. I am honored that I was able to be part of your life-changing experience. Always remember to call on Ram

Spirit when you need a firm footing. We are all here for you always, in every moment. You only need to ask for our help and we will be there."

Raguel then turned to Bacchus and Ezrael and said, "Bacchus my dear friend. I will see you again soon, I hope. Ezrael, thank you and please continue to watch over our Cleo." Bacchus and Ezrael both smiled and nodded back. Then Raguel turned and started climbing the mountain. He stopped to look back one last time, his mighty horns following the subtle bow of his head. The blue glow followed him as he turned back to ascend to the top of the mountain.

SACHAEL THE SNAKE

Cleo was feeling more joyous and peaceful than she ever had before. The smile on her face told the whole story. Bacchus was so happy for her. He said, "Cleo, what just happened is really nothing short of life-changing. I can see it in your smile and in your eyes. I am truly happy for you." "Thank you, Bacchus." said Cleo. "I feel so amazing! It's like a veil has been lifted. I know I have found the peace that you said you could help me find. Thank you, again. And to also know, and see, Ezrael is just out of this world. I had no idea what I didn't know. Thank you again Ezrael for saving my life. I love you so much." Bacchus smiled and said, "I think we could use a warmer climate now. Shall we proceed?" Cleo nodded.

The path opened up before them as it always did. But this time it seemed more luminescent. Hmmm, thought Cleo; another change. They turned to the path and began to make their way. Ezrael followed closely to Cleo. The sparse landscape they were in was transforming into a warm, arid field. The sun was out and it felt so wonderful. A few trees dotted the landscape and there was a lot of grass and small bushes interspersed. The air felt dry and warm. There was a breeze blowing and sounds of nature all around them. It was a stark difference to the snowy mountain.

Bacchus came upon a small bush and stopped. Cleo did the same, awaiting the next part of their adventure. It was only a minute before they saw it coming toward them. A black snake. It was over 7 feet long and it glided over the terrain with ease. Weaving back and forth, it crawled to Bacchus and Cleo. When she saw it, Cleo let out a scared but quiet yelp. Oh, I HATE snakes, she thought. Eww! Bacchus chuckled to himself. "Hello Sachael," he said. "Hello Bacchus!" said Sachael. "And this is Cleo! So nice to finally meet you, Cleo." Cleo gathered every ounce of courage and composure that she could and quietly said, "Hello Sachael."

Sachael was a large snake with shiny black scales that glistened in the sun. His eyes were pitch black as well but did not seem to be as sinister as Cleo would have imagined. His forked tongue flicked in and out of his mouth as he spoke. He coiled up into a tall spiral so he could see them better. Cleo cringed. "Cleo," said Sachael, "I understand how you feel about snakes and I would never mean to make you uncomfortable in any way. I am not a poisonous snake and I would never, ever do anything to hurt you." Cleo sighed and said, "Thank you, Sachael. I don't know where this fear comes from. I have never been harmed by a snake and I am sure you are really nice or Bacchus would not have let you come." Sachael and Bacchus laughed.

Sachael said, "Snakes have had a bad rap for a really long time. Some of that goes back more than 13,000 years. The earth was getting ready to go through a cycle of separation from All That Is. It was beginning to "go to sleep" for a very long time, at least according to your earth years. There were many beings from the galaxy on earth at that time. Some of those were from Sirius. And they brought light energy as well as dark energy. That is neither good or bad, it's just the polarity that was playing out on earth at the time. The Sirian dark energy was associated to snakes and serpents. There were many mystery schools on earth and some of those were hijacked for darker purposes. So, you see, snake energy became associated to the dark energy and it still carries that very old signature. And then, some of your religions cast us as a demon. We were seen as evil and portrayed as the very embodiment of temptation. So, most of your fear is actually born of very old group consciousness. And it's very wide-spread. I bet if you asked a hundred people about snakes, 90% of them would be scared or even terrified of snakes, but would never have even had one bad encounter with them. But in reality, snakes are really beneficial to the earth and humans. We help keep the population of rodents to a manageable level and minimize their ability to spread disease. And only about 10% of snakes are venomous, and that's so they can catch their prey, which is normally not humans."

"Wow," said Cleo. "Now I feel sorry for you. And I had no idea that stuff so old could still impact me and the world today. I guess I still have a lot to learn." Sachael said, "Please don't feel sorry. We accepted this a long time ago and have no issues with it. It is a human fear after all, nothing that impacts us. And you are always learning Cleo. The more you learn, the more you clarify your inner self. It never ends, and that's the really cool part about the Universe. You can see things in a new light and continue to reconnect with your true authentic self."

"Yes, I can see that," said Cleo. "Look how much I have learned just now. It really is an amazing game and adventure. I am curious about so many things now. And the day-to-day annoyances don't seem so big anymore." "And that adventure is now taking a whole new form," said Sachael. "Just like Israfel said, you are shedding an old layer of skin. The old parts of you, the beliefs that don't really serve you any longer, are being shed, and a newer you is emerging. And that is what Snake Spirit can help you with."

"So Sachael," asked Cleo, "how do I know if a belief is not serving me anymore?" Sachael replied, "You will know because of your awareness, Cleo. It is so important that you notice everything that happens in your reality. Because you are creating all of it. Notice in the things that you say to others. Notice in the things they say to you. Notice in the people that are drawn into your reality. Notice the things that happen in your life. Remember that everything is reflected in your mirror. Nothing is chance. It is all seen through the filter of your beliefs. And most of those beliefs have been with you for so long, they are like an auto-pilot. You are not even aware of the influence they are having in your reality. So, you must continue to observe everything. And then when you see what's in the mirror, with no judgment, you can choose to keep that belief or undo that belief. And there is no right or wrong here. Remember, that is human ego and duality that judges something as right or wrong; good or bad. When you can see everything instead, as an experience, with no judgment, then you are free to make clear choices in what you want and what you don't want, in that moment. And then you shed another layer."

"It sounds like it all goes back to the audience." said Cleo. Sachael nodded in agreement. "It is a wonderful way to play your game. And remember something else. And here you can also take your queue from snakes. Just as we remain close to the ground, so should you. Grounding is also so important for you as you continually move through the changes in your life. And I think you have learned a lot about staying grounded, right?" "Oh, yes!" said Cleo. "I think my favorite way is walking in the woods, but now I know I can also stay grounded through stillness." "Your wisdom is impressive, Cleo" said Sachael. "And I hope that you will also shed your fear of snakes. We really are very compassionate beings. Oh, and we aren't slimy either! Would you like to touch my body and see?" Cleo let out a nervous laugh and cringed again, just slightly. Then she thought about Lakshmi and her courage. And she started to look at Sachael from the audience. If this fear is really something that has come from others, then maybe I don't need to choose that belief any longer, she thought. As she saw the fear from a different perspective, she relaxed and took a breath. "You know what, Sachael," she said, "I think I would like to do that."

Sachael smiled, flicking his tongue in and out. He slowly uncoiled and his long body was now completely on the ground. He moved slowly toward Cleo so that she could reach him. His body was quite amazing and flexible as he shifted from side to side along the ground. It did not take long for him to reach Cleo. "You can touch my head or my body, Cleo." said Sachael. "Whatever you are most comfortable with." Cleo tentatively reached out and put her hand on Sachael's body, right behind his head. Instead of feeling something slimy, Cleo felt Sachael's body as warm and dry. It was very firm to the touch. She was surprised how different it felt than what she imagined it would be. She smiled and said, "Wow Sachael. It's not what I was expecting at all!" Sachael laughed and Cleo could feel his laugh ripple through his body. Cleo removed her hand. "Thank you Sachael," she said, "for helping me overcome my fear." "You are very welcome." said Sachael. "That was as good as a release ceremony!"

"What do you mean, a release ceremony?" asked Cleo. Sachael said, "A wise shaman and friend, Dr. Sssssssss, told me about a ceremony that you can do to help release things you don't feel serve you any longer. Would you like to hear about it?" he asked. "Yes," said Cleo. "I would love to know more."

"OK" said Sachael. "First, decide something specific that you feel you want to let go of. For example, let's say you want to release the anger you have toward your boss about selling her company. With a sincere intention, write it on a piece of paper. The wording is specific. Phrase it as 'I choose to release...' So, it might read something like, 'I choose to release the anger I have toward my boss for selling her company.' Now you need to find something in nature that will assist you with the release. Go out and find something that speaks to you, like a rock or a twig. Then ask the object if it would be willing to help you and serve as your effigy. If you get a clear signal of yes, then keep it. If not, find something else until you feel you have found the right thing. Take the object home with you and wrap the piece of paper that you wrote your intention on around it and leave it on your bedside table overnight. When you go to bed, say a prayer of gratitude for your spirit guides to help you dream into the paper and the object, what you are releasing. You may even have dreams about it that night. The following day, go back into nature and find a favorite tree. Ask the tree if it would be willing to help you do your release ceremony.

If the answer is yes, then dig a hole at the base of the tree – that is the grave. Thank your spirit guides, Grandmother Moon, the tree and Tree Spirit. Then read the words on your paper out loud and re-wrap the object with the paper. Remember the intention, hold it in your heart, and gently blow your intention into the paper and the object. Finally, put the paper and the object into the grave and light it on fire. Watch the flames and smoke rise up to Sky Father. After it has burned completely, bury the ashes and the object. Then say a final prayer of thanks. You can also include an offering to the tree, something like sage or sacred tobacco. Then observe what happens over the next day or two and watch for anything that comes to you in your dreams. Watch the magic happen."

"That sounds really good," said Cleo. "Thank you. I will definitely do that when I get back."

Bacchus and Ezrael smiled, seeing Cleo's excitement about the Release Ceremony. Bacchus looked at Sachael and said, "Thank you Sachael. What a wonderful way to end our visit. We are honored to have spent this precious time with you." "It was my gift and pleasure," said Sachael. "Cleo, I hope Snake Spirit wisdom has opened your eyes to new and wonderful things. We are all here for you always, in every moment. You only need to ask for our help and we will be there." Cleo smiled and said, "Thank you Sachael. I have learned a lot and I appreciate what you have taught me."

Sachael flicked his tongue and turned his head back to the bush. His body followed as he swerved left and right, moving silently along the ground. In a few minutes, he was completely out of sight.

THOTH THE TOAD

Bacchus turned to Cleo and Ezrael and smiled. Just for a moment, he looked at them standing side by side. He could feel the love radiating from them both and just wanted to savor that for a while. Cleo smiled back and said, "What is it Bacchus?" "Utter joy," said Bacchus. "We still have much to see and learn, Cleo. I think we should be on our way." Cleo nodded. Bacchus turned to the path as Cleo and Ezrael followed. The path moved away from the warm and arid landscape toward a luscious, green meadow. As they weaved their way through thick, tall grass, the path magically opened a part that was easy to walk through. The meadow was alive with sounds, smells and beauty. The melody of birds and crickets created a wonderful background noise, all merging together so no one sound was distinct. The smells were very dense and even heavy. It was earthy and moist. There were smells of decay. As they moved further into the meadow, the path led to a wonderful little pond. It wasn't very big, but the water was calm and crystal clear. There were rocks and twigs strewn on the ground around it, and a fabulous display of flowers by the banks of the pond. It was so serene with the sounds in the background.

Bacchus sauntered up to the side of the pond and stopped. He sniffed the air and smiled. Cleo said, "Oh, Bacchus. This is so beautiful!" "Yes, it is," replied Bacchus. "Cleo, would you do something for me?" "Of course," said Cleo. Bacchus continued, "Would you try the look in the water again? Given what you have been through now, I would like to see if you can now tell yourself that you really love you. Because I think you have a new-found sense of self and you should love that." Cleo smiled a wide grin and walked to the edge of the pond. She leaned over and saw her reflection in the water. And this time she didn't cringe. She smiled. And as she looked at her reflection in the water, she boldly said out loud, "I LOVE YOU". And she felt it. Ezrael put his hand on her shoulder and she could feel the energy surge through her body. She felt a power and humility that was even beyond what she thought could be. "I did it Bacchus! I said it and I meant it!" Bacchus bowed his head toward Cleo, feeling her joy.

As Cleo looked at the pond, she saw a flash of something to her right. She looked closer to see a small toad, half in and half out of the water. He was so cute! "Look Bacchus!" she said. "There's a toad!" Bacchus laughed and said, "Cleo, meet Thoth." "Oh! Goodness. Hello Thoth!" said Cleo.

Thoth raised his head slightly as the lower part of his jawline blew up into a bubble. The bubble was as big as his head. Then he made the strangest sound. As Thoth pushed air through the sac under his jaw, he made a high-pitched call that sounded like a trill. It lasted for about 10 seconds. Then the sac disappeared back under his jaw. He was a funny looking thing to be sure. He had a small squatty body and was shades of green and brown. He had black markings all over, spots and lines. His head looked like a triangle with a wide jaw and two eyes that stood prominently on top of his head. His legs were short and fat, with little fingers jutting out from his webbed feet. He had bumps all over his body that blended into his leathery skin. "Hello Cleo. Hello Bacchus. Hello Ezrael." said Thoth.

"Thank you for meeting me at my favorite pond. Isn't this the most magical place!" Bacchus nodded back to Thoth and said, "It is a wonderful pond indeed. Thank you for having us here, Thoth. I am so pleased to see you again." "As I am pleased to see you, Bacchus." answered Thoth. "My, my, Cleo. You have had quite the journey. So much magic, so many animals. A wonderful transformation to be sure. Perhaps we can all just sit and relax for a moment and think about everything that has happened so far. Contemplation is so wonderful. May I discuss with you Cleo as you relax and reflect?" Cleo said, "Yes that sounds nice. My mind and body are racing right now, in a good way. But I could probably use some time to reflect."

"Perfect," said Thoth. "Cleo, right now, you are probably feeling better than perhaps you have ever felt in your whole life. And there is nothing better than that. Know that you can never return to the girl that you were when you started this adventure. She has now become the full butterfly, the hawk, with mighty wings to soar beyond what you can even imagine. Know that your path is assured and it only gets crazy good from here. It's going to take you days to journal everything that's happened for you." Cleo looked at Thoth and said, "Well I hadn't thought about that. I don't really keep a diary or journal." "Then," said Thoth, "this is the time to start. Writing is so therapeutic. And the written word will sustain you when you have your down days. And don't be fooled, you will have down days. You are a human and all humans have dense emotions. On those days, you can review your journal and see just how far you have come. I know you have computers and phones that you can use to write with, but I recommend writing your journal by hand. It is a different experience, more grounded. Feeling pen to paper is such a good way to connect back to yourself. Write everything you feel, what you think, and it will clarify for you. It is very healing. Remember what Fairy the Fox said. Write down your intuitive thoughts so you can go back and hone your intuition skills. Review your journal often to remind you of the accomplishments you have made. That kind of internal reflection will help you contemplate and see how strong your skills really are. And writing something on paper does another thing. It brings your thoughts into reality. As you write, you are berthing the idea into the world. And when you read it back, you can feel what you wrote. And that is very powerful. To see and feel your words. You are in a very volatile time in your life right now. Some days you may feel unsettled. Use your writing and your journal to ground you and get you back to a place of wholeness."

"That sounds like really good advice," said Cleo. Thoth nodded his little head and then leapt out of the pool on to a rock. He jumped with such ease as his back legs propelled him forward and he landed with a bit of a croak in his voice. He still had some water spots on his body. He said, "Yes, thank you. Writing can connect you with your primal instinctual self. When you are ready, you can also do some automatic writing to feel a stronger connection to All That Is." Cleo looked at him a little puzzled. "What is automatic writing?" she asked.

"Oh," said Thoth. "It is something I think you will enjoy. You get your pen and paper ready and thank your guides for inspiration and creativity. And then you just write. Don't think about it, don't try to force it. Just write. Anything. And as you continue to write, you will get messages and inspiration. You'll be in a state of trance and you just let it flow. You may not even be conscious of what you are writing. Have fun with it! That's the best part. Then you can read back what you wrote. You may be amazed at what you find."

"That actually sounds like fun!" said Cleo. "I can see that you take writing very seriously. And I can see the power in what you are saying. I will definitely do that going forward." "Good," said Thoth. "It's an important part of your daily sacred work. Set aside the time to meditate and write every day. The more you do that, the more it becomes part of that auto-pilot of your subconscious that Sachael was talking about earlier. And that, Cleo, is a belief that you want to keep. We are all here for you always, in every moment. You only need to ask for our help and we will be there."

Cleo smiled and thanked Thoth for his wisdom and insights. Bacchus said, "Thank you, Thoth, for always bringing good things. I appreciate your time and wish you a wonderful day in the pond." Thoth croaked with a big smile on his face and said "Thank you Bacchus. I will see you again very soon." Then Thoth turned and jumped back in to the pond, basking in the beautiful ripples he just created.

URIEL THE UNICORN

Bacchus laughed at Thoth's return to the pond. He turned to Cleo and said, "OK, Cleo. Now we have something wonderful to see. Are you ready for the next big thing?" "Oh yes, Bacchus. But how could it get any better?" answered Cleo. Bacchus laughed again. "Cleo, what is yet to come is beyond your wildest imagination." He then turned to move away from the pond and meadow and pick up the new path. Cleo and Ezrael followed, both smiling broadly.

The path led away from the meadow as the landscape began to change. The trees started disappearing. The grasses slowly disappeared as well. The path became more and more barren as they moved on. As they ventured further, there seemed to be nothing at all. No nature, no sounds, no smells. Cleo thought what a strange place we must be going to. Up ahead, there seemed to be a veil in front of them that covered everything they could see. It had no start, no end. It had no top, no bottom. It was transparent but they could not see through it. There was a light behind it that seemed to be oozing out through the ethereal veil. As they reached what felt like the veil itself, Bacchus stopped. He turned back to Cleo and said, "Cleo, this is a very magical place we are about to enter. I hope it brings you incredible joy." Bacchus turned back to the veil wall and walked straight through it. Ezrael took Cleo's hand and followed.

As they entered into this magical place, there was an overwhelming feeling of peace and playfulness. The vibrations were actually palpable and the energy running through Cleo's body was electrifying. It was completely silent. But the brightness of this loving light was so intense that Cleo felt she had to squint. It wasn't as bright as the light she first saw when she and Bacchus entered the forest through the tree, but it was very close. There was no landscape. No color. No sounds. No smell. Only an ethereal feeling of nothingness. Bacchus walked a few more feet into the ether and stopped. Cleo and Ezrael stopped behind him. Then Bacchus lifted his head and waited. He stood completely still.

Out of the ether then came the most beautiful sound Cleo had ever heard. It was very high-pitched, but very pleasant to her ears. It wafted through the nothingness and filled the space with amazing harmonies and incredible voice. It was as if the most beautiful opera singer was doing her final aria. The notes were pitch perfect, the breath work was amazing and the song lulled you into the most wonderful, loving trance. Cleo could not see where the sound was coming from. So instead, she just closed her eyes and felt the sounds move through her body. It felt like waves and waves of love flowing over her. She felt alive, youthful and yet incredibly peaceful. She was so lost in herself that she barely heard Bacchus speak.

"Greetings, Uriel," said Bacchus. Cleo opened her eyes and was so amazed she could not contain herself. Before her stood the most magnificent unicorn! It was much larger than a normal horse. And of course it had a single horn coming from its forehead. The horn was made of the muted colors of the rainbow. It twisted into a spiral as it emerged from Uriel's head. And the glow, oh the glow! It was the most astounding aura of yellow, orange, and white light. Uriel also had large, fabulous wings. They were spread out to reveal the intricate feathers that were woven together. Like Ezreal's wings, there were shimmers of gold running through them while the rest was pure white, like his body. His mane was rather short and mostly stood up on his neck.

Cleo had to stop to catch her breath. She was in complete awe.

Uriel knew what Cleo's reaction would be. The Unicorns were used to that by now. So, he just let her settle into the space for a bit. Time was irrelevant, so it didn't matter how long they just "were". After a long while, Uriel said, "Hello Bacchus. So fun to see you again my dear one. And love to you, Cleo. It is our greatest joy to see you here with Ezrael. The Unicorns have a strong connection to the angelic realm and we love to see our angel friends." Ezrael took a deep bow and said, "And so it is my great pleasure to see you as well, Uriel."

Cleo took a deep breath and said, "Hello Uriel. Wow, this is way beyond my wildest dreams!" Uriel took a deep bow and said, "It is our honor to have you here. You have raised your vibration to be able to see us and we are so pleased you have found that power within you. Love to you, my dear one." As Uriel spoke, his horn seemed to channel the light that was all around and it began to glow.

Uriel continued after shaking his broad head. A surge of beautiful music rose in the background. "Cleo, we are pleased to show you some amazing things during your time with us. It's quite rare that we have the opportunity to spend so much time with a human. We are grateful to Bacchus for arranging this. Because you have raised your vibration, you now have access to many things in the non-visible world. So, let's take a little adventure, shall we?" Cleo was so excited she was shaking. "I would be so grateful to take an adventure with you, Uriel," she said.

"Good, my dear one. I think it would be most exciting to actually visit these non-visible things. Are you ready to take a ride with me?" Cleo couldn't speak, so she just nodded yes. "OK, climb up on my back and we will be off." Ezrael lifted Cleo up so that she could sit on Uriel's back. She sat right behind his neck, her legs straddling his immense body. His wings were spread out fully behind her. "Now grab my mane, let go of your worries and let's go play!" Cleo grabbed his mane with both hands as Uriel lifted off out of the nothingness. He flapped his large wings to ascend. The movement was so smooth that Cleo barely felt like they were moving. She started to laugh.

As Uriel flew upward, they flew out of the fog of nothingness into space. It was dark, but lit up by millions of stars. Cleo could see nothing below them but more space. But as they continued flying, she began to see planets. It was so quiet that Cleo had no trouble hearing Uriel as he spoke. "Cleo, do you know what your planetarian origin is?" "I didn't know I had a planetarian origin!" Cleo answered. "Well, then, my dear one, I shall show you," said Uriel. Uriel headed for a group of stars and planets up ahead. "We are going to the Pleiades," he said.

As they flew closer, Uriel continued. "All humans have a galactic origin, Cleo. Your origin started from the Lyran lineage, but your basic DNA is a combination of Lyran and earth primates. When that Lyran branch decided to leave earth, they joined with the pure Lyrans and started the Pleiadian civilization. And that is your true origin." Uriel was now in the Pleiadian star system so he stopped and hovered in the middle of the magnificent stars. There were seven stars grouped together and they glowed brightly with a luminous blue hue. "The Pleiadians have been through their own work to balance the masculine and feminine energies and raise their vibration and frequency. They did a lot of deep soul searching and inner work in order to make that shift. Now they are some of the most loving people in the Universe. That's where you get a lot of your tendencies for love and compassion for others on earth. And the Pleiadians are helping humans to remember their galactic origins and teach them how to do their own inner work so that they too can raise their consciousness and their frequency."

Cleo was trying to take this all in and remember everything that Uriel was saying. She repeated some of it out loud to help her remember. "So, I am part Lyran and part Pleiadian. And I get my tendencies from mostly the Pleiadian energy. That's why I have a loving and compassionate nature. Are all humans Lyran and Pleiadian?" she asked. "Well, dear one," said Uriel, "humans are a genetic mix of many galactic families. That is why there is such a huge diversity in your bodies, skin color, eye color and hair textures. We are amused when humans call others in various dimensions 'extra-terrestrial,' because humans are the most extra-terrestrial ones there are! One day you will all remember your galactic origins. It is part of your game on earth."

Cleo laughed at Uriel's attempt at a joke. "There are so many other realms as well," said Uriel. "Would you like to see?" "Oh, yes!" exclaimed Cleo. "Good, dear one. Then let's be off." Uriel flew through the stars and into another place of nothingness, only to emerge into the wonderful, playful realm of the sprites and fairies. "I think you have already met some of the fairies, Cleo." said Uriel. "Yes! They are so cute and so much fun. We saw them when we met Fairy the Fox." "Well, this is where they reside. They can come and go as they please, through several dimensions. And they are great fun. Remember Cleo, that this is all meant to be fun! Playing is so important for humans. It brings you joy, which is the highest emotion. It connects you back to all of this. The Universe, the Multiverse. The true nature of who you really are."

"And now, on to another realm!" said Uriel, as he flew away from the fairies. Next, they visited a very different realm. "This, dear one, is the realm of the dragons!" said Uriel. As they approached, Cleo could see all sorts of dragons. They were all different colors and their scales were luminescent and glistening. They were huge creatures! As they approached, Cleo could sense the love and peace of this place. "Wow!" said Cleo. "This is amazing! Look at all of the dragons!" "Yes," said Uriel. "The dragons came here when humans started to demonize them and hunt them. That was a long time ago in your earth years. But before that, humans had a very special relationship to the dragons. So even though they are no longer in physical form on the earth, you can still connect to their energy when you ask. They are happy to come to you and show you their incredible magic."

Cleo laughed to herself. I guess Bacchus was right, she thought. All of these things really do exist and I didn't believe him. Uriel laughed at Cleo's thought. "Yes, Cleo. All of it does exist, and more. Bacchus would never be anything but truthful. And speaking of Bacchus, perhaps we should get back, dear one. He and Ezrael will be waiting for you." Cleo nodded. Uriel turned and headed back to the Unicorn Realm. They arrived after one last fabulous flight through the stars. Uriel landed gently and stopped. Ezrael walked over and lifted Cleo off of Uriel's back and set her back on the ground. He could feel the excitement in her body and saw a new glow in her eyes. "Looks like you and Uriel had a grand adventure!" said Ezrael. "Oh, Ezrael!" said Cleo. "It was beyond my wildest imagination and it did bring me incredible joy!" And she looked over at Bacchus and laughed.

Uriel laughed along with them. "Cleo, remember this as you continue to connect to the light and feel the energy of All That Is. Be inspired, follow your joy, feel your power and play. That is what Unicorn Spirit can always help you with, dear one. We are all here for you always, in every moment. You only need to ask for our help and we will be there." "Thank you, Uriel." said Cleo. "This was so amazing!" Uriel bowed his head as his horn glowed even brighter.

Bacchus walked over to Uriel and looked up at him. "Uriel, you have been a wonderful galactic guide. We appreciate your time, your wisdom and your love. Until I see you again, I wish you joy." "Thank you, dear one," said Uriel. "You are always welcome. Ezrael, I'm sure I will see you soon as well." Uriel shook his head as the nothingness began to fill the space and he faded out into the void. The beautiful sounds of that amazing harmony rose up again as Bacchus, Ezrael and Cleo turned to leave.

VARUNA THE VULTURE

Bacchus nodded to Cleo and Ezrael to follow. As he walked away from the Unicorn Realm, he said, "Cleo, we are almost done with our adventure of discovery. But we have a few more friends and teachers to meet." He then turned to follow the new path as it unfolded. From the depths of nothingness, they began to see more signs of life. A stream appeared beside them that grew in width and depth as they proceeded. Some trees became visible as they entered an area with both wooded vegetation and grasslands. It was open and airy. They began to hear the familiar sounds of birds, squirrels, rabbits and chipmunks. The animal population was flourishing before them. Cleo still wore a huge smile from her ride with Uriel and she was still immersed in the joy she felt. As she walked with Bacchus and Ezreal, she asked, "Ezrael, is there an Angelic Realm as well? I saw the fairies and dragons but we didn't see any Angelic Realm." Ezrael nodded. "Oh, yes," he said. "There is a beautiful Angelic Realm as well. I think you know Cleo, that angels can be everywhere at once so we can support and comfort all that need us. But we always have a presence in the realm. And all of the angels are there, as well as the Ascended Masters." "Wow," said Cleo. "I would love to see that someday. I can imagine that it is amazingly beautiful. How many angels are there?" Ezrael laughed, "So many that you cannot count that high, Cleo! And there are so many different kinds. You heard something about the Archangels from Micheal. There are a lot of them. And then of course you know about the Guardian Angels now. But there are also lots of helper angels. There are joy guides, runner angels, healer angels, teacher angels, and SOS angels. And of course, angels can come in the form of animal guides too. I will teach you about all of the angels that you can call on for assistance when you need them. They are here for you all of the time and if you ask, they will come." "Oh my gosh!" said Cleo. "I had no idea! And what about the Ascended Masters that you mentioned. Who are they?"

"Ah, the Ascended Masters." said Ezrael. "They are very special. You are probably familiar with some of the names and others you may not have heard of. They were incarnate on earth at one time, and were spiritually enlightened beings. They came to show people what their potential is, the potential for all humans, as a guide and an example. You will know some of them like, Jesus, Buddha, Isis, Mother Mary and Lao Tze. But there are so many more. And you can call to them for guidance just like you would an angel." "Oh, yes," said Cleo. "I have heard of some of them. Ezrael, I want you to help me explore everything about the angels and ascended masters. Would you do that with me?" "Of course, Cleo," said Ezrael. "I am always here to assist you."

They had continued walking as they talked and now were standing beside a roaring river. The landscape around them was fully grown in and the colors and smells were wonderful. Bacchus had enjoyed listening to their conversation and was pleased to hear Cleo's interest in other realms. She is now even awakening to her galactic heritage and other Universal realms, he thought. And then he smiled.

Up ahead, next to a small bush on the edge of a clearing, Cleo saw a form lying on the ground. From where she was, she could see it was fairly large and had fur. She looked to Bacchus. "Bacchus, what is that over there on the ground? Is that our next animal friend, taking a nap?" Bacchus shook his head slowly. "No, Cleo. I'm afraid that it is not. Come, let's take a closer look." They all walked toward the furry form on the ground. As they approached, it did not move. At all. No breathing, no sounds. "Oh, Bacchus!" Cleo exclaimed. "It's a wolf! Is it dead?" she asked. "Yes, Cleo. Our friend the wolf is dead." Cleo looked at the dead wolf. He was completely peaceful with no marks of injury that she could see. He looked as though he had just laid down for a quick nap. "Oh, Bacchus. That's so sad. The poor thing," said Cleo. "Yes, it is always sad when we lose a loved one. Perhaps we can have Ezrael help its soul transition to All That Is."

Ezrael nodded and said a prayer over the wolf. "Ariel will be with him and help his soul ascend," said Ezrael. "Remember, she is the watcher over all beings in this natural world." Cleo began to cry. What a stark difference in emotions from when she was with Uriel to finding a dead wolf. "Thank you, Ezrael," she said. "Death is such a horrible thing to have to go through."

"Yes," said Bacchus. "Death evokes very strong emotions in humans. And some of that is because a lot of humans believe that death is the end. And it is the end for the body. Being separated physically from ones that you love is very emotional. But Cleo, now you know that the spirit can never die. It is eternal. The body is dead, but the life spirit still exists and will always exist. So, this wolf spirit will now ascend to All That Is and soon decide what next form it wants to take. It has gone back to the light. The light we saw when we started our adventure. Perhaps that will help you to see this as a transition and birth into another life." "Yes, I can see that." said Cleo. "But it's still sad."

Before Bacchus could answer further, they saw a great bird flying toward them. As it got closer, Cleo could see the immense size of this beautiful bird in flight. His wing span was at least six feet and he glided through the air with grace and ease. He was completely silent. "Wow," said Cleo. "That bird is so beautiful!" The vulture flew closer and was now more easily seen. Then he flew down to the ground and settled next to Bacchus. As Cleo could now see this giant bird close up, she cringed! Oh my gosh, it's so ugly, she thought. Eww.

Bacchus looked at the vulture and said, "Hello Varuna. Thank you for coming to meet us." Varuna nodded his bald head. He could not speak, but made raspy, hissing sounds. His communication was telepathic, since vultures don't have a voice box. 'Greetings Bacchus' he thought. 'I am pleased to see you all. And hello Cleo.' To her amazement, Cleo could 'hear' the vulture. She nodded toward him and said, "Hello, Varuna." He was an extremely large bird. The feathers that covered his body were black, with some white on the underside of his wings. His head was bald, which gave him an eerie look and feel. And the skin on his head was wrinkled and bumpy. He had big brown eyes and a very long beak, that curved down to a sharp point at the end. His legs were bare of feathers and instead were spindly looking with large claws at the end. Cleo cringed again as she saw Varuna up close.

'Cleo,' Varuna thought, 'I know you think I am beautiful in the air but ugly close up. Don't worry. Like Sachael, we are used to that human reaction and we are not bothered by it. It is part of your ego that makes judgments on things and likes to do comparisons. I am neither ugly nor beautiful. I just am. It is your emotion and belief system that categorizes me as ugly. And part of that belief system helps you believe that what we vultures do is gross. Eating dead animals. We get that too. There are so many beliefs in your world about death.'

Cleo was still stunned that she could "hear" Varuna but also saddened that her reaction to him was so negative. She remembered Sachael and the lesson she thought she had learned about judgment. Well, she thought, I guess I still have some work to do. 'It's OK Cleo,' thought Varuna. 'Remember that you are on a learning journey and sometimes it takes years to learn something. And that's also OK. You will eventually find the gifts in knowing me. You see, vultures are a necessary part of the whole ecosystem. Yes, we clean up dead animals. And that is so they don't contaminate other things. We are graced with so many unique things in order to fulfill our purpose. You think my bald head is weird and ugly, but do you know why my head is bald when other birds have feathered heads?' "No, I guess I don't." said Cleo. 'Well, it is so the bits of carrion, the dead animal, don't get caught in my feathers. If I had feathers all over my head, it would be a real mess trying to clean up after doing my work. It may sound gross to you, but we are specifically engineered to carry out our purpose. We can eat rotted meat that would be toxic to other animals. Just like Michael has that special DNA that makes him immune to cobra venom, vultures have special bacteria on our skin and in our intestines that allow us to digest dead flesh. This bacteria is extremely toxic to other animals, but not us. So, we can digest what other animals cannot. We do a great service to your world using the gifts built into our bodies from All That Is. And we can smell dead animals over a mile away. Death is inevitable, so we just help with taking care of it. And there is great beauty in that.'

"Yes, I can see that," said Cleo. "Actually, you really are amazing in what you do. I'm sorry I was not more understanding." 'Thank you.' thought Varuna. 'I appreciate your sincere desire to overcome your feelings about vultures. We are part of the circle of life, Cleo. Just like the roaring river beside us. Water sustains all life. It is sacred and should be treated as such. And just as water nourishes all life, the vultures ensure that death is also treated with reverence and respect. We seek out the opportunities to transform death, much like you can seek out opportunities to transform yourself. Just as we look for those opportunities from 10,000 feet, you can do the same for your life. Remember what Haniel said, take the higher perspective. And learn to see beauty where others cannot. You have a new awareness that most of the other humans don't have, Cleo. Release yourself to the winds of change and fly with us.'

Bacchus looked at Varuna and said, "Thank you Varuna for your insights and what you do for all of nature. You are very important and we appreciate you. And we are blessed that you will take care of wolf, as you do so, respectfully, for all dead animals."

'Thank you, Bacchus.' thought Varuna. Then Varuna turned back to Cleo. 'Remember Cleo, we are all here for you always, in every moment. You only need to ask for our help and we will be there. And now I must get to my work.'

Cleo thanked Varuna for his wisdom and contribution as she and Bacchus turned to leave wolf. Ezrael said a final blessing for wolf and Varuna before following them. As they left, the other vultures came to join Varuna in his sacred work.

WAHKAN THE WOLF

Cleo was still feeling sad about wolf as they continued on the new path. Bacchus could sense her emotions and said, "Cleo, would you like to know more about wolf?" "Yes, I think that would help me," said Cleo. "Did you know wolf?" Bacchus nodded. "I did know wolf and still know his spirit. He played a very special role in your world. If you would like to meet wolf spirit, we can do an animal spirit walk and you can talk with him." "Oh, that would be nice. Should we stop and do a meditation to speak to him?" Cleo asked. Bacchus answered, "Well, that is how we would normally connect to an animal spirit, but in this case, I think we should go and meet him. But to do that, we will need to travel to the Lower World." "What is the Lower World?" asked Cleo.

Bacchus began. "In Shamanistic and Native American practices, there are three worlds. They are all safe and they are all inhabited with spirit beings. There is the Upper World, the Middle World and the Lower World. The Upper World is very etheric. The animals there are mostly mythological ones, like dragons and Pegasus. The people are mostly spiritual teachers. It is a place like Haniel spoke of, to see the higher perspective. The Middle World is where you live most of the time. It is both physical and energetic. That is the world where you can experience both pain and joy. The Lower World is where we need to go. It is true nature, the nature that is unspoiled and pure. It is a world of healing and connects us back to the Universal web of life. It is where we go to meet the animal spirits."

"There is so much I still want to learn, Bacchus," said Cleo. "I'm ready to journey to the Lower World." "OK. Then let's be on our way," said Bacchus.

The three started down a new path. This path was winding and became less dense with vegetation and trees. As they continued, they could see, up ahead, the mouth of a cave. Cleo was a little apprehensive about entering a cave, but as she had seen so many times in her journey, everywhere Bacchus took her was safe. Bacchus said, "Cleo, the cave is safe and Ezrael and I will always protect you. You are about to enter a most magical part of your journey. Are you ready to proceed?" Cleo nodded, feeling a little better knowing that Ezrael and Bacchus would be by her side.

They entered the cave and the path led them down a small corridor. It was darker than when they were outside, but there was enough light to see. They continued. The path began to form a spiral staircase that led down into the earth. As they descended, Cleo could see the millions of years of rock formations that made up the walls and floor of the cave. She could see root systems from trees that spread out like an amazing network of cables overhead. And these roots were alive with life. Cleo could see the visible energy running through the roots and connecting the trees that must be above them now. It was a fabulous, intricate labyrinth of living energy. As they descended further, it began to get lighter. "Bacchus," asked Cleo, "how can it be getting lighter here since we are going down into the earth?" Bacchus stopped and looked back to Cleo. "Can you see the crystals that are all over the walls now? Those are the light that you are seeing." Cleo looked around to see the expansive crystals all around them. They were glowing with the most amazing, soothing light she had ever seen. "What is all of this?" asked Cleo. "These are the crystals that are most sacred to your earth." said Bacchus. "Crystals hold the information from past civilizations that have come and gone. Lemuria, Atlantis and many others that were helped and supported by the galactic federation. When these civilizations disappeared, their history and information did not. It was transferred to the crystals in the earth, awaiting the day when they could be awakened again. That day is now, Cleo. These crystals are becoming awake with the consciousness of Gaia. And they will light our way forward."

"I can't believe how bright they are, Bacchus," said Cleo. "It's like a bright lantern to show us the way." "Yes, they are amazing things.

And they also have a concentration on your earth like the ley lines we saw with Raguel. There are certain parts of your earth that have a large concentration of crystals. And humans can feel that connection when they are there, if they seek it."

As they continued to descend the spiral staircase, they saw layers of magma, rock, and things Cleo could not even describe. But at no time were they ever in danger and Cleo felt very safe, even as she was amazed at what she saw. As they turned the next corner of the spiral staircase, they entered into an open grassy area. It looked like what you would see on Middle World. "We have reached the Lower World," said Bacchus. "Take a minute to relax and soak in this new environment Cleo."

By this time, Cleo's head was spinning. She thought, how did we go from the earth core to a meadow! This is the coolest adventure ever! She looked around her. Within her field of vision, she could see a meadow, a forest, a beach, a mountain. Every kind of landscape she had ever known. She soaked it all in for a bit and then said, "Bacchus, how do we decide where to go?"

Bacchus said, "Well, when you are doing an animal spirit walk in your meditation, you will see the same thing. Then you will be led to go where the animal spirit guides want you to go. But today, we will go to the forest, where wolf spirit is." Bacchus began to head toward the forest. Cleo and Ezrael followed. They entered the forest and stopped beside a tree that had a large stump beside it. Bacchus motioned for Cleo to sit on the stump. "Now, Cleo. Ask Wolf Spirit to come."

Cleo closed her eyes and, in her mind, asked for Wolf Spirit to come. As she opened her eyes, she saw a wolf walking toward her. He was powerful and purposeful in his walk as he approached the trio. As he got closer, Bacchus said, "Hello Wahkan. We are honored to see you and thank you for coming." Wahkan continued to get closer and stopped when he was within a few feet of Cleo. "Hello Bacchus," he said. "I am pleased and honored that you have journeyed so far to see me. Hello Cleo. Hello Ezrael. I am happy that you are here and I am happy to spend some time with you." Cleo smiled back at Wahkan and said, "Hello Wahkan. I am so pleased to see you in this form instead of what we saw a little while ago." Wahkan nodded his approval. "Cleo, Bacchus said that you have some questions for me and would like to know me better. What questions can I answer for you?"

"Well," said Cleo. "I was wondering what happened to you. You looked so peaceful and it made me sad to see you there, on the ground." "Please don't be sad," said Wahkan. "As you can see, I am still the spirit I have always been and I am not in pain or sadness. When you transcend to the Lower World, it is beautiful and I am reconnected to All That Is, which is a wonderful thing. To go back to the light is a most peaceful way to be. But to answer your question, my purpose and mission was fulfilled on your earth, so I was ready to take a new form."

"So, if I may ask, what was your purpose and mission?" asked Cleo. "Of course you can ask," said Wahkan. "My mission was to protect a young boy who went through some significant trauma in his life. He was not always aware that I was there as his spirit animal, but I never left his side. And even through the car accident and him losing his parents, I was always there to protect him and guide him. And I think you know who that was, Cleo, don't you?"

Cleo held her breath for a moment, as she could sense the connection with Wahkan and her brother. Her intuition was firing. "Oh my gosh!" she said. "You were the spirit animal for my brother!" "Yes, I was." said Wahkan. "And I never left his side through all of that. I protected him spiritually and psychically, as all wolf spirits do. I helped him understand his self-esteem and integrity when he was feeling misunderstood by his friends. And did you know, Cleo, that he is going through his own awakening experience? Much like you. Not in the same way, of course, but no less transformational. And now he is ready for a new animal spirit guide. One that will take him from college to his next purpose. He is ready for a new animal spirit guide that will help him become who he is to be. And that is not me. So, I laid down and died, to be transformed into a new guide for someone who needs me."

"I am so pleased to know that you were there for my brother," said Cleo. "We both needed help, even if we didn't recognize it as animal spirit guides. But why can't you stay with him now? I don't understand that he doesn't need you any longer."

Wahkan said, "Animal spirits have many differences, depending on what you need at that time during your journey on earth. As you have seen with the animals that you have met on this journey, each animal brings a unique guidance and strength. So, as you move through your journey, you need different help. You have seen the various lessons that the animals have taught you, Cleo. And so, you can see how sometimes you need a different kind of support, protection and guidance. And you can have a number of animal spirit guides at the same time and through your life journey. And then you have a power animal. This is an animal spirit that is very personal to you and your personality and characteristics will mimic those of the animal spirit. Your brother needs a different kind of guidance and support now. And so, a new power animal has come to him to assist him."

"Oh, I see," said Cleo. "Well, what about me? Who is my power animal?" Wahkan and Bacchus both chuckled at Cleo's question. Then Wahkan said, "Just look beside you, Cleo. Through your transformation, Black Panther Spirit is your power animal."

Cleo looked at Bacchus and smiled. "Bacchus!" she said with excited tone as she jumped up from the stump she was sitting on. "Why didn't you tell me you were my power animal!" Bacchus laughed. "Everything comes at exactly the right time, Cleo. And now is the right time for you to know this. Always trust Universal timing Cleo. It is never wrong." Cleo smiled and then looked to Ezrael. She said, "Ezrael, you said that angels can come in the form of animal guides. Is that the same thing?" Ezrael smiled and was happy to know that Cleo remembered what he said. He spoke, "It is the same thing, Cleo. Angels will send love and blessings through the animal kingdom world. They will send inspiration through animals and send messages for you as well. Remember, at our source we are all one, All That Is. So, whether your message is from an angel, an animal spirit or an angel speaking as an animal spirit, it is all here to help you remember that you are part of All That Is, just like we all are." Wahkan nodded and said, "Yes, Cleo. We are all connected. And these valuable insights and teachings you are receiving are very important, so pay close attention. Have I answered all of your questions, Cleo?"

"Yes, thank you Wahkan. It was a great pleasure to meet you here in the magical Lower World. And thank you again for everything you did for my brother. I will be sure and tell him all about this when I see him next." Wahkan shook his head in acknowledgement. He said, "We are all here for you always, in every moment. You only need to ask for our help and we will be there." Then he turned to Bacchus and said, "Bacchus, my dear friend. I will see you soon and wish you all a magical end to your journey." "Thank you Wahkan," said Bacchus. "I will indeed see you again and I look forward to seeing your new form." Wahkan gave a subtle wink to Ezrael as he turned to leave.

XAVIER THE XENOPS

Bacchus turned to begin the ascent back to Middle World. Cleo and Ezrael followed his lead. As they neared the cave entrance, Bacchus looked back to Cleo and said, "Cleo, you saw the tree roots when we were descending. Take a closer look now." Cleo looked up to see the labyrinth of roots now above her head. "They really are amazing, Bacchus," said Cleo. "Yes," said Bacchus. "They symbolize the connection to all things. And they are connected to each other through their roots. Did you know that trees can nurse each other by sending electrical currents through the root systems? And, they will keep ancient stumps alive for centuries by feeding them a sugary substance through the roots. Their connection is very strong and that should be honored. Remember what you see here."

They reached the mouth of the cave and stepped back to the Middle World. Bacchus found the new path that led from the cave and began to walk. The landscape became quite tropical. There were large trees with lots of branches and vegetation and animals all around.

As the path led them by a large tree, they could hear a fast, chattering trill from one of the branches. Bacchus stopped and looked up. He smiled as he saw Xavier sitting on a branch, chattering. "Hello Xavier!" shouted Bacchus. Xavier looked down and saw the visitors. He stopped his chattering and called out to Bacchus. "Bacchus! So glad you are here! This is much better than that musty old cave!" Bacchus laughed. "Cleo," he said, "This is Xavier."

"Nice to meet you Xavier," said Cleo. "If I might say, you are so exotic! I don't think I have ever seen a bird quite like you." Xavier let out a trill and said, "Well, thank you Cleo. So nice to finally meet you. Yes, I am probably something you have never seen. I am a Xenops!" Cleo looked closer at this beautiful bird. It was only about 3 inches long but had the most beautiful coloring. His body feathers were mostly tan with some black and orange painted on his wings. His head had a white stripe under his eyes and a tan stripe over them. His little beak was wedge-shaped and the tip was turned slightly up. He had a rather long tail. "And you have good timing!" said Xavier. "I was just finishing up some foraging."

"Cleo," Xavier continued. "Wahkan was just talking to you about connectedness. What do you think he meant by that?" "Well," said Cleo. "We were talking about how angels and animal spirits were connected. So, I guess that's what he meant?" "Yes, indeed that is one part," said Xavier. "And weren't you also just talking about how the trees are connected through their roots?" "Oh, yes!" said Cleo. "That is amazing!"

Xavier gave a little chatter and fluffed his feathers. "Can you see how you are connected to all of that?" he asked. "Ummm," mused Cleo. "I feel like I'm connected to all of that, but I'm not sure how to describe it." "Yes," said Xavier. "It can be difficult to explain. Let's see if I can help. Think about your body. Are your fingernails connected to your kidneys?" Cleo thought for a minute, not sure where this was going. "Well, they aren't directly connected, I guess. But they are all part of my body." "Yes, that's right!" laughed Xavier. "You don't even really think about it at all, right? They are connected through your body systems and you don't really think about it. Now, what about your connection to the trees. Do you feel as connected to a tree as you do to your kidneys?" "Of course not," laughed Cleo. "Why?" asked Xavier. "Because they are separate from me," answered Cleo.

"Ah," sighed Xavier. "The separation game. Your egoic structure is so good at giving you the perception that you are separate. Your perception comes from what you can sense in the physical world. But that is such a small part of the bigger, higher perspective. Let's go back to when you and Bacchus were talking about your chakras. You learned what those were, didn't you?" "Oh yes," said Cleo. "Those are my energy centers in my body." "Absolutely," said Xavier. "In fact, that's what your whole body is made of, energy. And that's what everything in the Universe is made of, energy. And that's the same energy as All That Is. So, if everything is energy, then wouldn't everything be connected?" "That makes sense that it would be," said Cleo. "So," continued Xavier, "how would you be connected to all of the other humans?" "I guess it would be through the energy," answered Cleo. "Exactly!" said Xavier. "So how can you acknowledge that connection and make it stronger? Let's play a new game. Cleo, have you ever resented someone for spending money that you didn't have? Or have you ever felt resistant when someone you work with got a raise and you didn't? Or have you ever been jealous when you saw a couple in love and you were alone?"

"Well, to be honest, I have done all of those things," said Cleo. "And that's OK, Cleo," said Xavier. "No judgment here. Part of the game of separation from All That Is. And you all are very good at it! Now, remember that everything is made of energy. Everything. And all of what we just talked about is energy too. So, when you resent, resist and are jealous, you are only really blocking energy. Because energy can't flow where there is resistance. Now, let's play the next part of this game. And this part is all about allowing and receiving, so it's fun! Imagine that person who is spending their money. Now be happy for them, and say yes! Because that opens the flow for that energy to also come to you. Imagine the person who just got that raise. Woohoo! Be happy. Because that opens the flow for that energy to flow to you. You get the point. When you release the resistance, you allow that energy to flow to you as well! Isn't that cool?"

"Oh my," said Cleo. "I have never looked at things that way before. It makes a lot of sense and more than that, it *feels* right."

"Indeed," said Xavier. "Now one final part of this game. Oh, such fun! Now, feel your heart. You can put your hands over your heart if you want. Now feel your heart connected to everyone else on the planet. Say to yourself, 'Every heart on the planet has love for me. Every heart on the planet has love for me. And I have love for every heart on the planet.' Now feel your brain. Feel your brain connected to every other brain on the planet. Say to yourself, 'Every brain on the planet is working for me, inventing for me, coming up with new solutions for me. Every brain on the planet is working for me and my brain is working for everyone else on the planet.' And Cleo, when you can feel that, it is absolute, pure abundance. And it's there for everyone who chooses it. And because it's all energy, there is enough for everyone, because energy never goes away, it just changes form."

"Wow," said Cleo. "That just blew my mind!"

"Yes," said Xavier. "I thought you would like that. And there's more! It's not just the other humans. Everything on the planet is working in your favor. All of nature, the water, the animals, the plants, everything. Say it with me, 'Everything on this planet is working for me and I am working for everything on the planet.' Feels pretty good, huh?"

Cleo was smiling so broadly you could feel the energy from her aura expanding. She got it. In spades.

"But one question, Xavier," asked Cleo. "How am I working for everything on the planet. What do I have to do?" Xavier chirped a few trills of glee and said, "You are doing it now, Cleo! You are living in joy. And that's all you have to do! It's so easy and so much fun! Hasn't everyone on this adventure told you to be sure you are having fun and living in your joy? Lighten up, as they say. It's supposed to be fun!"

Cleo was laughing and feeling so connected. What an amazing game, she thought. Bacchus smiled at Cleo and let out a laughing grunt. He looked up at Xavier and said, "Xavier, that's an amazing lesson.

Thank you for what you have shared with us all." Cleo looked up and said, "Yes, Xavier. That's a lesson I will never forget. Thank you so much." Xavier trilled and said, "Cleo, we are all here for you always, in every moment. You only need to ask for our help and we will be there." Then he hopped up to another branch to start foraging again.

YARA THE YAK

Bacchus was laughing as he turned to leave. Cleo and Ezrael followed. "Oh Bacchus," said Cleo. "That was really amazing! I like Xavier a lot." Bacchus smiled. "That's great Cleo," he said. "We have a long way to go now, so I'm glad you have new energy to get there."

Bacchus started down the new path that unfolded before them. They all walked for a long time. They were chatting and laughing as they continued. Everyone was in such a good mood. The landscape was changing as they moved on. It was still humid from the tropical surroundings, but now the vegetation became sparse. There were hardly any trees to be seen and now they were mostly walking through open grasslands. It was expansive. The sun was out and it radiated off the ground. It was getting hotter.

Bacchus said, "Cleo, let me tell you about the other chakra that we didn't talk about before." Cleo smiled and said, "Oh, yes please." Bacchus continued, "the heart chakra you already know about. It's in your chest and it's your most important place when you want to feel love or feel closer to All That Is. This other chakra is right above the heart and in the center of your chest right below your collar bones. It is known as the Higher Heart Chakra and it is very special. It is the connection point for you to All That Is. It is the chakra used to free your ego through unconditional love, and it is your happiness point. Remember when Chamuel told you about the practice to pull the energy into your heart? At the time, you didn't really understand him. So perhaps now, you understand a bit more." Cleo said, "Yes, I remember being a little confused about what he was talking about. But working with all of the animals, I've learned so many other things. I think I can understand it a bit better."

"Good," said Bacchus. "So, when you use the heart chakra and the upper heart chakra together, you really have the power to transmute any of the denser emotions back to love. As you pull that energy back to your heart, you can use the infinity 8 between your heart and the upper heart. That is your thymus gland in your body. The thymus shrinks when you are stressed and anxious, and it grows when you are happy. So, it is also important for your immune system to have a happy thymus. Now, you can use your hand to run the infinity 8 between the two, and stay in your heart, loving and accepting all parts of you and all of your emotions. Then, you can send that love to the Universe and your higher self to manifest what you want. It is a very important tool and one that you will use often."

"Thanks, Bacchus. That sounds really good. And if I have questions, I can call on Chamuel to help me?" Cleo asked. "Of course," said Bacchus. "Or you can ask Panther Spirit," and he laughed. Cleo laughed as well.

As they made their way through the field, the sky began to get darker. The wind was picking up as well and there was emerging a very ominous feel to the place. Cleo looked at Bacchus and said, "Bacchus, is there are storm brewing?" Bacchus looked up as the sky grew even darker. "It appears that there could be." And before he could say anything else, it started raining. It was a light rain at first, nothing to be worried about. But as they kept walking, the rain became stronger and the sky grew even darker. The winds were now substantial, and Cleo had to concentrate to walk straight. Ezrael shielded Cleo with his immense wings, but they were blowing around too, and it didn't really do much to help Cleo. The sky turned pitch black and the rain started coming in sheets. They were all soaked completely through in a matter of minutes. The wind was howling so strongly now that they could barely walk against it. Cleo was now very scared and wondered where they should go to get out of the storm.

But there was no place to go. There were no trees to shelter under, no caves to crawl into, nothing. Just open field with no safety in sight. It was now raining so hard that Cleo could not see anything at all. She had to shield her eyes from the rain that stung her face. It was miserable. "Bacchus, what should we do?" she screamed. She waited for an answer. It did not come. "Ezrael!" she shouted. Again, there was no answer. She tried to look for them but could not see anything other than darkness and driving rain. Her fear was all she could think about. I'm all by myself and I don't know where I am or what I should do! she thought. She began to panic. Her heart was beating out of her chest, tears were streaming down her face and she had trouble even standing. The ground was completely saturated by now and it was getting harder and harder to even walk without sinking into the mud of the field. She had never felt so alone and scared in her life. Even when her parents died, it was not this level of sheer fear and abandonment.

Being able to do nothing else, she sank to her knees. Mud was everywhere and she became glued to the spot where she collapsed. Her mind was racing, her whole body was shutting down and she was nothing but tears. "Bacchus, Ezrael! Where are you?" she cried.

Bacchus was right beside Cleo, but she could not see him. Ezrael was standing next to her on the other side, but she could not see him either. Ezrael reached out for her, but she could not feel him nor accept his touch. He thought, even some storms you have to get through on your own.

From the distance, a very large animal was making its way to Cleo. She didn't seem to have any trouble navigating the winds and the rain, although Cleo could not yet see her. She was a yak. And she was powerful and strong. She had a very bulky frame and extremely sturdy legs. She had brown fur that covered her body, even though it was soaking wet. She had large horns on top of her head that were over 3 feet long and they were following the motion of her head, which was down slightly to combat the ferocious wind.

Cleo stayed on her knees and cried incessantly. She was totally lost and alone and scared out of her mind. She felt fear, immense fear. She felt despair rising up in her body. She felt abandonment rising up in her body. And it was so intense, she couldn't even cry any longer. Then, she heard a large booming voice. It seemed to come from nowhere and everywhere at the same time. And it was very clear. "Cleo, remember your heart," it boomed. "**The power of your heart is the heart of your power.**"

Cleo was trying to make sense of what she just heard. What was that, she thought! And as she sat there in the mud, she went to her heart. It was really hard because her mind was telling her that she was doomed, left alone and about to die. But she stayed in her heart and said over and over to herself, *the power of my heart is the heart of my power.* And as she continued saying it, she started to really feel the power of her heart. And as she felt that power grow, she stood up against the driving rain and wind. When she looked up, she saw the yak. It was right in front of her now. The yak looked at Cleo and said, "Grab my fur, Cleo. I will lead you to safety."

Cleo felt a wave of relief flow over her as she grabbed the yak's fur. The yak turned and Cleo went with her. They navigated the storm, the yak so strong that she gave Cleo the inspiration to move forward with her. As they walked, the wind began to die down and the rain slowed. Cleo could now see more clearly. As she looked around, she saw Bacchus and Ezrael right beside her. She was so relieved that she started crying again. But this time they were tears of joy. "Bacchus! Ezrael! Where were you?" she shouted.

Bacchus looked at Cleo and said, "We were here the whole time, Cleo. But your frequency was so low, you could no longer see us or hear us. But we never left you, nor will we ever leave you." At that point, the rain stopped completely and the wind died down to nothing. The sky began to get lighter. Cleo was still clinging to the yak's fur and when she realized that her hands were still clutching the yak, she let go. "Thank you!" she said to the yak. "You saved my life!"

The yak smiled and said, "No, Cleo. You used the power of your heart to save yourself."

Bacchus took a deep bow toward the yak and said, "Hello Yara. Thank you for your assistance." Yara looked at Bacchus and said, "Of course, Bacchus. I am always here for you and Cleo." Then Yara turned to Ezrael and said, "Hello Ezrael. So nice to see you."

"Cleo," said Bacchus. "This is Yara." Cleo smiled a deep smile and said, "Hello, Yara. Thank you again for leading me out of that horrible storm." Yara smiled and said, "Cleo, I know that was a really terrible thing for you to have to go through. I felt as though you lost all hope for a while." "Oh, I did!" said Cleo. "That was the scariest thing I have ever been through. How did that happen?" she asked. "I thought I had gained so many tools to help me weather any storm, but I was not able to weather that one on my own."

"Well," said Yara, "You were not alone. It only felt like that because you could not see what was right in front of you. And that was because the weight of everything you were feeling, the planetary forces that you were connected to, were such a low frequency, you momentarily lost your connection to your higher self and to love. That can be very strong when you are feeling alone and afraid. But you did use your power to get through it, even when you thought you had to do it on your own. I know that you have overcome a lot of personal challenges through this journey. And you are honored by all of us for what you have accomplished. But what you just went through was more than your personal challenges. What you felt was the challenges of the planet. All of the fear, rage and feelings of abandonment that the world is feeling right now, you felt during that storm. And the feelings of all of the people who feel those emotions were all with you during that time. And like Ezrael knew, some of these storms you have to go through on your own to get to the other side."

"I don't understand," said Cleo. "How could I have been connected to everyone on the planet? And how did I feel everything that they are feeling?" Yara said, "We are all connected, Cleo. Remember that all of that is energy and so we are connected through the energy. So, your emotions are not only yours, they are also the emotions of everyone on the planet. And because you can be influenced by everything, you felt those emotions. Through the energy. And as you claimed your heart power, you sent that power to all of the people on the earth. And you just made a difference."

"So, remember that when you are experiencing emotions, they may not all be yours. But when you transmute those emotions to love, like Bacchus was talking about earlier, through your heart and upper heart chakra, you can remember to include your community, your planet and even the Universe in that healing. And that, Cleo, is how you really change the world."

"Wow," said Cleo. "I guess I never understood just how powerful I really am until this moment." Bacchus smiled to himself and thought, it is done. Ezrael walked over to Cleo and gave her a huge hug. "I love you very much, Cleo." he said. "I love you too, Ezrael," said Cleo, as she returned the warm hug.

"And remember, Cleo," said Yara. "You can be alone but not feel lonely. Your guides are always with you, every step of the way. We are all here for you always, in every moment. You only need to ask for our help and we will be there."

"Thank you, Yara," said Cleo. "I think that may be the most important lesson of this whole adventure."

And with that, Yara turned and began her walk back across the muddy field.

ZURIEL THE ZEBRA

Cleo looked over at Bacchus and said, "Bacchus. I don't ever want to go through anything like that again." Bacchus nodded and said, "I understand. And as you use the tools you have learned today; you will feel the dense emotions less and less. But know this, Cleo. You will have days where you will be faced with immense challenges. Things will be happening in your life or on the planet that will draw you in to many stories about fear, anger, greed and abandonment. And you can now recognize that some of that will impact you and cause you to feel those same emotions. But, trust me when I tell you this. Those feelings will clear more quickly and you will emerge on the other side of them with grace. Because now you can see that from a higher perspective. And that makes all the difference."

"Thanks Bacchus," said Cleo. "That makes me feel better anyway."

"OK, good," said Bacchus. "Cleo, we have only one more stop. Shall we be on our way? And I promise there will be no storms." "Oh, I hate to see it end, but I'm ready Bacchus," said Cleo.

Bacchus turned to follow the path out of the mud of the field. As they moved on, things dried out quickly, as did the three of them. The sun was out in full force and they meandered through a wooded section before coming to the final spot. As the path led them to the final destination, it was sunny and hot. There were not a lot of trees and most of the earth was dry. There were some grasses under foot but the landscape was expansive. The few animals and birds they did see, looked as though they were trying to escape the heat of the sun.

After a while, Bacchus stopped, like he always did. Ready for the next animal to appear. And it did. From the horizon they saw a zebra trotting toward them. Behind him was a herd of zebras grazing on the sparse grass. The zebra walked over to Bacchus and said, "Well, my dear friend! So wonderful to see you all. What an incredible day!" Bacchus smiled and said, "Hello Zuriel. It is also wonderful to see you." He turned to Cleo and said, "Cleo, this is Zuriel."

Cleo smiled at the amazing animal and said, "Hello Zuriel. So nice to meet you!"

"Thank you, Cleo," said Zuriel. "I trust that you are recovering from the storm you just endured. And greetings to you Ezrael. You are looking bright after drying out from the rain." Ezrael smiled and said, "Yes, it was quite the adventure. But we have all come through it better than before." "No doubt," said Zuriel. "Adventures come in all shapes and sizes."

He continued, "Cleo, what an amazing day you have had. Such stark contrasts with all of the different animals and the things that have happened. But in the end, it was all in balance. And that's really important. And I know you have learned about all types of balance on your journey. They are all things that will continue to help you on your life path."

"Yes," said Cleo. "Like the balance of masculine and feminine energy. Or the balance of the physical life and the spiritual life. I've learned so much Zuriel." "Indeed, Cleo. We have all been pleased to teach you these fabulous things. Everyone is so unique and each person learns in their own way at their own time. Unique like the zebras. Did you know that all of the stripes on the zebras are different? Just like your fingerprints. We are all unique as well. And it is a wonderful thing."

"That's amazing!" exclaimed Cleo. "I would not have imagined that there could be so many variations of stripes that every one of you is different. Seems infinitely impossible!"

Zuriel laughed and whinnied as he shook his head. "There are infinite possibilities in all things Cleo. You just have to open your heart to all of them. Remember that there are always answers to things that you can't even imagine. So, if you are fixated on just one path or one solution, you close the energy to the other infinite possibilities available to you. And you can't understand that with your mind. It will always want to keep you steered on one safe path. But if you quiet your mind and go to your heart, ask your higher self to guide you, the endless possibilities open before you. Your heart always knows and will always lead you to the right next thing."

"Cleo, you look thirsty," continued Zuriel. "Can I get you some water?" "Oh, that would be so lovely," said Cleo. Zuriel nodded and turned. He raised his right front leg and shook his head. As he lowered his leg, an oasis began to spring up from the dry ground in front of him. Almost instantaneously, a beautiful clear oasis appeared. The water was crystal clear and looked very inviting. Cleo smiled and walked over to the edge of the water. She kneeled down and took a long drink. "Thank you, Zuriel," said Cleo. "That's just what I needed!"

Zuriel bowed forward and said, "Of course, Cleo. Water is so important. It is the essential elixir of all life. And water has consciousness. It can feel your emotions and your love. So always bless the water that you drink and know that when you send it love, it will return love to you. Respect water for everything that it brings to you and drink water often. It will replenish your body as well as your soul."

"Thank you, water," said Cleo. "I am grateful for what you have just given me."

"Water can also help keep you balanced, Cleo," said Zuriel. "Your human body is about 60% water, so always make sure that you keep hydrated. It is like the balance of the Temperance Card in the Tarot deck."

"Oh!" exclaimed Cleo. "Tarot? That's the evil card deck, right? The one that will make you crazy or align with the Devil!" Bacchus and Zuriel smiled. Zuriel said, "Cleo, that is a very outdated and inaccurate belief. Tarot and Oracle card decks are only used to get more self-insight and guidance. They are not evil and they will not conjure the Devil, even as he doesn't exist anyway. Tarot and Oracle cards are a very personal way for you to have another connection to higher guidance."

"Well, that's not what I have heard over my lifetime. I've heard that they are only used for future predictions and they are mystical and evil," said Cleo. "Well," said Zuriel, "sometimes humans in power make up stories to keep people from really connecting to their inner wisdom and divinity. I believe that this may be one of those times. Remember Cleo, you can choose your own beliefs now. You can see things from a higher perspective and you can choose what beliefs serve your higher purpose."

"So, are you saying I should get an Oracle card deck and start using it?" asked Cleo. Bacchus smiled. Zuriel answered, "You have free will, Cleo. You can do what serves you in the moment. I am only saying that an Oracle Deck can help you tone your intuition, allow guidance to assist you and it's something to have fun with. Remember, it's supposed to be fun. But I can assure you that if you do choose to read cards, there is no evil that will become you."

"Well, I don't know anything about them. What would I do if I had a deck?" Cleo asked. "First," said Zuriel, "the deck is for you. Therefore, you should spend time with it first before you start to use it. Read all of the cards and understand what the meaning of them are. There are so many to choose from now. There are cards that follow the traditional tarot cards, there are animal spirit cards, there are ascended master cards, and so many others. You will be drawn to the deck that will most serve you in that moment. And you can choose more than one deck if that is what you are drawn to. What matters is that you make a connection to your cards. It is part of your intuition and it is a link to your higher self. They are sacred and you should treat them that way."

"You can use them daily in your spiritual practice," Zuriel continued. "Just go to your heart and ask the cards, what do I need to know today? Then draw a card. It will have meaning for you in that moment. Then you can test it. Write down the cards you draw every day and track what they are telling you. You will probably start seeing themes and messages. The more you use them, the more comfortable you will be with them and the more they can tell you about what guidance you need. And just like you are magic itself, Cleo, you will start to see the magic in the cards."

"OK," said Cleo. "I can choose to change my belief about cards. Can we try it out now? Can someone draw a card for me?" asked Cleo. Zuriel said, "Yes, of course, Cleo. Ezrael, can you get a card deck for us?"

Ezrael nodded in agreement and drew a deck of tarot cards from his robe. He opened the cards and gave them a quick shuffle. Then he spread them in his hands in front of Cleo and asked her to draw a card. Cleo suddenly became very curious. First, that Ezrael had a tarot deck! Then, to know what her card would be. So, she reached forward and drew a card from Ezrael. She looked at the card to see that it was The High Priestess.

Cleo did not know the meaning of the card and so she showed it to Zuriel. "It's The High Priestess," she said. "Can you tell me what that means?"

"Of course," said Zuriel. "The High Priestess card is layered in meaning. It represents the divine feminine. And it is ruled by the number 2. That represents balance. The balance of masculine and feminine energy. And it also represents duality. If you look at the priestess, you can see that she wears a blue robe. That represents water. The robe flows like a waterfall and it is the source of all water found in the tarot deck. And she represents the sub-conscious. And how you get in touch with your sub-conscious is through your intuition. She is the symbol of intuition."

"And if you look at her robe, you will see that it is vibrating with energy. The energy that flows through everything. Now, notice that she is sitting between two pillars. Those pillars are the polarity of black and white. And she is the center pillar, again, representing balance between the polarity. And at the top of each pillar is a lotus flower. That represents the blooming of the feminine sub-conscious force."

"So, the High Priestess is guiding us to be aware of our own sub-conscious as well as the collective sub-conscious. She shows us that we are here to balance the masculine and feminine polarity. That could be you, Cleo, in a parallel life. An ancient priestess like Cleopatra. Finally, the High Priestess is a strong, independent woman. She may find herself alone, nourishing herself through her work. And she carries a deep love for harmony, beauty and balance."

"I think that is validation for you, Cleo, as to who you are now. After your adventure today, you are moving into a higher state of spirituality. I think you have drawn an appropriate card to represent everything that you have learned and experienced today."

"Wow," said Cleo. "Yes, I would say that really does sum up this whole adventure and where I am going from here. I guess there is something to card reading after all. And also, something I have learned and continue to learn; my beliefs are not always in alignment with who I am now. So, each time I have a reaction like I did with the conversation about cards, I should take a step back and just look at things from a higher perspective. And instead of immediately believing things I once knew, question them instead and be sure that is what I want now."

"Indeed," said Zuriel. "And I commend you again on your insight and perspective, Cleo. It is your path to greater awareness. You are magic, just like everyone else who believes. You will do great things, Cleo. You have now become the magic for others. You are a Wayshower. Just remember that you don't have to fix other people, just be who you are. Your authenticity will inspire and show others that they can choose the same thing. And in that way, we change the world one person at a time. And as you now know this as well, we are all here for you always, in every moment. You only need to ask for our help and we will be there."

"Thank you, Zuriel. This is a fantastic ending to a fabulous adventure and I am grateful for you and for the water," said Cleo. Bacchus turned to Zuriel and said, "Yes, thank you Zuriel. We are always inspired by your magic. I look forward to meeting again soon."

Zuriel whinnied and thanked them for their time. He thanked Ezrael for the help with the cards. Then he turned to join the herd behind him who had gathered at the oasis for a cool drink of water.

EZRAEL

Bacchus turned to Cleo and said, "Cleo, it is now time to get back. I think we should be on our way." Cleo sighed. "Bacchus, I don't want this adventure to end." Bacchus smiled and said, "Yes, it has been a great adventure. But your real adventure is about to unfold for you in ways you cannot imagine. For now, let's begin our journey home."

The path opened before them and began to lead them out of the dry and arid grasslands. Bacchus, Cleo and Ezrael walked along the path, slightly somber that their journey was at an end. The path led them to a wonderful forest. There were trees everywhere, so many different kinds. The animals of the forest were all busy doing their thing and there was a light, airy feeling to the whole place. The sun was shining through the canopy and it felt warm and inviting. The sound of birds, squirrels, and other forest animals were everywhere and it sounded so beautiful. Cleo smiled.

Bacchus led them to a small clearing. Within the canopy of the trees, this was a small but cozy place. As Bacchus, Cleo and Ezrael entered the clearing, Cleo saw a very large table set in the middle of the clearing. It was made from the trees of the forest in honor of Cleo. It was decorated with flowers, pine cones, crystals and nuts. Cleo had to stop and take in what she was seeing. As she stood there trying to understand, all of the animals from her adventure began to gather. It was a fabulous display of all of her teachers.

Cleo looked over at Bacchus and said, "Bacchus! What is all of this?" Bacchus nodded to Ezrael and said, "Perhaps you should ask Ezrael. He is the one who did all of this." "Ezrael!" Cleo exclaimed. "What is all of this?" Ezrael smiled and said, "Cleo, it's your birthday party!"

Cleo was so surprised! She didn't even think about her birthday after everything that had happened today. She was humbled at everything she saw. Ezrael said, "Cleo, please be seated at the head of the table.

There is a stump right there for you to sit on." Cleo laughed and took her seat on the stump.

As she sat down, she saw Ariel coming towards her, walking on top of the table. Her pink glow was still there and lit the way for her, as she made her way to Cleo. The other animals were taking their places around the table. To see all of her animal guides and teachers together was so overwhelming, that Cleo cried tears of joy. Bacchus sat next to Cleo and Ezrael sat at the other end of the table, opposite her.

Bacchus said, "Cleo, as in all animal spirit walks, the last thing that happens is that the animal gives you something to remember them by and represent their message to you. So, in that tradition, each of your animal guides has a gift for you, for your 'birthday'. We are all anxious to see what they have brought! Ariel, please begin."

Ariel now stood in front of Cleo on the table. Even though she was a large ant, she was still very small compared to the others. Ariel smiled and did a slight bow of her head to Cleo. "Cleo," she said, "You are now truly a queen. The queen you always were, but now know in your heart. You are powerful beyond your imagination and your words are gold. So, to remind you how much of a queen you are, I give you a crown. It is made from nature itself. It is vines woven together in love, with flowers and crystals imbedded in the circle. You are not only the queen of your team; you are a queen to yourself. Always remember your power and accept that with the greatest humility. You are loved beyond measure and your queen edict is to share that love with the world. Go forth and be you, as that is the greatest measure of a true queen. We are honored and humbled in your presence."

Cleo bowed her head at Ariel. Ariel then placed the crown on Cleo's head. Cleo felt immense gratitude and humility. "Thank you, Ariel," said Cleo. "This is such a special remembrance and I will always cherish your words of wisdom." Ariel smiled and said, "As I will always remember your fabulous journey, Cleo." Ariel turned and took her place at the first seat beside Cleo.

As Ariel took her spot, Barachiel flew over to Cleo. As he landed on the table in front of her, he said, "Cleo, you are even more beautiful than when I first saw you." Cleo smiled. "My gift to you is flower seeds. Take these seeds and plant your beautiful butterfly garden. Grow roses and beautiful flowers and invite the butterflies to come to you. Then, play and have fun with them. Smell the wonderful smells and see the beauty that you create. You are a butterfly, Cleo. Spread your wings and soar to heights you have never known before." Cleo remembered her scar and now, she had no feeling about it. She knew she was beautiful and she loved that. "Thank you, Barachiel," she said. "I will plant my garden and invite all of the butterflies to come and play with me." Barachiel smiled and flew over to the seat next to Ariel.

As Barachiel settled into his spot, Chamuel stepped forward beside Cleo. In his paws he held the most beautiful bleeding-heart plant. As he handed it to Cleo, he said, "Cleo, this is the bleeding-heart flower. You saw this when you first entered the magical woods. It is meant to remind you of how important it is to stay in your heart and feel unconditional love. Your heart is the power of you and you can use your heart to purify any emotion back to love. So, use this flower to always remind you of how important it is to stay in your heart as much as you can. For that is the way to enlightenment and inner peace and joy. Remember that your default state is unconditional love. It is really who you are. We all love you immensely and so you should do the same with yourself and everyone else." Then Chamuel smiled and took a step back. Cleo smiled a smile of unconditional love and thanked Chamuel for his gift. Now she understood what he had told her not so long ago. Chamuel turned to take his place at the table.

As he settled into his spot, Daniel was waiting to see Cleo. He walked up beside her and nodded for her to hold out her hand. When she did, Daniel dropped something from his mouth into her palm. She looked down and saw a perfect acorn. Then she looked up and smiled at Daniel. Daniel said, "Cleo, my gift to you is an acorn. Not only is it meant to remind you of the special woods where we first met, it is also the symbol of new beginnings, patience and compassion. You are now on your new beginning and you will find the most amazing things ahead of you. But the acorn will remind you that patience is important. Like the small acorn will ultimately grow into a beautiful oak tree, it will take years and years. Your journey will also take years, so be patient with yourself. And always remember to be compassionate with yourself and others. You will be learning and changing just like them. Let it remind you of your heart chakra and your compassion for your brother. And let it symbolize the strength of the mighty oak tree, the same strength that is within you." Daniel then bowed his head one last time to Cleo as his antlers followed the movement. Cleo said, "Oh, thank you Daniel. This is a very special gift and one that I will cherish and carry in my heart." Daniel looked at Cleo and said, "Yes, good. Always remember the power of your heart, Cleo. That is where your true strength and power lie." And then he turned to take his place at the table with the others.

Cleo was feeling so wonderful with all of her new gifts. What a fabulous birthday, she thought. She looked up to see El Morya running down the path toward her, his feathers flying all around him as he stopped in front of Cleo. El Morya fluffed his feathers and then handed Cleo a small hand mirror. Cleo looked into the mirror and smiled. El Morya said, "Cleo, congratulations on your fabulous adventure! And happy birthday! I am so pleased to be able to see you again. I give you a mirror as my gift, but it is really from your inner teacher. Of course, I know that you can now look in that mirror with love for yourself and that is so amazing. But it is really to remind you that everything you see is your mirror. First, remember the unbreakable law, 'what you put out is what you get back'. Let the mirror remind you of that often. Do your reality creation consciously by observing what you are putting out. But also use the mirror as a reminder that everyone and everything in your life is there for a purpose. Your inner teacher is showing you things through those interactions. Sometimes those are meant to reflect who you are being at that moment. Sometimes they are reflecting what you could be. And sometimes they are reflecting what you don't want to be any longer. Be aware in every moment, Cleo. That is the best lesson I can teach you." Cleo bowed her head gratefully toward El Morya and said, "Thank you, El Morya. And that is a very powerful lesson. One that I will always remember, I promise." El Morya bowed his head to Cleo and then moved to take his place at the table.

As El Morya was moving away from Cleo, Fairy was moving toward her. She came with a lovely smile on her face and handed Cleo her gift. It was a small pine cone, one that would fit in the palm of her hand. Cleo smiled. Fairy said, "Cleo, my gift to you is a pine cone. And, it symbolizes something very special. You see, inside your brain between your 3rd eye chakra and your crown chakra is the pineal gland. Imagine this as your pathway to your intuition, your connection to All That Is. And it looks like a pine cone! And the more you use it and activate it, the more of the pine cone opens to reveal new connections to the most magical things. You are magic, Cleo. Never forget that. And use your intuition so that you can see the magic in your life in every moment. Because every moment is magic, Cleo. Every moment." "Oh, thank you, Fairy," said Cleo. "What a thoughtful gift this is. It will always remind me of my pineal gland and the intuition I have yet to unlock. And I promise to have fun with it!" Fairy smiled and laughed and then moved to take her place at the table.

As Fairy took her place at the table, Gabriel made her way to Cleo. Cleo looked down to see her coming toward her. Gabriel smiled and with a soft whistle said, "Oh my! It's so bright here, hahaha." Cleo laughed as well. "Cleo," continued Gabriel, "my gift to you is a coin. And on this coin is etched the Yen and the Yang, the balance of masculine and feminine energy. Carry this coin with you in your pocket to remind you that you can draw on both of these energies when you need to. Use it when you are hesitant to speak your truth, to remind you that you can speak with integrity, using your masculine power of being firm in your convictions and your feminine power of compassion for those you are speaking to. Keep that balance in your life and you can never go wrong." "Thank you, Gabriel," said Cleo. "It is a great remembrance of that balance and I will carry it with me always. It will be my talisman for staying balanced." Gabriel smiled and moved to take her place at the table.

As Gabriel took her place, Haniel flew down from the open sky, and with a screech, landed in front of Cleo. She was such an amazing and beautiful raptor, and even more so, up close. With her bright yellow talon, Haniel handed Cleo her gift. Cleo looked into her palm and laughed. Haniel smiled and said, "Cleo, it is wonderful to see you again. I did so enjoy our flight together. My gift for you is a sweet gum ball! This is to remind you of the different perspectives there are to see, and our glorious flight through the sky. First, that sweet gum ball looked so prominent from where we started on the ground. You could see the prickly, round balls all over the ground. But when we were in flight, those prickly little details just disappeared. Your focus changed from small and limited, to broad and infinite. So let this always remind you that there is always a different perspective, if you are willing to look." Cleo remembered back to the flight she took through Haniel's eyes and smiled. "Thank you, Haniel," said

Cleo. "That is a flight I will never forget! And the sweet gum ball will always remind me of it and the greater perspectives that are available to us all. My sincerest thanks." Haniel nodded her head and took her place at the table.

As Haniel found her place, the sound of music began to emerge. It grew louder and had such a strong rhythm that everyone at the table began to tap their various feet, talons, and hooves. Heads were bobbing, antennae were waving and feathers were fluffing. Then, down the path beside the table, Israfel came dancing toward Cleo. He was electric, donning a new pair of sunglasses, with a stride and wiggle that made everyone laugh. Cleo could feel the music running through her and began to swing her legs to the beat. Israfel danced over beside Cleo and looked over at her with a huge grin. "Gotta keep it real, Cleo!" he said. Cleo laughed and Bacchus chuckled. "Cleo," said Israfel, "My gift to you is a silver musical note charm. It has diamonds, emeralds, rubies and sapphires encased in the charm. This is to remind you how important it is to dance and sing! It is your joy. And remember that joy is a choice that you can make at any time. Music is the language of your soul, so listen to it and turn up the music loud when you want to get back to your joy. Start your day with a little tune and it will set the whole 'tone' of your day, hahaha. And never forget that you can still find music and joy when you are shedding the layers that will come." Cleo was so surprised and pleased with Israfel's gift. "Thank you so much, Israfel!" said Cleo. "This is so beautiful! I will wear it with joy!" As Israfel turned to find his seat, the music subsided.

As Israfel headed to his seat, Jeremiel sauntered up beside Cleo. Like Bacchus, he was graceful and smooth as he walked. Cleo smiled at Jeremiel, remembering the race that he and Bacchus had. Jeremiel held up his paw and handed Cleo his gift. "Cleo, my gift to you is a topaz gemstone," he said. "The topaz is a powerful crystal and it symbolizes compassion, love and affection. Let it remind you that compassion and forgiveness will always win over fear and hatred. Like we talked about, everyone is on their journey and whatever they are doing, and whatever you do, it is the perfect thing at the perfect time. So, live your life in love and compassion for yourself and let others do the same. The color of the topaz, the gorgeous yellow and brown, should also remind you of me and my beautiful fur color." And then Jeremiel grew a big grin on his face. "Oh Jeremiel," said Cleo. "This is a beautiful stone and it will indeed remind me of the compassion and love that you spoke about. And I will never forget you or your gracious lessons." Jeremiel bowed his head slightly at Cleo and then turned to find his seat at the table.

As Jeremiel settled into his place, Kalani slowly made her way to the head of the table to greet Cleo. She was so graceful in her movement; it was very calming. When Kalani reached Cleo, she gave her a warm smile. Cleo smiled back. "Cleo," said Kalani, "my gift to you is a eucalyptus leaf. As you know, eucalyptus is such an important part of a koala's life, but did you know they have a meaning as well? The eucalyptus leaf is used for purification. It can bring a wonderful cleansing effect as well. In fact, for many indigenous cultures, the eucalyptus leaf is considered holy, representing the division of the underworld, the earth and heaven. So, you can burn the eucalyptus leaf to cleanse your space as you meditate. Let it be a reminder to you of how important it is to relax, refresh and be still. Quiet your mind and go to your heart. Practice often and it gets better and better." Cleo remembered the meditation that Kalani taught her and immediately felt calmer and more peaceful. "Thank you, Kalani," said Cleo. "This is such a genuine gesture and reminder of our lovely meditation experience. And it smells soooo good! I will cherish this and always remember your calming influence." Kalani smiled and turned to find her place at the table.

As Kalani settled into her seat with a yawn, Lakshmi came to greet Cleo. Her gait was so smooth and she seemed a little more refreshed than when Cleo last saw her. Cleo smiled and said, "Lakshmi, it's so nice to see you. Where are your cubs?" Lakshmi laughed and said, "One of the other lionesses has graciously agreed to cub sit." Cleo nodded and laughed. Lakshmi bowed her head toward Cleo and ask her to remove her gift. Cleo looked at Lakshmi's mane and saw an eagle feather. She reached over and delicately removed it. Lakshmi said, "Cleo, my gift to you is a sacred Eagle Feather. In the indigenous culture, the eagle feather symbolizes the highest, bravest and strongest. Let this sacred symbol remind you of the courage it took for you to start this adventure in the first place, and the courage that you developed along the way. You can now stand high with your strength and bravery, just like the eagle feather. Remember to keep the strength of what you want in your focus. Do not focus on fear and lack. Your abundance and joy are in *your* hands, and no one else's. Create that abundance and remember that it comes in all shapes and sizes, so never discount anything All That Is sends you." Cleo reverently brushed the eagle feather against her face. It was so soft. She smiled and said, "Thank you, Lakshmi. I can feel the special power of this feather and it will always remind me of my courage and my power, just like yours." Lakshmi smiled as she elegantly turned and took her place at the table.

As Lakshmi settled into her seat at the table, Michael jumped over to land at Cleo's feet. He did one small flip to keep his energy high. "Hello, Cleo. And happy birthday. We are all so pleased to see how much you have learned on your adventure and we honor you for taking that leap of faith." Cleo smiled at Michael as he handed her his gift. "My gift to you is a silver charm angel wing. Let it remind you that your angels are always there for you, especially Ezrael. They love you unconditionally, as that is the only way they can love. When you are feeling self-doubt, remember to see yourself through their eyes. And you will then see the true nature of who you are. Know that you are always protected and always safe with your angels. And have fun with them. They love to laugh and dance and play. They know the true meaning of joy. And when you need a little more courage, reach to them, and Mongoose spirit." Cleo had a small tear of joy run down her face as she held the angel charm. It was so delicate. Then she looked to the other end of the table at Ezrael and smiled even bigger. "Thank you, Michael," said Cleo. "This is such a special gift. I will wear it next to my heart, where all of my angels live." Micheal's blue glow began to encompass his whole body as he nodded to Cleo. Then he turned and took his place at the table.

As Micheal was seated at the table with the others, Netzach made a rare appearance as she made her way to Cleo. When Cleo saw her, she jumped slightly and said, "Netzach! You are out of your sanctuary! Will you be OK?" Netzach smiled and said, "Yes, with the help of Ariel and Michael, I have the protection I need while I am here. Thank you for asking, Cleo." "Oh, good," said Cleo. "We don't want anything to happen to you!" Netzach smiled as her long tongue peaked out from her mouth. "Cleo," said Netzach, "my gift to you is a humble one. But it is mighty in its message. I give you a small twig from the sanctuary. This is to remind you of the plight of the numbats and all endangered species. We need help and support from the community and the world to live and thrive again. And all animals deserve the opportunity to thrive. And we know you will be part of that support system. But the twig also reminds you to start small. You can do the smallest thing and make a large impact. And when you combine all of the small things, the small twigs, you can build incredible things. Remember the animals, Cleo. They are such an intricate and important part of your world. Honor them for what they contribute." Cleo had tears in her eyes as she listened to Netzach. "Be assured, Netzach," said Cleo, "that I will do whatever I need to help you and the other animals. I can think of nothing that would bring me more joy. Thank you for this reminder. I will cherish it, as I cherish you." Netzach smiled at Cleo's words and made her way to her place at the table.

As Netzach climbed up on her seat, Orion flew down and landed in front of Cleo. He looked quite different in the daylight, but no less magical. Cleo smiled, remembering her conversation with Orion about little green men. She laughed to herself. "Cleooooo," hooted Orion, "my gift to you is something very special. Please hold out your hand." Cleo held out her hand toward Orion. In her palm, Orion put a small star. It was the most amazing combination of light, stardust and pure magic. Cleo could not contain herself while she looked at this magnificent thing. Orion continued. "Cleo, my gift to you is a small star. This star is to remind you that miracles are everywhere and happen in every moment. What you thought was impossible is just a thought away. Magic is everywhere, Cleo. You just need to believe, open and allow it into your life. And it is to remind you that there are friends in the stars, waiting to help you and teach you what they have already learned. Take advantage of their wisdom and ask them for help. They are waiting to be of service. And finally, let this star remind you of me, as I came from the stars and return to them. Never forget that *you* are magic and miracles, Cleo. Never forget." Cleo was still star struck, but looked at Orion and said, "Wow. This is such an impossible, but completely possible, gift. Thank you, Orion. I don't even have the words to describe what this means to me." Orion hooted back with a smile and flew over to his seat at the table.

As Orion landed in his spot, Cleo saw Phanuel making his way slowly down the table towards her. Everyone else was laughing and saying, 'we're going to be here a while!' Phanuel laughed as well and then flew the rest of the length of the table to land in front of Cleo. Then he turned his head ever so slowly to the others and had a small chuckle. Cleo reached out her hand for Phanuel to climb on. He gracefully obliged. "Cleo," said Phanuel, "my gift to you is a watch." As Phanuel held out the watch to Cleo with his long forearms, Cleo laughed, knowing that Phanuel did not operate based on time. "But this is a special watch, Cleo," said Phanuel. "Look closely." Cleo looked down to see that the watch did not have any hands. It was completely blank of hands and numbers. "This is a watch with no time and no hands. And that is to remind you, Cleo, that time only exists as a perception on earth. There really is no time, only this now moment. And even though you operate with time in the 3rd dimension, know that you have the power to dissolve time as a perception. You are that powerful. And then, live your life in the present moment. Savor everything, notice everything and understand that you are an infinite being, and so time is really a small construct in the overall infiniteness of your soul life." Cleo laughed softly and said, "Thank you, Phanuel. What a unique gift. And I could not think of anything more appropriate to remind me of our *time* together." And they both laughed a hearty laugh. Phanuel climbed down from Cleo's hand and flew over to his seat at the table, as everyone laughed and cheered him doing so.

As Phanuel settled in his place at the table, Quan Yin flew over to land in front of Cleo. It was quite the feat, because of what she held in her foot. She reached her foot out to Cleo to hand her the gift. "Cleo" said Quan Yin, "my gift to you is a gavel. It represents judgment and is meant to remind you that judgment is only in the eye of the person who is dispensing it. Because judgment is a very personal thing. So, remember the gavel when you feel like someone is judging you. Look at it from a higher perspective and know that it is always about them, and not you. And then you can have compassion for them and not take what they say to you to heart. For you now know who you really are, and their judgments can hold no weight for you. But also remember that judging yourself is a useless thing. Everything that you do and experience is just that, an experience. It is not right or wrong, that is your ego. It is just an experience meant to teach you. So, love it and accept it as that and then grow from there." Cleo took the gavel and said, "Thank you, Quan Yin. Sometimes that is indeed a hard thing to remember. So, it is good that I can have this gavel to remind me when I get caught up in what other people think. And it will always remind me of you and the other quails." Quan Yin flew up to land at her place at the table.

As Quan Yin took her place at the table, Raguel made his way beside the table to see Cleo. He was a mighty site with the horns, but this time there was no snow on his face. He stood beside Cleo and she could feel his warmth, his love and his balance. Raguel nodded to Cleo. "Cleo," he said, "my gift to you is a rock. But this is a very special rock. It comes from the mountain where you had such an incredible awakening. There is magic in this rock. It will help you toward your purpose. When you meditate, hold it in your hands and feel the vibration of the mountain." Raguel handed Cleo the rock from his split hoof. As Cleo reached out to take the rock, she could instantly feel the vibrations and magic of the mountain. She looked at the rock and saw something else. There was a fossilized image of a ram horn in the rock. She gasped. "Yes, Cleo," said Raguel, "That is indeed a ram horn engraved in the rock. And that is to remind you of me, but also to remind you that your world is really like a spiral. And as you ascend, you will do so in a spiral form, just like my horns. You don't have to understand that now, but you will come to understand in time. Until then, just let it remind you of Ram Spirit." "Thank you, Raguel!" exclaimed Cleo. "That was a very memorable part of my adventure. Looking death in the eye and then being saved by Ezrael is something that I will, of course, NEVER forget. And I will use the rock as a symbol for my purpose to help the animals." Raguel smiled and nodded back to Cleo. Then he turned to take his place at the table.

As Raguel found his seat, Sachael slithered down the path beside the table to Cleo. He looked even bigger in this semi-enclosed place, but Cleo no longer did the 'cringe thing' or the 'Eww thing'. She was way past the fear of snakes at this point, and she smiled slightly; not only to see Sachael, but also at her ability to overcome a fear that was not even hers. When Sachael reached the head of the table, he climbed up the table leg and coiled in front of Cleo. Cleo smiled again. "Cleo," said Sachael, "my gift to you is a charm of the caduceus." He lowered his head slightly so that Cleo could see the charm on Sachael's neck. She reached out and took the charm. "As you can see," continued Sachael, "the caduceus is two snakes, interwoven together. It is a powerful symbol of health and healing. It is to remind you that snakes can also bring a positive message to the world and to you. Remember that we are very compassionate beings. And as you continue to shed your layers of beliefs that no longer serve, you are healing. Wear it when you do your release ceremony to remind you of the power of your intentions. And finally, wear it for others who are still struggling with ancient beliefs that they don't even know about or understand. Wear it in love." "Oh, Sachael," said Cleo. "Thank you so much for this wonderful reminder. I am so grateful to you for teaching me about fears and beliefs. I will never forget you, Sachael. And I will now look at all snakes differently." Sachael let out a faint hiss and then turned to wind his way down to the table top to his seat.

As Sachael climbed down to his place on his stump, Thoth came hopping down the table to Cleo. When he reached her, his jawline blew up into his chin bubble, and one last time, he trilled. Everyone laughed. Cleo laughed as well. Then Thoth said, "Cleo, happy birthday! My gift to you is a pencil. Use this pencil to start your journal, and then never stop. Remember how important it is to write things down on paper and then see them come to life! Your journey will last a lifetime, so imagine how much you will learn, see and experience. Then, perhaps one day, someone will get your journals and write a book about your fabulous adventures. Writing is primal for all humans, so join the club and have fun with it!" Cleo laughed and said, "Thank you, Thoth. I can't wait to start writing all of this down. It will be part of my daily routine and I'm sure it will deliver benefits beyond what I can even see now." Thoth croaked and then turned to hop back down the table to his seat.

As Thoth hopped down to his stump, the most magical and beautiful music came from everywhere. It was mesmerizing. Everyone turned to each other and said, "Here comes Uriel!" and then they all laughed together. Uriel walked down the path beside the table to Cleo. He looked so different now, not in the nothingness where Cleo first met him. But he was even more beautiful as he emitted the most gorgeous light and sense of playfulness. Cleo smiled even bigger when she saw Uriel coming. Uriel walked up to Cleo, his wings spread out, the gold in them glistening in the sun. Uriel nodded his head and said, "Cleo, dear one. My gift to you is a map of the galaxy. It contains all of the places that we visited on our flight and so many more. Use this through your lifetime on earth and beyond. It will open your eyes to worlds that you know nothing about now, but perhaps someday will visit. And the Angelic Realm is on the map, so you can visit that with Ezrael one day. Remember that there is so much magic in the world. Open your heart to it, dear one, and you will see incredible things!" Cleo looked at the map. It was filled with so many places she had no idea about, but was thrilled to think she could visit them one day. Then she saw the Angelic Realm on the map. She looked at Ezrael across the table and held up the map and pointed to the Angelic Realm. Ezrael laughed and nodded his head in affirmation to Cleo that they would visit that realm one day. "Thank you, Uriel!" shouted Cleo. "It will be my greatest joy to see the multi-verse and experience all of these amazing places. If it is anything like our flight, I'm sure I will be astounded." Uriel shook his head in agreement and turned to find his place at the table.

As Uriel found his place, everyone looked up to see Varuna flying down from the sky. He was truly the most incredible looking raptor in the air. He flew down to the group, completely silent. Then he landed on the table in front of Cleo. He was huge, standing on the table. So huge, he had to look down to Cleo. As he did, Cleo chuckled at his bald head. Varuna looked to Cleo and without speaking, communicated with her telepathically. "Cleo," he thought, "my gift to you is a small bone. This bone is meant to remind you that the death of the body is inevitable, but the spirit lives forever. So even as you grieve the death of a loved one, know that they are always taken back to the light and will be transformed into many other forms through infinity. We are all energy, Cleo, and energy can never be destroyed – it only takes other forms. I hope this will comfort you as you deal with death through your human journey." "Thank you, Varuna," said Cleo. "It will be of great comfort, I'm sure. It is the perfect gift from you, and I am grateful for what you do, and what you have taught me." Varuna nodded his bald head and turned to fly over to his place at the table.

As Varuna found his place, Cleo waited, as she knew Wahkan would be coming. But she didn't know how he would appear, since he was only an animal spirit now. As she pondered this question, she felt an energy behind her. She turned around to see Wahkan materialize before her eyes. After an initial startle, she smiled. Wahkan moved beside Cleo. He reached his paw to Cleo and dropped a crystal in her hand. "Cleo," he said, "my gift to you is a clear quartz crystal. This is from the caves that you journeyed through on your way to the Lower World. It has the most powerful and transformative energy of all crystals. This is to remind you that there is so much magic everywhere in the world, especially in places you don't even know about. And it is meant to represent the powerful love I have for your brother and for you. Never doubt that. And finally, it is meant to remind you that death is just another form of transformation. So, hold this crystal when you meditate and know that it will amplify your access to All That Is and to your higher self. And know that animal spirits will always be with you and guide your way when you allow them to do so." Cleo held the crystal tightly in her hands. She could feel the energy of the crystal flow through her body. "Thank you, Wahkan." said Cleo. "This is so beautiful and it's even more so because it came from you. I will always remember what you did for my brother and for that, I am forever grateful. I will use this crystal as I meditate, and know that it is the purest form of love." Wahkan nodded and then walked over to take his place at the table.

As Wahkan settled into his place, Xavier flew over and landed in front of Cleo. He was so small. He looked up at Cleo and she could see that he carried something in his beak. He dropped it in front of Cleo and then gave a fast, chattering trill. "Cleo," he said. "My gift to you, on this very special day, is a charm of the infinite knot." Cleo picked up the charm and looked at it. It was amazing the way that the silver threads of the charm wove in and around itself to really form what looked like an infinite knot. Xavier continued, "This is a most sacred symbol of what we spoke about earlier. Everything is connected. Everything. The energy ties it all together and connects you to everyone and everything on the planet and in the Universe. Let it always remind you that your heart and your brain are connected, and as everything is being done for you, you are also doing everything in return. So, live your joy, Cleo, so that you are sharing that with the Universe. And never underestimate what an impact that has across the earth and across galaxies." Cleo smiled a large smile as she held the charm. "Thank you, Xavier," she said. "This is so beautiful and so meaningful. And to know that I am connected to you, and all of the wonderful animals here, as well as everything on the planet and the Universe, is something that will still need to sink in for a while." Xavier trilled, and then flew over to find his place at the table.

When Xavier was settled at his place, Yara slowly made her way to Cleo on the path beside the table. She was such a commanding presence as she approached, that Cleo felt her strength all around, just as she had done during that horrible storm. It made her even more happy to see Yara again. As Yara reached Cleo, she stopped beside her and handed Cleo her gift. Cleo reached out to Yara to receive an unusual amulet. As Cleo studied what Yara had given her, Yara said, "Cleo, my gift to you is the Egyptian heart amulet. It is very ancient and even more meaningful." As Cleo looked at the amulet, she saw a small stone with a pitted surface. It was shaped like a round heart with handles on either side to represent the arteries, and it had a blind eyelet at the top. "This amulet," continued Yara, "represented to the Egyptians that the heart was the source of human wisdom and emotions – in fact it was the soul itself, instead of the brain. I know that this will always remind you that the power of your heart is the heart of your power. And Cleo, that is the most important lesson that you have learned today. Always go to your heart. Always. And then love and adore everything about you." Cleo had tears streaming down her face as she looked at Yara. "Yes," she said. "That is something that I will always remember and always do. I *know* that my heart leads me to everything I need. Thank you, Yara. It is the lesson I came here to learn." Yara smiled back at Cleo and then turned to take her place at the table.

As Yara found the next to the last place at the table, Zuriel trotted down the path to Cleo. He smiled as he approached Cleo and said, "Cleo, it's good to see you again so soon. I feel like we just left each other only a short time ago, hahaha." Cleo laughed and said, "Yes, Zuriel. It was a short time ago, indeed, but I'm so pleased to be able to see you again." Zuriel handed Cleo her gift and said, "Cleo, my gift to you is a very special one. And, I know, something that you will love and cherish always. It is your own oracle card deck. And when I say, 'your own,' I really mean that. It is a deck of all of your animals that you have met today on your fabulous adventure. We all have our pictures there for you to remember us, as well as the message of what we talked about during our time together with you. Use this deck each day. Ask your heart and your higher self, what you need to know for the day, and then draw your card. Not only will it help guide you for the day, it will also make you smile and laugh, seeing our faces again." Cleo took the card deck and began to look through all of her new cards. She smiled, chuckled and even cried as she saw all of the animals in print. She looked up at Zuriel and said, "Oh Zuriel! This is the most special thing ever! I don't know how you did this, but I open my heart to all that seems impossible. You know I will cherish it always." Zuriel nodded and whinnied and headed to the last open place at the table.

Bacchus walked back over to Cleo and said, "Cleo, our adventure is now at its end. But we have plenty of time to stay here for a while and play. I'm sure everyone would find immense joy in that."

Cleo nodded. "Thank you, Bacchus. I can think of nothing I would love more right now than to stay and play!" Then she turned to face everyone seated at the table. Her heart was so full, it felt like it would explode. As a tear ran down her cheek, she said, "I think I need Gabriel to help me find the words to tell you all just how incredible this day has been. I could not have imagined what realm I was about to enter, and now I cannot imagine leaving it. Each of you has touched my heart in a very special way and I will never forget any of you. I am a very different person now, and I have all of you to thank for that. And incredibly, this is just the beginning! So please be assured that I will be doing plenty of animal spirit walks when I get home, and I know that each of you will come when I ask. So, with a heart full of love for you all, I give you my upmost thanks and reverent respect." Then she bowed her head to them all as she wiped away the tears.

Everyone at the table was, of course, touched by what Cleo said. They all returned her love with grunts, hoots, trills, howls and croaks. It was a symphony of sounds that all crescendoed into the most beautiful music Cleo had ever heard. Even better than Uriel's! Then everyone began talking and laughing. Israfel turned up some tunes and a few of them started dancing. Cleo passed around her new oracle deck so that everyone could see their picture. They all pointed to them and each other and laughed some more. They snacked on the bounty that was spread before them on the table and Ezrael had even brought some eucalyptus leaves for Kalani. They played and laughed for what seemed to be hours. No one really wanted to leave. But, one by one, each animal had a place to be, and a thing to do, so they said their good-byes to Cleo, Bacchus and Ezrael, and slowly made their way back to their homes.

When all of the animals had departed, Cleo, Bacchus and Ezrael sat for a few minutes in silence. It was hard to take in everything that had happened. Then Bacchus said, "Cleo, I will leave you now as well. Ezrael will take you back and make sure you are safe along the journey. And he will help you back to your world. But know that I am always with you, and I will be honored to continue to be your power animal for as long as you need me. And my spirit will always be alive in your heart. It has been my greatest honor and privilege to see you find your power and your joy. Never forget how very special you are to me, and to the world. You have a great mission ahead of you, and lots of fabulous adventures to experience. And I can't wait to see it all unfold. I love you very much. And I wish you the greatest joys in the smallest pleasures."

Cleo got up from her stump seat and hugged Bacchus so tightly he could hardly breathe. "Bacchus," said Cleo, "I can't imagine the day when I won't need you. What you have done for me, and with me, is beyond anything I could have imagined or hoped for. This is truly the most special birthday I have ever had, because I have now been given the gift of sight. Seeing the oneness of everything and All That Is and to know I am part of that. And you, my dearest friend, made that possible for me. So, I will see you in my dreams and tell you everything, even though you will probably already know it all. I love you very much too. Thank you, Bacchus, for this fabulous adventure." She hugged him one last time before he turned to Ezrael and said, "Ezrael, please see our little girl safely home." And then he turned to follow a new path. But he did not look back. He did not need to.

Cleo turned to Ezrael and fell into his arms, tears streaming down her face. Ezrael held her tightly for as long as she needed to cry. Then he looked at her and the table full of gifts and said, "Cleo, I have one last gift. And it is from me. From his robe, he pulled out a beautiful silver necklace chain. And on the chain hung a single pearl. It glistened in the sun. It was flawless. Cleo gasped. Ezrael said, "This is your new necklace, to carry all of the charms you received today. But already there is a pearl, from me. This pearl symbolizes perfect love, the love I have for you. It is the tear of an angel. It represents the tears I cried for you, before you knew me. I have wanted you to know me for so long. I have been patiently waiting for this day. And now I cry no more." The light that emanated from his face was almost blinding. Cleo smiled at Ezrael and said, "Ezrael, this is the most beautiful thing I have ever received. And that's saying a lot, given all of these wonderful gifts I received today. But the best part is that I don't have to say goodbye to you. And that is my greatest joy." And she smiled a tender smile at her loving guardian angel.

"So, how am I going to carry all of these wonderful gifts with me?" she asked. Ezrael smiled and said, "Well, first we will put all your charms on your necklace. Then we can put the rest of the gifts in my little silk pouch here." And from his robe he pulled out a silk pink pouch. Cleo laughed in amazement. "This is a special pouch, Cleo. It will encase all of the gifts in a protective bubble so that nothing gets hurt or destroyed as we walk." "Well, of course!" laughed Cleo. Ezrael threaded all of the new charms on Cleo's necklace and then placed it around her neck. She felt like such a queen! Then he helped her gather the rest of the gifts and place them in her new silk pouch. Then finally, he took the crown from her head and placed it in the pouch. "OK," he said. "I think that's everything. Are you ready for us to make our way home?" he asked. Cleo smiled and nodded.

They walked side by side, all the way back to the edge of the realm of the woods. When they arrived, Cleo looked up to see the tree with the heart in it. But on this side of the realm, the heart was much larger. Ezrael looked down to Cleo and said, "Cleo, when we get back to the other side, you will not be able to see me as you do now. I will, of course, always be at your side, but the density of the 3rd dimension prevents me from being able to materialize like I do here. But when you raise your frequency, you will be able to see me, even though others will not." "That's OK Ezrael," said Cleo. "I *know* you are always there." Ezrael smiled a radiant smile and said, "OK, are you ready? Take my hand and let's get you home." Cleo grabbed Ezrael's hand as they jumped into the tree heart.

When they emerged on the other side, Cleo could no longer see Ezrael, but she could feel his presence. She took a breath in relief. Reorienting herself now back to the real world, she pulled out her phone to see what time it was.

As she looked down at the phone, she gasped.

It was 11:12.

READER'S GUIDE

Cleo
Cleo is representative of the goddess energy from Cleopatra. She represents the energy of a warrior as she discovers and addresses the traumas and difficulties in her life. She transforms into a great warrior queen.

11:11
The angel number 11:11 means that you are one with the Universe, the angels, and the ascended masters. Align with the highest good and you will bring love into the world.

Bacchus
Bacchus is a black panther who symbolizes the unleashing of desires and awakening to the kundalini forces. Black panthers symbolize a time of imminent awakening. The name Bacchus is taken from the mythical figure, Bacchus, who was nursed by panthers. He has a chariot that is pulled by black panthers.

Ariel
Ariel is the Archangel that oversees the natural world. She inspires through nature and helps us deepen our relationship with animals, natural elements, and plants. Part of her purpose is to reveal destinies.

Ant
Ant spirit teaches us how to get to work and see things through to completion. It shows us how to use teamwork and conveys diligence, will power and patience through our inner power. The queen ant is always giving to others.

Barachiel
Barachiel is the Archangel of blessings. His name means 'God has Blessed'. He has rose petals scattered on his clothing to symbolize the Universe's sweet blessings showering down on people. He brings prosperity and good fortune to those that call to him.

Butterfly
Butterfly spirit teaches us to get ready for big changes, just as the caterpillar ultimately transforms into a beautiful butterfly. It symbolizes spiritual awakening when the time is right. Butterfly also reminds us to lighten up and not to take things too seriously.

Chamuel
Chamuel is the Archangel of love and adoration. He helps us open our hearts to love and breaks down the barriers we have around our heart. He helps us heal our emotional wounds and pain that hold us back from loving ourselves. He helps us feel unconditional love in our hearts.

Coyote
Coyote spirit helps us look for lessons in the drama that we have in our lives. He helps us forgive ourselves for our mistakes and instead see the mistakes as gifts that come from those experiences. Coyote spirit also reminds us that laughter is truly good medicine and that it is OK to be playful. He challenges us to think about the things that we have pushed down or hidden from ourselves.

Daniel

Daniel is the Archangel of marriage and union. He brings feelings of love and helps us open our heart chakra. He helps heal old wounds from relationships and helps us release old baggage.

Deer

Deer spirit teaches compassion for ourselves and others. It brings a sense of calm. It helps us seek safe situations and teaches us to trust our instincts and intuition. Deer spirit also tells us that we are ready for an exciting adventure.

El Morya

El Morya is an Ascended Master that helps us remove energy that is not for our highest good. He represents courage, power, forthrightness, and self-reliance. Liken him to King Arthur. He helps us connect to our inner teacher.

Emu

Emu spirit teaches us to put aside judgment and open ourselves to new ideas, while maintaining a sense of fun and light-heartedness. It is associated to the element of Earth and represents survival and adaptability as well as the joy of discovery.

Fairy

Fairies are beings of magical power. They signify love, magic, and springtime. They are complicated beings that slip in and out of several different realms. They love to test and play games with themselves and each other.

Fox

Fox spirit teaches us about trusting our intuition and using our intelligence and ingenuity. It teaches us to not let the negative things that other say about us, affect us. Fox spirit represents slyness, mystery, and adaptability. Foxes are also known to have super-natural abilities.

Gabriel

Gabriel is the Archangel of revelation. She teaches us how to find our voice, communicate with integrity and courage. She has the power to announce Divine will to man. She is the feminine Archangel of the moon, birth, and communication.

Gopher

Gopher spirit teaches us to look under the surface and get to the truth that could be buried and hidden. It has symbolic ties to secrets, Earth history and feminine energy. Gopher spirit also symbolizes communication and individuality, represented by the ultrasonic ability to communicate with other gophers.

Haniel

Haniel is the Archangel of intuition. She is the angel of joy, and her name means 'Joy of God'. She is associated to the moon and moon energy. When you look at the moon, it is Haniel reminding you to listen to your inner guidance. She teaches us to honor our emotions.

Hawk

Hawk spirit teaches us to look at things from a broader perspective. It comes to inspire us to fly higher than ever before and trust your inner guidance and higher self. Hawk spirit also teaches us to eliminate distractions and stay focused on the task before us.

Israfel

Israfel is the angel who blows the trumpet to signal the Day of Judgment. He is the angel nearest to the Divine and translates the Divine's commands to the other archangels. He is the angel of music and has a warm embracing presence with a golden glow.

Iguana

Iguana spirit teaches us to bring things into balance between our responsibilities and relaxation. Iguanas have very keen eyesight, and they are always watching everything. As they grow, they shed their skin. Iguana spirit teaches us to release our old "skin" for personal growth, or risk being caught in skin too small and therefore be bound to the past. Iguanas love music and Iguana spirit teaches us to do little things every day to experience joy.

Jeremiel

Jeremiel is the Archangel of forgiveness. His name means 'Mercy of God'. He helps us look back on our lives and gain clarity. He brings forgiveness so we can move forward in a fearless and powerful way. His messages come in dreams and visions, and he gives us the ability to let go of judgment.

Jaguar

Jaguar spirit teaches us to focus on what we want and stay with it. It foretells an experience of awakening or deeper psychic vision. Jaguar spirit teaches us to find our inner strength and regain our power. It encourages us to face change without fear. Jaguar spirit shows us the strength we have within, that we have yet to recognize.

Kalani

Kalani is a Hawaiian name that means 'the heavens', coming from the Hawaiian "ka", meaning "the" and "lani" meaning "heaven." The name evokes images of the beautiful, tropical paradise of Hawaii. The name is also associated with serenity, peace, and a connection to nature.

Koala

Koala spirit brings calm to your life. It is perpetually at peace with itself and its surroundings. Koala spirit teaches us to meditate with deep breathing so that you can restore your mental and emotional clarity. Koala spirit can also be a precursor for the development of psychic gifts.

Lakshmi

Lakshmi is the Hindu goddess of all of prosperity. That includes fertility, fortune and well-being. Lakshmi can be invoked for guidance on wealth and prosperity. She teaches health, happiness, joy, success and opportunities. She will help energize gratitude.

Lion

Lion spirit teaches us to follow our hearts rather than our heads and to hold your head up with dignity. Lion spirit shows you the courage that is always with you and that you can tap into whenever needed. Lion spirit is associated with regal grace and power. The lioness spirit teaches how to nurture and protect the weak. It can teach you how to banish fear, remain humble and use your power.

Michael

Michael is the Archangel that is the ruler of the angelic realm. He is a fierce protector, especially of light workers. He helps us surrender negative feelings and emotions so we can align with source, unconditional love. He radiates a blue color and carries a sword for defending all.

Mongoose

Mongoose spirit teaches us to show courage when we are faced with fear. It shows us how to stand our ground in the face of fear and not to run away from challenges. Mongoose spirit also helps us stay positive and not lose hope in an adverse situation. It can support you in dreaming of the life you desire and make plans and act on them without hesitation. Finally, this spirit helps block negative energy.

Netzach

Netzach is part of the Kabbalah. Kabbalah is an esoteric method, discipline and school of thought in Jewish mysticism. Netzach implies two Hebrew words: nitzachon – victory over our fears and nitzchiut – eternity. Netzach embodies endurance, fortitude, and patience to follow through on your passions. It is leadership and the ability to rally others to a cause and motivate them to act.

Numbat

Numbat spirit symbolizes the endurance to not let anyone or any challenges distract you from your dreams. Numbat spirit inspires you to be a better version of yourself. People with this spirit animal are generally introverts and find they spend time alone, even though family is of great importance to them. Finally, Numbat spirit people love to walk in nature.

Orion

Orion is the Archangel of manifesting miracles. He helps us connect to All That Is and reminds us that we are one with everyone and everything. He helps create the most magnificent things in our lives. He is associated with stars and constellations. He has powerful cosmic energy. This is also a reference to the constellation of Orion and the 3 stars of Orion's belt.

Owl

Owl spirit reminds us to tap into our great intuitive wisdom. By quietly observing your environment, you can watch and listen for signs and omens that will answer your questions. Owl spirit can help you uncover your hidden qualities and talents and bring them to life. It symbolizes wisdom, clear vision and insight as well as guide you into the unknown.

Phanuel

Phanuel is the Archangel of truth. He is known as the 'Face of God'. He is the angel of repentance and hope, encouraging people to pursue an eternal relationship with God, overcoming guilt and regret. He is seen as the angel of judgment. Phanuel reminds us that if you trust and desire for good, and you believe your desire is attainable, it opens the door for the desire to be delivered to you.

Praying Mantis

Praying Mantis spirit has strong ties to meditation and is very spiritual. It teaches us to be in nature, be very still, and listen to your instincts. Mantis spirit brings good omens and represents good luck and blessings. The key messages of Mantis spirit are mindfulness, patience, awareness and spiritual stillness. It is highly connected to clairvoyance and clairsentience.

Quan Yin

Quan Yin is the goddess of pure compassion and love. She can lead someone to a place of peace and harmony. She is a prominent figure in Buddhism and Taoism. She is all-seeing and all-hearing. She teaches that you should not let your wellness be affected by someone else's behavior or by the outcome of a situation that cannot be controlled.

Quail

Quail spirit comes when you have embarked on a new spiritual quest and it comes with higher knowledge. Quail spirit teaches that if you are being criticized, you should not respond directly; learn to re-direct the attention. It will help you discover a greater sense of yourself and encourages you to act on a long-held dream. And once you start, you must ensure you do not put the spark out.

Raguel

Raguel is the Archangel of peace and harmony. His name translates to 'Friend of God' and it is his role to make peace and to provide strength and balance on Earth. He emanates an aura of blue and has symbols of snow and ice to portray him, as this represents a cooling effect for overcoming difficult situations.

Ram

Ram spirit represents that there may be something out of balance or harmony in your life and encourages us to discover what it is and take steps to correct it. Ram horns grow in a spiral and represent the circular nature of life, death and rebirth. Ram spirit also shows us how to achieve balance and sure-footedness.

Sachael

Sachael is an angel who has a bright loving presence and is very protective. He can bring hope, inspire clearing and ultimately healing and can cut through negative emotional energy. He helps you reconnect with the authentic version of yourself and your soul purpose. He is also connected to streams of wealth, success, harmony and material gain. Because he is associated to the planet Jupiter, he can also inspire you to grow, evolve, take risks and expand.

Snake

Snake spirit represents significant personal and spiritual growth. It represents shedding your old skin or your old self and transforming into a new version of you. Snake spirit is a powerful symbol of transformation and regeneration. It often marks the ending of one journey and the beginning of another with newfound strength and wisdom. It reminds us to stay grounded as you move through these changes.

Thoth

Thoth was an Egyptian God known for many things, among them, the knowledge for how to connect to Universal Intelligence. He is the god of writing, divine magic and the moon. As a powerful spiritual guide, Thoth can help us understand magic and the power of the human will, to complete whatever you set out to do. He was able to control time and space. Animals were sacred to him.

Toad

Toad spirit can help us clear past emotional issues and connect with our most primal self. It shows us that it would be a good time to withdraw, be in solitude and explore emotional or spiritual matters. Toad spirit helps us form a deeper connection with our feelings and therefore, can help purge negativity from our lives and lead us back to healing and purification.

Uriel

Uriel is the Archangel of truth and light. He is known as 'God's light'. Uriel brings the energy and the harmony of the sun to us so we can feel youthful and playful. He also helps us feel balanced and focused. Uriel can show you how to step into your power and how to share your gifts with the world.

Unicorn

Unicorn spirit invites us to pursue our creative interests. It also shows us how to notice signs from other Nature spirits. Unicorn spirit is about playing and having fun. It also helps us suspend our disbeliefs and connects us to the invisible world of imagination. Unicorns sing a beautiful song that emits the frequency of love.

Varuna

Varuna is a Hindu god-sovereign and divine authority. He is the god of sea and rain. He rules the sky realm and upholds cosmic law. He is associated with all types of water, as well as the clouds and rain and is known as the King of Waters. He is a great sustainer of life by providing rain for the crops.

Vulture

Vulture spirit symbolizes the power of patience because there is no need to rush their choice. Vulture spirit also represents time to clear up clutter in your life, figuratively and literally. It also symbolizes dramatic rebirth. And because the vulture does not have a voice box, vulture spirit represents the lesson of walking the walk, instead of talking about it. Keep your word and show people your true nature through your deeds.

Wahkan

Wahkan is a Lakota Sioux name meaning 'Sacred'. The name Wahkan embodies a sense of reverence and spirituality, reflecting the deep connection the Lakota Sioux people have with the natural world and the divine. It symbolizes the sacredness and mystery that permeates the understanding of the universe. It is often given to individuals who are believed to have a special connection to the spiritual realm and possess wisdom beyond their years.

Wolf

Wolf spirit is aligned with you if you have a strong sense of family and you are affectionate with your friends and family. It teaches valuable insights that may be coming your way and it shows us how to maintain our self-esteem and trust our inner knowing. Wolf spirit is always protecting, both spiritually and psychically.

Xavier

Xavier is an Arabic name meaning "new house" or "bright". The name means the deep thinker, intuitive and imaginative. It also symbolizes being idealistic and wise.

Xenops

Xenops spirit is associated with service and guiding souls. It represents wisdom and social connectedness. It is a symbol of health and spiritual protection. Xenops is the bird of joy and reminds us to live our joy as much as we can. Its spirit and message are powerful for insight and nature's majesty.

Yara

Yara is the name of a Brazilian goddess. Yara is the water spirit and has green hair and fair skin. Yara name means strong, independent and beautiful person.

Yak

Yak spirit is the epitome of ruggedness and strength. Yak spirit can help when you might lose hope. It shares its tools to carry you to ensure your survival. When conditions turn cold and unforgiving, Yak spirit helps you find your way out of the storm toward victory.

Zuriel

Zuriel is the Archangel of vitality and magic. His name means 'Strength of God'. He rules over the zodiac sign of Libra, which means he brings balance and order. He is the patron of magicians and mystics. He has a strong connection with water and can create an oasis or fountains of spring water for the thirsty.

Zebra

Zebra spirit represents balance. His stripes are black and white, like yin and yang, and embody balance. No two zebra stripes are the same, representing the individuality of people. Zebra spirit helps us see things in more than one way and helps us see that there are infinite ways to address a problem or issue to bring it to resolution. If you are struggling with your sense of self, Zebra spirit can help you hone your vision and path and embrace it.

ABOUT THE ILLUSTRATOR

The pictures in this book are so important, because they truly bring the characters to life.

And they are amazing. So, I would like to introduce you to the artist that made them happen.

The illustrator is **Cedric Perret**. Cedric is a Swiss imaginative creator, who gives life to a range of fantasy and surreal concepts using AI and design tools. His gallery is extensive and worth a visit!

If you can dream it, he can draw it!

Cedric does commission work and is a true joy to work with. If you have ever wanted to have your picture with your dragon, you should contact him.

Cedric can be reached at the following sites:

- Facebook: VisualDreams.art (https://www.facebook.com/visualdreamsbycp)
- Website: www.VisualDreams.art
- Email contact: contact@visualdreams.art

ACKNOWLEDGMENT SECTION

This section is to acknowledge the numerous people who shaped this book as well as my continuing education into all things metaphysical. It is also for guiding the reader to the many resources available for more information and exploring.

Overall, the animal spirits information comes from *Animal Spirits Guide* by Dr. Steven Farmer. This is a must have book for anyone interested in learning more about the wonderful world of animal spirits and shamanistic practices. www.drstevenfarmer.com

The angel references and information mostly come from Kyle Gray. He has numerous books and classes about the angels and how to develop a connection with them. His book, *Angel Numbers,* was the source of the meaning of 11:11. www.kylegray.co.uk

Finally, my exposure to a lot of these resources listed below came from an intriguing series on GAIA called *Interview with E.D.* (Extra-Dimensionals) produced and filmed by Reuben Langdon. www.Interviewwithed.org.

GAIA is a streaming service that contains a unique blend of Yoga, Meditation, Personal Transformation and Alternative Healing content. It's affordable and it's amazing! www.Gaia.com

And finally, a special call out to Georgia Jean and The Circle of Light. A truly fabulous adventure into learning how to really do all of the stuff outlined in this book. www.circleevolution.com

The rest of this will follow the chapters by name so that you can quickly reference what you are being drawn to through the animals. Explore and enjoy!

Barachiel the Butterfly

Self-love. Saying 'I love you' in the mirror.
   You Can Heal Your Life – Louise Hay www.louisehay.com
Akashic Records
   The Akashic Records Made Easy – Sandra Anne Taylor www.sandrataylor.net
   Interview with E.D. - Emily Harrison (Season 3, episode 9) – www.theakashicacademy.com

Chamuel the Coyote

Audience awareness
   The Golden Lake: Wisdom of the Stars for Life on Earth – Lyssa Royal-Holt www.lyssaroyal.net
   Interview with E.D. – Lyssa Royal-Holt and Hamon (Season 2, episode 18)
Reclaiming energy to your heart

   Circle Evolution – Georgia Jean www.circleevolution.com
   Interview with E.D. – Georgia Jean (Season 2, episodes 11 & 12)

Daniel the Deer

The Chakras
    Psychic Navigator – John Holland – www.johnholland.com
Your heart has a brain
    Dr. Joe Dispenza – Rewired (A Gaia series) – or www.
drjoedispenza.com
Releasing emotions from the palm of your hand
    The Wisdom of the Council – Sara Landon https://resources.
saralandon.com/
    Interview with E.D. – Sara Landon (Season 2, episodes 22 & 23)

El Morya the Emu

Higher Soul and creating your reality
    Roxanne Swainhart – The Odyssey of Ascension www.
odysseyofascension.com
    Interview with E.D. – Roxanne Swainhart (Season 1, episodes
16 & 17)

Fairy The Fox

Intuition and how to develop it
    Psychic Navigator – John Holland – www.johnholland.com
    Energy Speaks - Lee Harris - Lee Harris Energy - https://www.
leeharrisenergy.com
    Interview with E.D. – Lee Harris (Season 2, episodes 7 & 8)

Gabriel the Gopher

Speaking Your Truth
    Kyle Gray - Certified Angel Guide Class – www.hayhouse.com

Haniel The Hawk

Different perspectives and living your joy
Lee Harris - Lee Harris Energy - https://www.leeharrisenergy.com
Circle Evolution – Georgia Jean www.circleevolution.com
Ego
A New Earth – Eckhart Tolle - https://eckharttolle.com/

Israfel the Iguana

Shedding layers of old beliefs
Roxanne Swainhart – The Odyssey of Ascension www.odysseyofascension.com
Deep Clearing – John Ruskan - https://www.emclear.com/

Jeremiel the Jaguar

Forgiveness and who we really are
The Dream, the Journey, Eternity and God – Sara Landon and Mike Dooley
https://resources.saralandon.com/
https://www.tut.com/

Kalani the Koala

Meditation
Circle Evolution – Georgia Jean www.circleevolution.com
Dr. Joe Dispenza – www.drjoedispenza.com
Deep Clearing – John Ruskan - https://www.emclear.com/
Gaia - www.Gaia.com - All Meditation videos
Empower You App – Unlimited Audio and guided meditations

<u>Lakshmi the Lion</u>

Spiritual Guides
>*Animal Spirit Guides* – Dr. Steven Farmer - https://drstevenfarmer.com/
>*Spirit Animals as Guides, Teachers and Healers* - Dr. Steven Farmer - https://drstevenfarmer.com/
>*Healing Ancestral Karma* - Dr. Steven Farmer - https://drstevenfarmer.com/

<u>Michael the Mongoose</u>

Meeting your guardian angel
>Kyle Gray - Certified Angel Guide Class – www.hayhouse.com

<u>Netzach the Numbat</u>

Numbat Sanctuary – Australian Wildlife Conservancy - https://www.australianwildlife.org/wildlife/numbat/
(Yes, there really is a numbat sanctuary)

<u>Orion the Owl</u>

Galactic Origins
>*The Golden Lake: Wisdom of the Stars for Life on Earth* – Lyssa Royal-Holt www.lyssaroyal.net
>Interview with E.D. – Wendy Kennedy (Season 1, episodes 1 & 2)

<u>Phanuel the Praying Mantis</u>

The history of Mantis Beings
>Interview with E.D. – Robert and Jacquelin (Season 1, episodes 28 & 29)

Interview with E.D. – Elizabeth April (Season 2, episodes 19 – 21) https://elizabethapril.com/

Quan Yin the Quail

Basic human instincts and duality
Circle Evolution – Georgia Jean www.circleevolution.com

Sachael the Snake

Snake phobia
Interview with E.D. – Lyssa Royal-Holt and Hamon (Season 2, episode 18)
Beliefs and their veil to your reality
Roxanne Swainhart – The Odyssey of Ascension www.odysseyofascension.com
The Release Ceremony
"Dr. Ssssssss" - Dr. Steven Farmer - https://drstevenfarmer.com/

Thoth the Toad

Journaling and automatic writing
Lee Harris - Lee Harris Energy - https://www.leeharrisenergy.com
Dr. Steven Farmer - https://drstevenfarmer.com/

Uriel the Unicorn

Galactic heritage and the Pleiades
The Golden Lake: Wisdom of the Stars for Life on Earth – Lyssa Royal-Holt www.lyssaroyal.net
Interview with E.D. – Lyssa Royal-Holt and Hamon (Season 2, episode 18)

Dragons and Unicorns
>   Interview with E.D. – Prageet & Julieanne (Season 3, episode 16 & 17)   https://www.thestargateexperienceacademy.com/

<u>Varuna the Vulture</u>

Angelic realm and angels
>   Sonia Choquette https://soniachoquette.net/

<u>Wahkan the Wolf</u>

Shamanism and the Animal Spirit Walk
>   *Animal Spirit Guides* – Dr. Steven Farmer - https://drstevenfarmer.com/
>   *Spirit Animals as Guides, Teachers and Healers* - Dr. Steven Farmer - https://drstevenfarmer.com/

Crystals
>   Interview with E.D. – Wendy Kennedy (Season 1, episodes 1 & 2)

<u>Xavier the Xenops</u>

Connectedness to everything
>   Circle Evolution – Georgia Jean www.circleevolution.com

<u>Yara the Yak</u>

Higher heart and thymus gland. Infinity 8 purification.
>   Circle Evolution – Georgia Jean www.circleevolution.com

"The power of my heart is the heart of my power"
>   (One of my favorite quotes and mantras of all time)
>   Direct quote from the Z's, channeled by Lee Harris - Lee Harris Energy - https://www.leeharrisenergy.com

Planetary consciousness and healing
   Circle Evolution – Georgia Jean www.circleevolution.com

<u>Zuriel the Zebra</u>

Infinite possibilities
   Circle Evolution – Georgia Jean www.circleevolution.com
Water has a consciousness
   Dr. Masura Emoto - masaru-emoto.net
   Veda Austin - vedaaustin.com
Tarot Cards
   Theresa Bullard – Gaia – Mystery Teachings of the Tarot
   https://theresabullard.com/

OTHER TITLES BY ANNE POLLARD

Fabulous

Fabulous is an inspirational autobiography about the decade leading up to an amazing personal transformation. It explores the life gifts from The Universe during those ten years and how they molded the author. Themes of friends, animals and music are woven through the journey that spanned sadness, happiness, debt, abundance, failed relationships, laughter and ultimate joy. It is meant to serve as an inspiration and reference for those looking for happiness, abundance and peace.

Everyone has been through hard times and good times. This book tries to help you see those times from a different perspective, and one that might just lead you down the road of your own transformation to a life of happiness. And since everyone's definition of happy is different, we can all try and strive toward the happy for each of us. Because in the end, isn't everyone's ultimate goal in life to be happy? And when you find your happiness, you help change the world.

WHAT'S COMING!

Be sure and watch for more of Cleo's Fabulous Adventures!

The Realm of The Dragons

The Realm of The Unicorns

The Realm of the Angels

The Realm of the Fairies

Printed in the USA
CPSIA information can be obtained
at www.ICGtesting.com
CBHW051440101024
15668CB00009B/137